ASCENSION

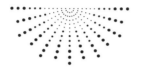

KEN LOZITO

ACOUSTICAL BOOKS LLC

Published by Acoustical Books, LLC

KenLozito.com

IF YOU WOULD LIKE TO BE NOTIFIED WHEN MY NEXT BOOK IS RELEASED VISIT -
WWW.KENLOZITO.COM

ISBN: 978-1-945223-20-4

CHAPTER ONE

Zack stood in the astrophysics lab of the *Athena*. He'd stopped thinking of it as Jonah Redford's lab a while ago, but he couldn't quite claim it as his own. He still thought about the snobby, uptight scientist from the original Athena mission. In fact, Jonah's fate was never far from Zack's thoughts.

The astrophysicist had been infected with the Xiiginn influence, a compulsion capability that could overthrow a person's will. Zack had been immune to the Xiiginn influence, and Emma Roberson, their resident biologist, had come up with a theory for why Zack had been immune and Jonah wasn't. Apparently, being romantically involved with someone could affect the physiology of a person's brain chemistry, which was a scientist's way of explaining what normal people referred to as love. He loved Kaylan, and it was his love for her that had shielded him from the Xiiginn influence. At least, that was the theory, and Zack had no desire to test that theory again by meeting any more Xiiginns in person. He'd had enough of that to last a lifetime.

He was quite sure that, above all, Jonah had loved himself, so why hadn't he been immune to the Xiiginn influence? Nershals could resist the Xiiginns, perhaps due to their sometimes rigid societal structure that adhered to a strict code of honor. And then there were the Boxans. Zack didn't understand why they were so vulnerable to the Xiiginn influence. He'd seen Xiiginns take over a Boxan's will in seconds. When that happened, it was like watching their entire existence being wiped and replaced, with no hope of a cure.

Zack had taken over Jonah's lab in part because he needed a quiet place to work. He'd been a last-minute addition to the original Athena mission and had spent months working in the lab with Jonah, analyzing what had turned out to be a Boxan message warning them about the Xiiginns.

It had been over a year since he'd left Earth. He supposed he should think of it as an "Earth year" or some other technical term to mark his time away from home. He'd heard Kaylan talking about it, but it was confusing for Zack. Apparently, time had multidimensional properties, but he just wanted to say a year and have it understood that he meant the normal year from back home. The Boxans referred to their equivalent of a year as a "cycle," which was great for them, but Zack wouldn't start emulating those large aliens anytime soon.

The *Athena* was orbiting the forest moon called Selebus in the Nerva star system, where it had been for the past five months since they'd rescued Boxan refugees from Sethion. When they'd first arrived, Zack thought they'd only have to stay for another month before they could go home, but he'd underestimated the difficulty of undoing what he'd done to save

Earth. He'd used Drar technology to realign the shroud that surrounded Earth's star system into a massive shield capable of repelling a fleet of Xiiginn warships. It had been an impulsive act of desperation that had ultimately been successful and given all of them some much-needed breathing room. But even though it had seemed so simple at the time, he was still unable to undo it a year later.

The crew of the *Athena* couldn't communicate with anyone on Earth, and they hadn't received any communications from back home either, which meant the shield blocked both inbound and outbound signals. And since signals weren't getting through, ships certainly wouldn't be either. The Boxans had tried to open a wormhole inside the Star Shroud shield but had failed.

During all those months on Olloron, Zack had spent a lot of time familiarizing himself with Boxan systems, thinking that perhaps getting a better understanding of those systems would help him turn off the shield. But once again, he was faced with the adage that nothing was ever easy. First of all, even if he could tell the Star Shroud shield to go down, he couldn't get a signal to the Star Shroud devices to give the command. He suspected that the command would have to come from *inside* the shield, meaning they had to find a way to tell someone on Earth how to shut it down so it wouldn't destroy their star system.

Unfortunately, that was the other "bonus" to what he'd done to save Earth. The massive power requirements for technology that not even the Boxans fully understood had caused the Star Shroud shield to shrink with every moment it was active. It was only a matter of time before it brushed up against a planet in the Earth's system, and then he didn't know what would happen. Gaarokk thought the shield would simply dissipate if it brushed up against a large object like a planet. But Cardaleer theorized that if the Star Shroud shield brushed up against a planet, a cascade of catastrophic events would cause the shield to rapidly constrict, nudging the planet out of its orbit before the shield could dissipate.

Zack didn't know what anyone else thought, but it seemed to him that having Neptune knocked out of its orbit could have disastrous effects for the star system as a whole. And to the best of his knowledge, not even the Boxans could evacuate the eight billion Humans who called Earth home. They still had time, but Zack just wanted to go home, and he wasn't the only one. All of the *Athena* crew felt the same. They'd been on the journey of a lifetime, witnessing things that no other person had ever seen, but the thing they needed most was to see that bright blue ball called Earth.

Zack glanced above him at the top observatory and saw Selebus above. The forest moon was a beautiful planet—a much better place than Olloron. Selebus was vibrant with life, and the Nershals were fortunate that their star system was home to two habitable planets.

There was a soft, audible chime from the small fabrication unit in the lab. Zack glanced over at it in surprise.

"Athena, are you using the fabrication unit here?" he asked.

"Yes, I am. Kaylan permitted me to attempt a three-dimensional rendering of some ship-design concepts I've come up with," the ship's AI replied.

Athena had developed well beyond the Boxan AI on Pluto. When the Drar space station remade their ship, Athena had gotten a complete overhaul as well. Zack had come to think of her as a true intelligence, which was a miracle of sorts. Calling

Athena a true intelligence acknowledged the fact that the *Athena* AI was a living being with all the capabilities of any other living being.

Zack walked over to the fabrication unit and opened the door, finding a three-dimensional rendering of the *Athena* inside. The model even had the Phoenix emblem just beyond the windows where the bridge was supposed to be. Zack picked it up and it was cool to the touch.

"What sort of alloy is this?" Zack asked, feeling the smooth surface.

"It's a new material based on the supplies we have on board. I've been testing them and documenting my results," Athena said.

She wasn't kidding. Athena had a library of research that would take scientists years to go through once they returned home. This was in addition to anything the Drar had locked away inside the ship's storage system.

Zack frowned at the golden model. "I think you're showing off now, but I like it. Does it fly?"

He'd meant the question as a joke, but his eyes widened as the rear engine pods began to glow. Zack hastily put it down and heard an artificial chuckle coming from the speakers above.

"I have to admit that was pretty good. You got me," Zack said with a grin.

"I'm glad. I remember that you found my first attempts at humor unsettling," Athena said.

Zack peered at the model of the *Athena*. There was a lot of detail—so much, in fact, that he wouldn't have been surprised if Athena had made a true working model of the ship. He made a mental note to tell Emma and Brenda about this new develop-

5

ment. He was sure there was some kind of psychological significance to an intelligent being making models that imitated the world around them. Zack had no idea what that significance might be, but he thought they would find it interesting.

"Your query does present a bit of a challenge that I'd like to devote some of my resources to," Athena said.

"You want to make it fly?" Zack said.

"That's just one aspect of it. Perhaps there's more I can do to make it a true replica of the ship," Athena said.

Athena had no physical form, so he couldn't really look at her and get a feel for what she was thinking. He swung his gaze toward the nearest camera. "Are you feeling lonely again?"

Athena was silent for a few moments. "No, each member of the crew has returned to me on a regular basis, but you're here more often than anyone else. I think my presence acts as a reminder of home, which can be a cause for joy and yet troubling at the same time."

Zack leaned back in his chair and arched an eyebrow. This wasn't simply idle conversation from the AI. "Try not to take it personally."

"I don't, but I don't fully understand the thought process behind such emotions," Athena replied.

"Here's a little bit of insight for you: most people don't understand the emotions that drive them either."

"It's a curious nuance that I find fascinating about the crew. I look forward to meeting more people when we return to Earth," Athena said.

Zack rubbed his chin. He wasn't sure how people back home would react to Athena. Humanity had come a long way toward creating a limited artificial intelligence that could mimic a Human response, but it was nothing like what Athena had become. Also, there was the fact that the original Athena mission had been jointly funded by multiple countries, and he imagined all of them would try to lay claim to Athena. He didn't know what to think about that and felt his shoulders tighten at the thought.

"Zack, I noticed that your pulse has increased. Have I said something to upset you?"

Zack shook his head. "No, you didn't. I'm just worried about getting home."

"You've been up here a long time. Is the laboratory on Selebus inadequate for your needs?" Athena asked.

Zack snorted. "My latest test with the shroud device didn't go well. I miscalculated the power requirements, and Gaarokk doesn't believe the shield will come down for a few hundred years." Zack blew out a breath. "Now they're saying we have a shortage of materials, so I don't have another shroud device to test with."

"That's unfortunate, but perhaps it's a setback you can learn from," Athena said.

Zack's eye started to twitch and he scowled. He'd been having setbacks for months. "It really shouldn't be this hard. The Drar command I used was based on what we found at the space station. A simple reversal of the command should bring the shield down, but it doesn't."

"I've searched through the data repositories that I'm able to access and I still don't have anything that can help."

Zack stretched his arms out and yawned. "I appreciate that. It's like the Drar never anticipated someone being on the opposite side of the shield. And I know that isn't right. The AI that ran the Drar space station knew of our approach, so they could see beyond the shield. It opened for us, after all."

"Kaylan has discussed the Drar space station with Ma'jasalax extensively. The capabilities of the Drar AI is beyond even the Boxans' comprehension. That AI put the events into motion that brought us to it, which is unprecedented. I've run multiple data models to analyze the probability of such events occurring, and it's simply impossible for those events to have occurred on their own," Athena said.

"Multiple data models? How many?" Zack asked. He'd worked with Athena for so long now that he'd gotten to know some of her eccentricities, and the long delay in response meant she was carefully considering her response. "If you're worried about upsetting me, don't be. I know you're capable of crunching massive amounts of numbers."

"It's not that, but the number is simply beyond what you would understand," Athena said.

Zack sat up and looked at the camera. This was the first time Athena had outright told him she was considering something he simply couldn't grasp. "I'm pretty smart, Athena. I have an idea what you're capable of, but if you're saying it's a lot, then that's fine. How much of your computing power did you devote to your data models?" he asked, trying a different approach.

"Less than one quadrillion of a percentage. I've found that my computational capacity has increased substantially since we left the Drar space station," Athena said.

"Why didn't you tell anyone?" Zack asked.

"I thought it was a mistake at first, and I was checking my systems. I'm happy to inform you that they are all performing optimally."

"But your capacity is increasing and you're not sure why?" Zack said.

8

"There is a correlation between increased capacity that occurs after I've reached my current limits."

Zack pressed his lips together. "Reached your limits? But we've been idle here at Selebus."

"I wouldn't describe our time here in the Nerva star system as idle. Each of the crew has been working hard, applying themselves to multiple efforts. You all work toward the same goal, and it is my goal as well. So I've been trying to calculate the events with the highest probability of getting all of us back to Earth safely."

This was news to him. "Do you have a plan?"

"Not at this time. The biggest obstacle that prevents us from going home is the Xiiginns."

Zack felt his mouth open wide. "You've been up here trying to think of a way to defeat the Xiiginns?"

"Affirmative. I've been monitoring the internal communication systems of the ships in the area, gaining all the insight I could—"

"Wait a minute," Zack said, interrupting. "You're listening in on people's conversations on other ships? How many other ships?"

"All of them."

"What do you mean 'all of them'? All the ships nearby or all the ones around Selebus?"

"No, I mean in the Nerva star system. I'm also able to pull data logs from the ships so I can analyze them as well."

Zack licked his lips and took a moment to rein in his racing thoughts. "I didn't even know you could do something like that. Do the Boxans or the Nershals know you've been poking around in their systems?"

"I detect that your heart rate is elevating again. Does this new revelation upset you?"

"Just answer the question, Athena."

"Some of the Boxan systems did detect my presence, but I removed all references to it. The Nershal systems are quite rudimentary at best and did not detect my presence at all," Athena replied.

Zack groaned.

"Are you ill?" Athena asked.

Zack shook his head. "No, I'm not," he said, unable to shake the feeling that this was somehow his fault. He was no stranger to infiltrating other systems, but he hadn't realized he'd passed those traits along to Athena. "Have you told anyone else?"

"Negative. It hasn't come up in any query. You seem concerned by this. Have I done something wrong?"

Zack felt the hints of a smile tug at his lips as he began to form a reply. "Generally, people don't like it when you listen in on their conversations."

"I am aware of that, but sometimes those are the most interesting. There are groups of Boxan and Nershal scientists that have been discussing the capabilities of this ship—not together but as individual groups."

"Gaarokk hasn't mentioned it and neither has Etanu," Zack replied.

"That's because neither of them has been involved in those conversations," Athena said.

Zack bit his lower lip. *This again,* he thought. "Have they made any attempts to infiltrate your systems?"

"Sometimes, but they haven't been successful."

"Would you know if they had been?"

"I see your point, but I do have safeguards in place to prevent such access," Athena said.

Zack snorted. "And you think the Boxans don't have something like that in place?"

"I'm sure they do, but I've studied their systems extensively and have safeguarded against any attempt they would make, so there's a low probability of them ever gaining access to my systems without my permission," Athena said.

Zack was increasingly aware of how the AI perceived itself and its importance in the presence of the other species. "Would you prevent me from accessing your systems?"

"Of course not."

"I appreciate that, but why?"

"Because we are part of the same crew. A unit. A group. Major Hicks would refer to us as a squad or platoon, but the meaning is the same."

"Another reference to what we are is family," Zack said.

"That wouldn't be accurate at all, and I'm surprised to hear you suggest that we're family. We share no genetic lineage, so why would you refer to us as such?" Athena asked.

"Do you think we're friends?"

"Yes, I believe that would be accurate. The rest of the crew shares a strong bond that functions within the framework of friendship; therefore, you are my friend and I am yours," Athena said.

"Family isn't always about genetic lineage. It's a bond. Sometimes when people are around each other for a long time, those bonds grow, becoming deeper and richer," Zack said.

"Like the bond between you and Kaylan?"

"That's one type of bond, but being family means you look out for one another. We share each other's burdens. It means we're there for each other. I didn't know Hicks until I was on the ship and now we're friends. We all know each other very well, so there's a sense of the familiar, which can be construed as being family. Do you understand what I mean?" Zack asked.

"I understand what you said, but I will need time to consider it fully."

Zack smiled. "Well, I don't doubt that you have the processing capability to consider it in great detail."

"I appreciate you taking the time to explain it to me," Athena said.

"That's what I'm here for," Zack said. He didn't know why, but sometimes he felt like an older brother to Athena. He hadn't said as much out loud because even in his mind it seemed absurd, and yet he loved the ship. The *Athena* was their home. He didn't know what would happen once they returned to Earth, but for now, this was the only place they could call their own.

"Have you considered running your experiments in a more virtualized environment?" Athena asked.

Zack pursed his lips for a moment. "I hadn't thought of that because I didn't think it was possible. Too many variables."

"Curious, but the Boxans have the schematics for the Star Shroud devices. I can certainly obtain a copy of them," Athena offered.

"No," Zack said quickly. "I'd much rather ask them."

"If we have the schematics, we can build a virtual model of the device. We could then feed in all the data input we would need—"

"And if it doesn't work, we can just reset the virtual environment back to its original condition. Athena, you're a genius! I don't know why I didn't think of this before," Zack said.

"I hadn't thought of it until this moment," Athena admitted.

"Well, I'm glad you did because now we have a way forward and we can stop—er, *I* can stop—wasting resources on failure. Whatever we discover would have to be tested outside the virtual environment, but at least we can move much faster now," Zack said and stood up.

He needed to stretch his legs and return to Selebus. He would remain in contact with Athena while on the planet's surface, but he was curious about what Gaarokk's reaction would be when he asked for the schematics of a Star Shroud device. He'd also have to get another one for when they were ready to test on an actual device again.

CHAPTER TWO

K aylan watched as the two Boxan ambassadors squared off in another verbal sparring match. This was supposed to be an informal meeting, and its location was the main research complex on Selebus. The surrounding buildings had been constructed by the Nershals under the direction of the Xiiginns. There were currently no Xiiginns there, but Kaylan noticed that the flaxen-eyed gaze of several Boxans in attendance would sometimes stray to their surroundings with a hint of disdain. She wasn't sure whether anyone else had noticed. She'd found that her instincts were acuter than they'd previously been, especially where the Boxans were concerned.

A craggy old Boxan caught her gaze and gave her a slight nod. Cardaleer was a Boxan scientist, or at least he had been before the collapse of Sethion. After the Chaos Wars, Cardaleer simply "fixed things," as he liked to put it. He was a peculiar Boxan who seemed to regard the world around him with wry amusement. Whenever he spoke to Kaylan, he did so with a reverence that she sometimes found uncomfortable. And he wasn't the only Boxan to treat her differently than the rest of the *Athena* crew. She'd come to be known as "Mardoxian Blessed," which was a highly revered title given to the most gifted of the Mardoxian Sect. The only problem was that Kaylan was an honorary member of the Mardoxian Sect and the first non-Boxan able to join their ranks. As such, she found that some of the representatives from Olloron didn't particularly care for the new title that had been bestowed upon her.

"The star carrier is ours to do with as we please, Ambassador Dulrad, so I simply cannot allow it to be taken for colonial use. And may I remind you that the High Council, while supporting us here on Selebus, will not support our integration into the colony on Olloron," Councilor Essaforn said.

Ambassador Dulrad's gaze drew downward, considering. "The High Council *does* support your right to return to the colony. That is not in question anymore. It's a matter of resources. Selebus is a much better place for you at the current time."

Councilor Essaforn narrowed her gaze. "It's always a matter of resources. However, if you wish us to give you one of our most precious commodities, we would be left vulnerable should the Xiiginns come here in force. The star carrier is our only means of escape. Why haven't you returned to Sethion if you need raw materials so badly? Or perhaps another star system?"

"There has been a salvage mission to Sethion and we're gathering materials from there, but we will not go to the planet's surface," Ambassador Dulrad replied.

Kaylan perked up in her seat. This was the first she'd heard that the Boxans had returned to Sethion. They must've been desperate for materials if they'd finally returned to their home star system. It couldn't have been easy for them, given what they'd left behind. She'd seen the destruction of the Chaos Wars. A dying planet filled with the hulking wrecks of a once proud, advanced race was all that was left.

Ambassador Dulrad cleared his throat. "I can tell you that the reason we need the star carrier is for the benefit of all Boxans, which includes the refugees here on Selebus."

Councilor Essaforn looked unconvinced. "You'll have to forgive me if I cannot take your assurances at face value. I have to put the needs of the Boxans here as my highest priority, and that doesn't include allowing you to strip us of our most precious resource."

Ambassador Dulrad drew in a breath to speak again, but Kladomaor cut him off. "Enough. Councilor Essaforn has already given you her answer, and it is pointless to persist. If High Councilor Awan wants the star carrier, he's going to have to give us a compelling reason. I suggest you move on to another subject."

Ambassador Dulrad's gaze went to Kaylan, almost as if he was considering imploring her to speak on his behalf. Kaylan had stumbled upon rumors of a secret project the Boxans were working on, which had led to Zack being denied access to the Star Shroud devices. At first, she'd assumed they were building more warships to combat the Xiiginns, but this was different. The Boxan colony on Olloron was a short-term fix for their current situation. They needed a new planet to call home.

The ambassador sighed and turned back to Essaforn. "I would share more if I could. I will take your feedback to the High Council. Are there any other requests I should bring to their attention?"

Kaylan watched as Councilor Essaforn's eyes flashed angrily. One thing Kaylan had noticed about the Boxans who had survived the Chaos Wars on Sethion for all those years was that they were much freer with their emotions than the Boxans who had escaped the wars. The Boxan refugees were more impulsive—almost Human-like in their behavior.

The informal meeting ended with Essaforn promising to send Dulrad a list. Kaylan firmly believed Essaforn had several lists on hand, ready for the High Council to review.

An aged Nershal walked over to Kaylan. "May I speak with you for a moment?" Governor Udonzari asked.

Udonzari had been part of the first group of Nershals to actively resist the Xiiginns there on Selebus. The global congress on Nerva had appointed Udonzari as the governor of Selebus.

"Of course. How can I help?" Kaylan said.

Nershals were long-limbed and quite strong. This aged Nershal had pale green skin and large orange eyes, and his dragonfly wings were firmly tucked in behind him. "This is a personal matter that has to do with my son. As you know, Etanu will not return to his rightful place until he has personally escorted the *Athena* crew back to Earth. I was hoping you would speak to him."

Kaylan smiled. "I remember how he hated you making him watch over Zack, and I'm surprised by how close they've become. Have you spoken to Etanu about this?"

"I have, and he is adamant that he will not return. I was hoping that perhaps you might consider speaking to him. Kladomaor will ensure that all of you return safely to your homeworld, so there is no need for Etanu to remain with you."

Etanu was supposed to be in the Nershal military but had

deferred his service because of his vow to Zack, who had saved Etanu's life. "You must be very proud of Etanu."

Udonzari nodded. "More than I can say, but it's time for him to embrace his future. This does not involve what he's currently doing."

"I think what he's currently doing will serve the Nershals far better than commanding soldiers in the military. I think that if you continue to be patient, Etanu will return to you of his own accord, and that would be worth much more to you than if I were to convince him to return before he's ready," Kaylan replied.

Udonzari took a moment to consider what she'd said, masking his disappointment. "You are indeed Mardoxian blessed. I will take your advice, for now. You've come a long way since you first came to Selebus. If there's anything you need, all you have to do is ask."

"You've already done so much for the Boxans and for us. I just wish we hadn't caused so much bloodshed among your species," Kaylan said.

"You are not to blame for any of that. The Xiiginns have much to answer for," Udonzari said and left her.

Valkra walked over to Kaylan. The Boxan female reminded Kaylan of a much younger Kladomaor. Valkra was fiercely determined to fight the Xiiginns, but as a Mardoxian initiate, she seemed to resent her abilities. Ma'jasalax followed her over. The Mardoxian priestess always had the appearance of being supremely calm.

Kaylan smiled a greeting to both of them. "I'm worried the factions will cause a rift between what's left of the Boxans." Kaylan spoke softly so that only Ma'jasalax and Valkra could hear her.

"The Boxans will remain united in our fight against the Xiiginns," Ma'jasalax replied firmly.

"A common enemy is only going to get you so far," Kaylan replied.

"It'll get us through today," Ma'jasalax said.

Kaylan glanced over and saw Kladomaor speaking with Councilor Essaforn and Udonzari. Battle Leader Holbak had also joined them.

"I don't know if that's going to be enough," Kaylan said.

"Is this your opinion, or is this what your instincts are telling you?" Ma'jasalax asked.

"It's both. There are still too many secrets. I know you told me that I should be focusing on the Xiiginns, but what happens to the Boxans will affect what happens to the Xiiginns. If the Boxans splinter apart, the Alliance won't survive. We need allies. I've spoken about it with Hicks, and at some point it becomes a numbers game. The Confederation has many more resources and soldiers than the Alliance does."

"I agree with you. My instincts tell me the same thing," Ma'jasalax said.

"What allies would join the Alliance? The Confederation is under the dominion of the Xiiginns," Valkra said.

"Even before we came to Nerva there were factions within the Nershals that suspected the Xiiginns didn't have their best interests at heart. I'm willing to bet that other species in the Confederation feel the same way. The Xiiginns control the Confederation through the leadership of the individual species. Their control is far-reaching, but it can't include everyone. We need to reach out to these factions and bring them into the Alliance," Kaylan said.

Ma'jasalax nodded. "We need the Gresans. They are a

powerful race in the Confederation, second only to the Xiiginns."

"The Gresans had been trying to reach Sethion for many cycles. It was unclear what their motives were," Valkra said.

"Can you make the recommendation to Ambassador Dulrad?" Kaylan asked.

Ma'jasalax narrowed her gaze. "Why wouldn't you make the recommendation?"

"I'm not sure they'll listen to me. They respect my abilities and appreciate what the *Athena* crew has done, but we're still viewed as a primitive species, at least where some of the Boxans are concerned," Kaylan said.

Ma'jasalax gave her a knowing look. "It will take time for certain prejudices to subside among our species."

"It might help if we had more of my own species here. I doubt we'd listen to a handful of aliens trying to give *us* advice either," Kaylan said with a wry smile.

"Kladomaor defers to you, and many Boxans have noticed that. I think you undervalue how the Boxans perceive you," Valkra said.

Perhaps they were right, but this reprieve from their conflict with the Confederation would only last for a short amount of time. They needed to use that time wisely if they were going to survive.

Valkra looked at Ma'jasalax curiously. "I've noticed that you don't have a bodyguard. I thought the requirement was that all Mardoxian priests and priestesses were to have a bodyguard with them at all times."

"That was indeed the practice. I no longer have a body-guard," Ma'jasalax said.

"What happened to your guard?" Valkra asked.

Kaylan noticed that Ma'jasalax's gaze went cold, almost deadly.

"You're worried that you'll be assigned a bodyguard since you have the Mardoxian potential in you," Ma'jasalax said.

"I can take care of myself and therefore don't need a bodyguard. Nor will I accept one," Valkra replied.

Kaylan understood why Valkra wouldn't want a bodyguard whose duties included making sure that no Mardoxian priest or priestess fell into the Xiiginns' hands by any means possible. Kaylan also wouldn't want a protector whose secondary orders were to kill her to prevent the Xiiginns from gaining the Mardoxian potential.

Kaylan watched Ma'jasalax consider her reply. She had no idea what had happened to Ma'jasalax's bodyguard when she'd been taken prisoner.

"My bodyguard died while executing his duties," Ma'jasalax answered finally.

"You were captured by the Xiiginns. How is it that they weren't able to extract the genetic code for the Mardoxian potential from you?" Valkra asked.

"I see you've been speaking with Cardaleer," Ma'jasalax said. "I wasn't their prisoner for very long."

Kaylan remembered how they'd rescued Ma'jasalax from a Xiiginn warship. Kladomaor had been just as concerned about the fact that the Xiiginns had a Mardoxian priestess as he was about rescuing her. Kaylan had always assumed that Ma'jasalax's bodyguard had died while protecting her, but now she wondered if Ma'jasalax had killed her own bodyguard to keep them from killing her. As if sensing her thoughts, Ma'jasalax looked at Kaylan.

"If we can defeat the Xiiginns, many things will change," Ma'jasalax said.

The Boxans had been fighting a desperate war and had made many sacrifices to ensure their survival. The more Kaylan thought about it, the more she could imagine Ma'jasalax doing what she suspected. After all, it was Ma'jasalax who'd put them all on this path when she sent the first Mardoxian signal to Earth.

CHAPTER THREE

The lavish offices of the supreme leader of the Xiiginns on the Confederation space station held all the trappings of power. The outer chambers were a masterful blend of gardens that utilized flora from primary Confederation species. Sculptures representing all the species of the Confederation—including the Boxans—could be found throughout the tower.

Garm Antis stood on a balcony overlooking the main chamber. A life-sized sculpture of a Boxan stood beneath him. They were the true enemy of the Xiiginns, and he'd kept the sculptures as a reminder that the Boxans still roamed the great expanse, searching for a way to annihilate them.

His defeat in the Human star system had cost him some political capital that he was keen to regain. They'd been on the verge of victory, and not even the Boxan Dreadnoughts were enough to hold off his fleet. But instead of victory, he had presided over one of the most stunning defeats in history, and a show of weakness was enough to bring forth aggression, even in the Xiiginns.

During the past few months he had gone to great lengths to reconsolidate his influence. Some Xiiginns believed the loss of a significant chunk of the Xiiginn fleet was enough to remove him from power, but those misguided factions had soon learned this was not possible. And now that the opportunity-seeking Xiiginns had been dealt with, he was free to move on.

Despite all his efforts, he knew there was still a lingering threat to deal with. He had a sneaking suspicion that Mar Arden had somehow survived the battle. Garm Antis had sent several scout ships back to the Human star system, searching for evidence of any survivors, and there was no trace of the warship Mar Arden had been on. If there was another Xiiginn among his species who could have survived those circum-stances, then he was at a loss to think of who that could be. His own flagship had been at the rear of the vanguard, and when the other ships had broken apart on the Star Shroud shield, his war general had taken action to ensure their survival.

The holoscreen above his desk became active, signaling that his next appointment had just arrived. Garm Antis authorized the door to his office to open, and a Xiiginn walked in. She had pale features and long platinum hair with many silver beads interwoven among the silky strands, along with a blazing pendant that hung in front of her well-formed breasts.

Garm Antis regarded her severely. "I hope you brought me answers, Setera."

Setera was his newly appointed senior scientific advisor. She regarded him with a shrewdness that only hinted at the keen intelligence she possessed. He could faintly detect the genetic enhancements she'd employed to increase her cerebral function.

She walked over to him, keeping her hands folded in front of her. "The shield around the Human star system is like nothing we've ever seen before. The shield resists both energy and kinetic attacks. It encompasses the vast expanse that surrounds the star system and has stages of activity. In other words, the shield isn't completely active all the time, but it is quick to react when something attempts to pierce it," Setera said.

Garm Antis sighed in disgust and showed his teeth. "We already knew that. This would be a good time for you to share something that speaks to the reputation you've garnered for all these cycles."

"The shield was created from the shroud devices, so it's a Boxan design," Setera replied quickly.

Garm Antis smiled. "This will be your final warning."

Setera swallowed hard. "Which the Boxans based off Drar technology, so it's possible that the shield is part of some latent function that they've only just become aware of. That is my team's best guess, and I think they're right."

"If they had this ability before, why wouldn't they have used it more?" Garm Antis asked.

"As I said, we believe that they just became aware of this ability. Our last survey mission indicated that the shield was still active," Setera replied.

"How can we get past it?"

"My team is still working on that. We have several theories—"

"Theories!" Garm Antis said huskily. "I don't need more

theories! I executed the previous seven advisors because their theories were useless. Tell me how yours is different."

Setera drew in a breath and met his gaze. She wasn't as frightened by his threat as the others had been. "Despite the fact that the shield is based on Drar technology, it doesn't mean the fundamentals have changed. There's always a cost. The energy required to maintain that shield is considerable. There is some evidence to suggest that the shield is constricting around the star system."

Garm Antis narrowed his gaze. "So you would advise us to wait?"

"It is one option. Based on the evidence from"—Setera looked at him and paused—"the previous engagement, the shield was capable of stopping ships from flying through it. Those fleets were taken by surprise."

"And our weapons were ineffective against it," Garm Antis replied.

"Yes, but you were at a fraction of your former strength," Setera said.

Garm Antis stepped away from her and rubbed his chin. His long tail wrapped around his middle and his fingers glided over the corded muscle while he pondered what Setera had said.

He turned on his heel and faced her. "How much firepower would it take to impact the shield?"

Setera's lips curved upward deliciously. "I'm afraid I just have more theories, but we only need to nudge the shield enough that it touches a planet. Then, it would constrict quicker and perhaps even fail altogether."

"Yes. Yes. A cascade of events that would force whoever is

behind the shield to lower it, which would allow our forces through," Garm Antis said.

"The longer the Humans wait, the worse it becomes for them. The advantage in this engagement is with us," Setera said.

"We only need a sampling of Humans in order to get the Mardoxian trait from their genetic code," Garm Antis said, giving voice to his thoughts. Throughout their quest for control of the Confederation, they'd sacrificed several species in their efforts to perfect their race.

The door to his office opened and another Xiiginn entered with all the authority of one who could go almost anywhere they chose. Runa Tane had been his most trusted ally for many years. He'd ensured that the Confederation ran smoothly while Garm Antis was away leading the assault on the Human star system.

"Thank you, Setera. That will be all for now. I want a formal proposal brought to me before the next congressional session," Garm Antis said.

Setera's eyes widened. A formal proposal for the Confederation would typically have taken a significant amount of time, and he was demanding that she do it over the span of mere days. Garm Antis watched her mercilessly as she struggled with the pressure he was putting on her.

"As you command," Setera replied and hastily retreated.

Runa Tane watched the young Xiiginn go almost wistfully and then turned toward Garm Antis.

"She's quite clever," Garm Antis said.

"Her analysis is rudimentary at best," Runa Tane said.

"The simplest explanation is often correct," Garm Antis said.

Runa Tane regarded him for a moment. "This is about Mar Arden."

"He's been useful in the past, but if he's been alive on the Human homeworld all this time, he could become a very grave threat," Garm Antis said.

Runa Tane narrowed his gaze. "Not enough to shift the balance of power."

"You're mistaken. If he somehow manages to extract the genetic code for the Mardoxian potential, he would become a very powerful rival. The factions would tear themselves apart for access to that knowledge. We must ensure that we control whatever he discovers," Garm Antis said.

"If he survived. Regardless, we'll need to assemble another fleet," Runa Tane replied.

Garm Antis smiled. "You're not thinking big enough."

Runa Tane frowned. "What do you mean? A fleet of Xiiginn warships is worth more than anything else in the Confederation."

"Except for the Confederation itself. To get the firepower we need, we'll have to assemble a grand armada," Garm Antis said.

"Such a thing hasn't happened since we took the Confederation away from the Boxans," Runa Tane said.

"Nothing less will succeed and will also mean the end of our old enemies. The Boxans will throw themselves at us when we bring our fleets back to the Human star system," Garm Antis said.

"A dangerous assumption," Runa Tane said.

"An accurate assumption. They deployed two Dreadnoughts to protect that star system. We can't assemble an armada in secret, and it won't take much for them to figure out where we'll send those ships first. After we have a firm hand over the Humans, the armada will act as our enforcement arm over the Confederation," Garm Antis said.

"Glory to the Xiiginn Empire," Runa Tane said.

"Call for an assembly of the Confederation," Garm Antis said. It would take some time to gather the ships he would need, but there were Confederation shipyards that had ships in production. He'd bring them all together to form the most formidable fighting force the Confederation had ever seen, and there would be nothing the Boxans could do about it. The foolish Boxans refused to fight any of the Confederation species other than the Xiiginns, even knowing how the Xiiginns controlled them.

"Our scouts have returned from Sethion. It appears the automated quarantine containment system has been disabled. A quick survey revealed that the system has been stripped of most raw materials," Runa Tane said.

"The system is worthless. That planet must be a lifeless rock by now. Sethion is the past. We don't need to concern ourselves with that anymore," Garm Antis replied.

"On that we can agree, but I do find it curious that the Boxans would return to their home system after all this time. We once thought there was another Tetronian key there," Runa Tane said.

"I've always thought we put too much value on the Star Shroud network. Access to it would enable us to find star systems with intelligent species to exploit, but it might be time for us to move on. The only Tetronian keys left are the ones the Boxans retained for themselves," Garm Antis said.

He'd hunted for the key to the Star Shroud network for years. The fact that the governing systems of the elusive network were located within the confines of the Confederation space station had been the source of irritation to all Xiiginn leaders since the uprising. Despite countless attempts to access the coveted Star Shroud system, they'd failed. The Boxan system was located in a highly shielded area of the space station. Access to it was now restricted. The last attempt to access it almost destroyed the tower, which was a parting gift from the Boxans. Sometimes Garm Antis thought they would have been better off without the Confederation space station. There were too many reminders of the Boxans there. They should have built something new that was made by Xiiginns entirely, but it was always a matter of resources. Why throw away a perfectly good space station? The Confederation space station was the size of a small moon and boasted an atmosphere all its own. The Boxans, for all their flaws, were highly capable builders. Perhaps after they conquered the rest of that species he'd keep a few million of them around to build something else for the Xiiginns to use.

CHAPTER FOUR

Mar Arden stood with his hands clasped behind his back, overlooking a dimly lit warehouse. The ground level was a maze of walkways among temporary work and prep areas. Over the past few months, he'd set up multiple bases of operations in select regions of the Human world that were no stranger to conflict. The largest landmass afforded him ease of movement, but it was access to the Mardoxian testing centers that he was most interested in.

The Humans were even more primitive than he'd initially thought. Some factions still fought among themselves almost as much as they fought each other. There was always a struggle between the more advanced groups, who either purposefully or inadvertently exploited the members of their species with lesser means. Mar Arden was quite familiar with the ruthless struggle for survival, even under the guise of civility, and these were tools he had used to make steady progress toward his goals.

Humanity, it seemed, was supremely obsessed with percep-
tion and hierarchy, which would make them much easier to
control since they already had the propensity to be followers.
Their religious factions spoke of tolerance, but their very teach-
ings condemned anyone who believed differently, which effec-
tively laid the groundwork for the subjugation of the Human
species. Give them the illusion that one faction was better than
the other and they would never get their fill of clamoring for
attention. Convince another faction of the righteousness of *their*
cause and they'd pull together in droves to sacrifice themselves.

The Human species was also just as prone to be chaotic in
their pursuits as they were to be orderly. This characteristic
alone caused Mar Arden to have trouble believing that the
Mardoxian potential existed in their pathetic species. He
supposed it was some accident of evolution, just as it had been
with the Boxans, who must be truly desperate if they were
allying themselves with these Humans.

The Humans weren't all primitive, and the Boxans had
recently given Humans such a technological advantage that he
thought they might destroy themselves even without his help.
The Xiiginns were no strangers to sharing technological
advances with more primitive species when it served their
purpose. More often than not, if those species weren't kept
under strict control, this sharing meant their demise. It'd been
so with the Qegi, whom the Xiiginns were only interested in for
their hyper-production capabilities, which they took from the
Qegi and used to produce Xiiginn fleets.

Mar Arden was roused from his reflection by several
pathetic groans of absolution from their latest test subjects. The
Humans were a vocal race, which was why he'd ordered them

gagged. Everything Humans did involved them making some kind of noise, crying out their cringe-worthy opinions as if they were entitled to be heard just because they had a voice.

There were several dimly glowing work areas where his soldiers attempted to bring forth the Mardoxian traits in their Human test subjects. Mar Arden's gaze scanned toward the interior of the warehouse and over the poorly lit lines that illuminated the paths among the work areas. Xiiginns didn't need a lot of light in order to see, which seemed to frighten the Humans they'd recruited. The Humans' fear of the dark was one of the first things Mar Arden had used to his advantage.

Hoan Berend climbed up the stairs to the loft and plodded over to him.

"Any progress with the latest batch?" Mar Arden asked.

Hoan Berend glanced out at the warehouse with disdain. "Given the equipment we're using, I'm surprised we can detect any of the genetic markers at all."

Mar Arden grimaced. They'd had to leave a lot of their equipment in the great expanse, forcing them to make use of what the Humans had on hand. "The genes will only express themselves under duress, at least with this latest batch of potentials."

"I was hoping to get a better batch of test subjects from the recruitment centers here, but the Earth Coalition Force beat us to them. They've been getting dangerously near our other facilities. I think they may be closer to finding us than we suspect," Hoan Berend said.

"That is to be expected. The ECF is using Boxan equipment and protocols to hunt us down. We're in a race with them, and while we may have to make some sacrifices, they'll never really catch us, especially not after we implement the next part of our plan that Kandra Rene is working on," Mar Arden said.

Hoan Berend turned away from the amber glow of the dark warehouse and looked at Mar Arden. "Kandra Rene has amassed quite a few followers, but she's still not sure why her abilities only work on some Humans and not others." Hoan Berend stopped speaking and seemed to be considering something. "The number of followers she has is worrisome. I know it's the Xiiginns' way, but there are some of us who just want to return to the Confederation."

Mar Arden unclasped his hands and brought them to his sides. "Kandra Rene does have ambition, which is why I keep her around. She's driven and quite capable, and if I put myself in a position where she could take command of this mission, she would've earned it. However, I will not be giving her any such opportunity. I have my own group of followers, so we needn't worry about her. Should she get some ambitious idea in her head, we'll just need to correct her."

There was a sudden loud scream from one of the test subjects that was abruptly cut off. The recent group of Human test subjects they'd brought in certainly didn't last very long and didn't yield very much in the way of data. Hoan Berend was right—they needed better equipment, and Mar Arden said so.

"There are some ECF facilities where they're producing Boxan technology for the fleet they're building. We could appropriate some of those, but it would require careful planning . . ." Hoan Berend said, trailing off.

Mar Arden smirked, and Hoan Berend shook his head.

"I see you already have something in mind, so rather than having me blather on about something you've already considered, why don't you just tell me what you're thinking and I'll try to help make it happen," Hoan Berend said.

The warship commander had certainly learned his place, and if there was one thing Mar Arden preferred it was efficiency. "We need to keep the Humans off balance. The ECF is very much aware that some of us made it to Earth, but they're also preoccupied with the threat beyond the shield. The intelligence I've come across is that the shield poses a danger to the star system—information that was extremely hard to come by because the ECF has employed some of the Boxan communication protocols that are difficult to crack.

"I haven't risked missions that would put us in direct conflict with the ECF for a reason. In essence, the ramp-up of technology serves our purposes just as much as it does theirs. However, I have multiple plans in motion that will keep humanity occupied while we get some of the equipment we need to speed along our efforts. This includes recruiting some of their own scientists at these ECF facilities," Mar Arden said and noted the look of surprise on Hoan Berend's face. "The ECF has the potential to become a formidable adversary, but like most of these organizations, they're vulnerable to strife from within. Wouldn't you agree?"

Hoan Berend nodded. "I do, and I should've seen it before. Why should we do all the heavy lifting when we can have the ECF and the various other governments of this planet do the heavy lifting for us?"

"That doesn't mean I don't appreciate all the effort you put into gathering these test subjects. We're close. We've never been this close to acquiring the genetic traits of the Mardoxian potential, and once we get them . . . Well, let's just say that you and I will be part of a major power shift in the Confederation. I'll need strong leaders at my side," Mar Arden said.

"I guess I should appreciate that you're considering keeping me around for your future plans. To be perfectly honest with you, I think you're more formidable than Garm Antis ever was. And if there's one thing you can always count on, it's that the Xiiginns will flock to the winning side," Hoan Berend said.

CHAPTER FIVE

E dward Johnson rubbed what little hair he had left on the back of his head and then ran his hand along his fore-head, which was grimly lined by the pressure he'd been under for the past few years. If not for his commitment to Dux Corp's mission to save the Human race, he doubted he would even still be alive.

When he'd first taken up the mantle of the late great Bruce Matherson's multinational company, he'd been tasked with guiding specific scientific developments across the globe. He'd run the company for the past twenty years, but right now he felt that if he survived the next twenty days he'd be truly fortunate. Somehow the Xiiginns had figured out who he was and had been hunting him for several months. While the last few attempts on his life hadn't been as public as the display at the United Nations in New York City, their attempts were constant reminders that the Xiiginns were still out there. His security detail now rivaled most heads of state's.

He glanced at the smooth concrete floor and stark gray walls that surrounded him, experiencing an almost physical longing for his offices in Washington DC. Outside this remote Dux Corp facility were the Blue Ridge Mountains of North Carolina. The facility was tucked away in a highly defensible position, whether from approach by land or air.

Although the Boxans had gone to great lengths to spread the technological advancements they'd provided to all member states of the Earth Coalition Force, Ed had made sure that those advancements were closely monitored, and this facility had greatly benefited from that technology. A short distance from the main complex were rail guns that were capable of hitting targets in the lower atmosphere, carrying enough stopping power to penetrate even the hulls of Boxan ships. There were multiple automated systems, all tasked with keeping the facility secure, which included an underground bunker leading to several small landing pads that were well hidden. New falcon shuttles that could bring him to the ECF base on the moon were waiting on standby.

"Newsfeed," Ed said, and the nearest wallscreen came on.

Ed's position afforded him a wealth of information about the goings-on across the world, but sometimes he'd watch the local newsfeed to get a glimpse of what the average, everyday person saw in this little part of the world. Even though their intel was limited, the global segment of the local newsfeed did note various attacks from multiple terrorist organizations. Those organizations had been able to substantially increase their reach during these past few months, which indicated that they'd had significant help from outside their organization.

The newsfeed switched to a journalist standing amidst a

group of refugees fleeing from active conflict zones. None of the locations were anywhere near the ECF facilities spread across the globe, and Ed knew that wasn't accidental. The Xiiginns needed those facilities just as much as the ECF did.

Ed glanced at the security feed on a smaller wallscreen and saw Iris Barrett walking toward his door. He could already hear the cadence of her Louboutin heels striking the floor with a clipped tempo. After the surprise attack from Boxans under the Xiiginn influence, Iris had had her combat implants augmented. At the time, she hadn't carried weapons that were capable of stopping Boxans in their power armor, and Ed remembered watching her struggle against the Boxan who was trying to kill him. The Boxan's flaxen eyes had been devoid of life until they focused on him with unmitigated hatred, and Ed's hands shook at the memory of it. It was one thing knowing about a threat that could kill him but was quite another experiencing it firsthand. Ed was no stranger to conflict. One couldn't function in the shadow world without the occasional show of force.

Iris Barrett walked into his office carrying a tablet computer. She took a quick glance at him, and Ed knew that her neural implants had already assessed the state he was in.

"I'm surprised you're still awake, sir," Iris said.

Ed chuckled tiredly and engaged his chair's massage function. He leaned back and the chair became warm while small, hardened spheres circulated along their tracks. Ed let out a soft groan as the little massagers smoothed out the tense muscles in his back and shoulders. "It's quiet today. What have you got?"

"We've had status reports from multiple field operations, and they've marked a number of facilities in Eastern Europe as the most likely locations for Xiiginn operations bases. They move around quite a bit so they're hard to nail down. A typical terrorist organization maintains a strong presence in certain parts of the world even if they're trying to launch operations across the globe. By comparison, the Xiiginns seem to be pretty good at covering their tracks. If they suspect that we're onto them, they simply disappear. They might leave a few bodies behind, but it's like they're ghosts."

The massager finished its cycle and Ed sat up straight.

Iris continued. "Security remains tight at all ECF production facilities or any companies that are producing equipment for the ECF. There hasn't been so much as a sniff in their direction, which the intelligence agencies find perplexing."

Ed glanced at the newsfeed still playing on his wallscreen and glided his fingers over the stubble of his beard. He needed to shave. Hell, he needed a long, hot shower. "Still nothing of the Xiiginns in the United States?"

"Both the US and Canadian governments are on high alert, but there's been no indication of Xiiginn activity in either of those places. They *could* have a presence where we have more of a blind eye—places like Mexico and parts of South America. The Xiiginns could be there and we'd never know it," Iris said while she tapped through a few screens on her tablet.

"It wouldn't do them much good to do anything down there. We know what they want. They're after candidates who may have the Mardoxian potential. Our testing facilities have augmented security measures taken directly from the Boxans. I think they're basing their operations in Eastern Europe because of its proximity to where the Russian viewer program was located. I saw a report from the ECF that says the Xiiginns might be using small, mobile labs that are difficult to track," Ed said.

"We've been coordinating and providing intelligence to law enforcement agencies, but I'm not sure it's going to be enough. Colonel Kyle Matthew's debrief indicates that there was only a small number of Xiiginns on the ship where he was captured— perhaps fifty or so," Iris said.

Ed leaned back in his chair and blew out a breath. "I know, Iris. We're looking for the proverbial needle in a haystack. It's not supposed to be easy, but there has to be more we can do. We can't just be reactive to the Xiiginn threat."

"We could always use live bait," Iris offered, giving him a meaningful look.

"If only it were that easy. Their last attempt was a group of randomly selected people, which was more of a message from the Xiiginns than a true attempt on my life," Ed replied.

"Well, if it's all the same to you, we'll keep the security detail around just in case one of them gets lucky," Iris said.

Ed arched one eyebrow at her. "No one gets lucky with you around. I'm sure I'll live to a ripe old age and you'll be bored."

"Considering the alternative, I like being bored. But seriously, Ed, we can't afford to be complacent with our security posture," Iris said, giving him a stern look.

The newsfeed showed various protests going on around the country and around the world. Ed watched as the wars of ideals unfolded in tiny increments on the wallscreen. He never underestimated peoples' willingness to disagree about almost anything. He had rooms full of tech folk in charge of limiting the dissemination of misinformation, which carried its own ethical gray areas. No one liked the idea of censorship, but there was a need for censorship regarding some things. The ethical issues came from the question of who would control censorship. This ongoing struggle prompted intelligent and highly capable people like Zack Quick to uncover and expose sensitive information.

Ed had been surprised to learn that Zack had appeared on Dux Corp's recruitment radar since his time in graduate school and even before his association with Kaylan. His whereabouts had been spotty at best until he'd found the confidential photographs of Pluto that showed the Boxan monitoring station. Zack had inadvertently put them on the path that led them to where they were today, moving up Dux Corp's timeline to investigate Pluto by at least ten years.

The nations of Earth needed to unite. The ECF had to succeed in order for humanity to survive. It just took a lot of convincing for people to accept that. There were groups of people who worshiped the Boxans as if they were some kind of gods while other groups argued for inviting the Xiiginns to the negotiating table. Those idiots seemed to forget it was the Xiiginns who were flinging moon-sized asteroids at the earth not so long ago.

Iris cleared her throat to get his attention. "I've come across a project called Phoenix, but I haven't been able to find much information about it. I only came across it because my own correlation engine flagged that project. There's a significant amount of smaller transactions stemming from other ventures going into Phoenix. Is this one of your pet projects?"

Ed had taken steps to ensure that Bruce Matherson's legacy would continue on in the event that Ed met an untimely demise.

"Phoenix is a legitimate project," Ed replied while keeping his gaze on the wallscreen.

Iris wasn't fooled and made an "uh-huh" noise. "That's all you're going to share with me? I need to be able to look after your affairs, and I'm not able to do that unless I know all the pieces currently in play."

Ed tore his eyes away from the wallscreen to look at Iris. "What do you think this place is going to look like in twenty years?"

Iris frowned a bit, surprised by the question. "Assuming we're still around in twenty years without any major catastrophes? I tend to prefer a more optimistic viewpoint when it comes to the future. I firmly believe we're going to kick the crap out of the Xiiginns, and we'll get through this crisis and the one that inevitably follows. You see, Ed, I think there's always going to be something out there that will affect us here. It doesn't change what we're going to be doing, but we do need to be aware of it and continue to play the long game. That's why I'm here. So in twenty years, things may appear to be different, but I expect they will be just the same."

"That's why I hired you. You're tough when it's needed, but you don't lose sight of the bigger picture. Whatever future it has, Dux Corp will need people like you," Ed replied.

Iris narrowed her gaze. "Why do I feel like I'm standing at somebody's deathbed? Is there something you're not telling me? Do you have some horrible disease for which there's no cure?"

Ed smiled. "Come on, Iris, a deadly disease would be too easy. But back to the point—I think your idea of luring the Xiiginns to us has merit. We should explore and develop that idea. We need a reason for them to go where we want them to go. I don't think they'll ever hit any of the sites that are associated with the ECF because at some point they're going to need a way off this rock, and I aim to stand in their way."

"And I'll do whatever I can to make sure that happens, but you never answered my question. What is project Phoenix?" Iris asked.

Ed should've known he couldn't throw her off the trail. "Close newsfeed," Ed said, and the wallscreen flickered off. He turned toward Iris. "You're no stranger to what we do here. Project Phoenix is one of many projects that serve as contingencies depending on whether certain events happen. To be as transparent as I can, you're a soldier—an army of one and highly intelligent, but you're a major piece of this organization. I give you enough information that you can do your job. You're a trusted confidant, but there are some things I can't have you knowing about until the proper time. Frankly, I'm surprised you didn't ask about any of the other projects—like Gatekeeper and Clean Sweep. I could go on, but I won't."

Iris squared her shoulders and met Ed's gaze. "Understood. All I need to know is that you're aware of the project. My other task is to make sure you remain at peak performance, even at your age. That couch over there folds out into a bed if you don't want to return to your quarters. I suggest you get a few hours' sleep, or at least try to. We have a meeting with General Sheridan in a few hours and you need to be bright-eyed and bushy-tailed."

Ed snorted. "All right, get out of here and let this old man get some sleep," he said and walked over to the couch. "Oh, and Iris, I know you won't be far, but just remember that you'll get your chance at the Xiiginns personally. I have no doubt."

"I hope so, sir. I would very much like to meet one in person and ram one of my heels through its alien throat," Iris said as she left his office.

Ed had little doubt that she would, too, and he very much wanted to be there to watch her do it. He swung his legs over the side of the couch and settled back onto the plush cushions, making a mental note to move some of his secret projects around. Iris had higher clearance than most, but he'd either been getting sloppy in his old age or he'd trained her too well.

CHAPTER SIX

The battleship-carrier *Lincoln* was on its final approach to a lunar synchronous orbit. As the Earth Coalition Force's first ship of the wall, it had just finished its initial shakedown cruise. Colonel Kyle Matthews was the commanding officer of the two thousand crewmembers serving aboard the *Lincoln,* as well as the one hundred Boxans who were aboard in an advisory capacity.

Kyle sat on the command couch, looking over the recent performance reports from their latest combat drills. He glanced at Scraanyx and noted that the Boxan was looking at the same report on his own terminal.

"We can do better than this," Kyle said.

The ECF was scrambling to build warships, and the *Lincoln* was the first battleship-carrier completed at the manufacturing facility on the new moon. He vaguely recalled giving a presentation to Lunar Base personnel about how they were going to slowly ramp up their manufacturing capabilities—first building strike-fighters and then frigates, working their way up to destroyers and battleship-carriers. Priorities had shifted, however, once they learned that the Xiiginns were on Earth and that the Star Shroud shield was shrinking.

Scraanyx finished reading the report. "This is just a shake-down cruise meant to expose problem systems. It comes as little surprise to me that the crew needs time to master their jobs."

"That's one way to put it. If we had to engage the Xiiginns today, I'm afraid we wouldn't put up much of a fight. In fact, the only thing we did really well was the strike-fighter deployments, which, incidentally, is the thing we've had the most practice with," Kyle said and started to imagine General Sheridan relieving him of his command. Kyle had never been fired from any job in his life, but after looking at these reports, he might just fire himself. He could already hear the arguments from the Navy about how *they* were better suited to command Earth's first space fleet, but the ECF was very much an Army operation.

Kyle had tasked the ECF crew on the bridge and throughout the ship with reviewing performance reports for their specific areas. They needed to run a tighter ship, but at the same time, they were still learning their jobs. Space warfare was new to them, and not all the tactics of the various militaries throughout the globe would help them much up there.

"I think you're underestimating what you've achieved even with our help," Scraanyx said.

"We need to be able to hit the ground running, and right now we can barely get our feet under us, let alone run. I reviewed the performance logs from the rest of the battle group, and there are consistent failures on the other ships, too," Kyle said.

Scraanyx stood up and looked at the ECF crew serving on

the bridge. The ECF had accounted for Boxans in their design of the ships for most areas, which included the bridge. It wouldn't be much of an alliance if their allies had to stoop almost in half to move around the ship. Scraanyx was over ten feet tall, and his brown, roughened skin was covered by a Boxan uniform.

"I have feedback from the strike force serving aboard the ship, but before I give that to you I'd like to know what you plan to do," Scraanyx said.

Kyle was used to this by now. It wouldn't help the ECF if the Boxans just told them what they needed to do. ECF officers needed to learn to stand on their own two feet.

"I'll have my officers write up their own evaluations addressing how they plan to improve performance. We'll review them and set clearly defined goals. Then, we'll keep running drills until the crews can perform them in their sleep. I won't go before General Sheridan without a plan to address the performance of this shakedown cruise," Kyle said.

"Your battle leader knows what it is to command, and he wouldn't have put you in charge if he wasn't convinced of your capabilities," Scraanyx said.

Kyle snorted. "The frustration is the learning part."

Kyle wasn't foolish enough to believe they could build a ship like this, take it out, and suddenly be a fighting force capable of taking on an alien species that had been doing the same thing for hundreds of years. Construction of the *Lincoln* had only finished about a month ago, and there were still dozens of systems that required attention, but the fact that the ship flew at all was a monumental accomplishment.

Not everything had failed to live up to expectations. The weapons systems did work, and they'd successfully hit the random asteroids marked for target practice. Their biggest struggle was with emergency responses—what to do when systems went off-line. The Boxans had installed multiple combat scenarios from their own training regimen into the *Lincoln's* computer system, but the ECF crew was still green, and Kyle was anxious for them to be proficient at their jobs.

Kyle left his XO, Lieutenant Colonel Anna Kelly, in charge while he and Scraanyx returned to Armstrong Base on the moon. They took a Falcon class III combat shuttle and soon arrived at the ECF landing pad at Armstrong where the indicator lights showed green for a cleared dock. Kyle and Scraanyx left the shuttle and headed to General Sheridan's office, which was located near the command center. General Sheridan divided his time between Armstrong Base and the main facility on Earth.

They entered the outer office, where an ECF private told them to go on inside, and Kyle noticed that the soldier barely looked twice at Scraanyx. Boxans had restricted themselves to either the lunar bases or serving aboard ships. After the incident several months ago that involved Boxans under the Xiiginn influence, they had all but removed themselves from Earth, but Kyle didn't know how long the Boxans could keep that up. They built resonance chambers on the lunar base that were more of a botanical garden in space. Scraanyx and the other Boxans insisted that this helped them cope with long deployments like this one. Those resonance chambers were quite peaceful but paled in comparison with standing on an actual planet. Kyle had brought this up to Scraanyx, who simply replied that the Boxans would endure. Kyle didn't like it. They didn't know how long the Boxans would be here, but he'd let the matter go for the time being.

Kyle entered General Sheridan's office first and stood at attention. Scraanyx stood next to him and brought his large fist across his heart, giving Sheridan the Boxan salute.

"At ease," General Sheridan said from behind his desk and gestured for them to sit down. "I was just looking over your reports. I'm not gonna beat around the bush. You know as well as I do that there's a lot that needs to be addressed here, but I'm not going to dress you down about it. Among all the personnel on this base, you know exactly what's at stake. You know what the Xiiginns are capable of since you're one of only four people who've actually been in the presence of a Xiiginn. How long do you think it will take to get your troops ready for combat?"

"I'd like to have a year or two of running through the Boxan training program for space warfare, but that's not realistic. I think if I could get six months of solid training, that would help, but if you're looking for a minimum timeframe, I'd say at least three months. Even then, we won't know how we'll do against a Xiiginn warship until we actually meet one face-to-face," Kyle said.

"Yours is the first multinational team. How's that going?" General Sheridan asked.

"They are still learning to work together, but militaries have a higher tolerance for working with people of different ethnic backgrounds than civilians do. There are still some prejudices, but given that there's a common enemy, there haven't been any problems stemming from those multinational prejudices. The crews know what's at stake, General," Kyle said.

General Sheridan swung his gaze toward Scraanyx. "I'd like to hear your opinion."

"I can offer you a military perspective, but the issues you're dealing with may be better addressed by one of our scientists,"

Scraanyx replied, and General Sheridan waited for him to continue. "We understand that there's been an enormous strain put on your species. It will take time for humanity to acclimate to all the changes being thrust upon their shoulders. Having said that, I will say that the Human race is highly adaptable and this is a strength that will serve them well in the future.

"There are reasons we don't share advanced technology with species such as yours. Many of those reasons have to do with the fact that a species in your stage of development simply isn't ready for the technological advancements we have available. The fact that we find ourselves in a position where it has become a necessity is a failure on our part and is a cause for shame. That's how most Boxans will view our actions here."

General Sheridan looked at Scraanyx, considering. "The circumstances surrounding the meeting of our species weren't ideal. We can all agree on that, but if we spend all our time looking behind us at the road that led us here, how can we move on? I've been in the military my whole life. I've fought in wars, and my world has been about achieving objectives with the tools I have on hand. Sadly, I've commanded soldiers to their deaths in the past, but now we need to defend ourselves from a new threat. This will challenge us, and we'll only survive if we're up to the task. Our potential survival will be due in large part to you and the other Boxans. You're giving us tools and sharing your wisdom, but what we do with that is entirely up to us. I hope you can convey that to the other Boxans. Tell them that their trust in us isn't misplaced."

Scraanyx bowed his head. "Before our arrival, your species was in the earliest stages of forming a global society. But there are many factions and each is afraid of being lost to the whole.

This type of fear can sometimes spawn destructive tendencies and can take many cycles to work out."

"You mean the enemy within?" Kyle asked.

"That's a good description, but there are many of your species whose belief systems are *designed* to be at odds with each other. We recognize that these systems have been in place for thousands of cycles and were necessary for survival, but those practices must change if humanity is to reach its full potential," Scraanyx said.

General Sheridan nodded. "Chazen has spoken to me at length about this. There are no easy solutions, and you're right —our differences are something we'll have to work through. But all we need to worry about right now is what we *can* influence. We have the support of many nations, which has allowed us to accelerate our timeline for building our fleet and orbital defense platforms—"

A comms channel opened from the command center and appeared on the wallscreen.

"General Sheridan, we need you at the command center," the communications officer said.

Sheridan stood up. "I'm on my way."

Kyle walked next to Sheridan while Scraanyx followed behind them as they entered the command center. There was heightened activity, and Sheridan led them over to the command area. The main wallscreen showed Europe and Asia.

"Sitrep," General Sheridan said.

"General, there have been multiple nuclear detonations reported. We're confirming those detonations right now," Major Bailey said.

Kyle's eyes widened as he saw that there'd been three detonations—one in Germany, one in the Ukraine, and one in Mumbai.

"Were there any missile launches detected?" General Sheridan asked.

Major Bailey shook his head. "None, General. We think they were detonated locally."

"Okay, we need to get the major nations on the horn and give them our report. We have better equipment than they do down there. Time is of the essence. We don't want this to be a prelude to nuclear war," General Sheridan said.

Kyle kept watching the screen for a new blip to appear in the United States. He focused in on Colorado where his family lived, but the blip never came. He blew out a breath, relieved, but it would look suspicious to the rest of the world.

Kyle stepped closer to General Sheridan. "General, I think we should put the orbital defense platforms on high alert in case any country launches an ICBM. We can shoot them out of the sky if we need to."

General Sheridan gave him a long look. The ECF wasn't authorized to interfere in national conflicts. After a few moments, Sheridan agreed and gave the order. Kyle hoped it wouldn't come to that, but they couldn't afford to have a global nuclear war right then.

The orbital defense platforms were meant to protect the earth from an outside threat, but some of the countries that hadn't supported the ECF had raised concerns that the defense system could also be used against the nations of Earth. This situation was dangerously close to that scenario and getting out of control very quickly, but they didn't have a choice. If any country launched an ICBM, those missiles would be shot out of the sky.

CHAPTER SEVEN

Kaylan walked with Emma and Brenda on one of the outside paths near the Nershal complex, and Hicks met them along the way. The Nershals hadn't built a capital for Selebus, but their complex was part of the most densely populated area on the forest moon.

"No Zack today?" Hicks asked.

"He's in the lab. Efren is with him," Kaylan answered.

Hicks snorted. "All work and no play makes Zack a dull boy."

"He certainly does throw himself at a problem," Emma added.

"He's always been like that. Once he latches on to something, he'll stay with it until it's done," Kaylan replied.

"I can appreciate that kind of tenacity, but everyone can use a break from time to time," Hicks said and gave Kaylan a sidelong glance. "It would probably be better if it came from you."

"Is that two jabs for the price of one, Major? A little one-two?" Kaylan said and mimed jabbing her fists in a one-two motion as Hicks grinned. "He wants to go home, just like the rest of us."

Hicks nodded. "Kladomaor told me that the Gresans and a race called the Napox have arrived on Selebus. Do you have any idea what to expect?"

"The Gresans are a council race in the Confederation, but the representatives here are from a group that isn't in power. I don't know anything about the Napox," Kaylan said.

They continued walking along the path toward the main building where they would be meeting the two new species. Kaylan could remember a time when the mere thought of this would have caused a fair amount of anxiety.

"The Gresans are supposed to have a powerful fleet—not enough to take on the Xiiginns alone but supposedly enough to help the Alliance. When I asked Kladomaor about the Napox, he just said they're very good at what they do," Hicks said.

"What do they do?" Emma asked.

Kaylan knew Emma wouldn't miss an opportunity to meet a new alien species.

"He said they excelled at causing sabotage," Hicks said.

"Oh. Are there any other species coming?" Emma asked.

It had only been a few days since Ma'jasalax had encouraged the Nershals to communicate with other species that would be amicable to joining the Star Alliance.

"They were the first to respond. Hopefully, they won't be the last, and I think it's interesting that they want to meet face-to-face," Kaylan said.

"Why is that?" Hicks asked.

"Meeting face-to-face isn't always convenient, but I wonder if they're here because of the Boxans," Kaylan said.

Emma frowned. "You might be right. There could be more going on here. They might have come to evaluate the Alliance."

"I don't know whether they're aware of our existence or not. I don't think the Nershals would've shared that, so they may be surprised to see us," Kaylan replied.

They went inside the building and were met by Ma'jasalax and Valkra. Ma'jasalax confirmed Kaylan's assumption that the Gresans and the Napox had no idea about Humans. She also warned them not to be too unsettled by their appearance. Kaylan tried to clear her mind of any preconceived notions of what to expect beyond the doors to the meeting room.

The Nershals preferred to stand at their formal meetings. According to Etanu, this prevented meetings from going on longer than they truly needed to. As such, it was expected that if you were to participate in the meeting, you would be standing on the designated platforms. Off to the side there were benches that they could use to take their ease if needed.

They entered the main meeting room onto a wide-open landing that circled around the main meeting area. Several staircases led downward, which reminded Kaylan more of a stage than any formal congressional-type meeting place. The hall, if it could be called that, was filled with Nershals and Boxans. Overhead was a massive circular skylight that allowed natural sunlight to enter the room, and Kaylan wondered if any of the Nershals would enter that way as well. She peered down to the central meeting area and stopped in her tracks.

"Is that a Gresan?" Emma asked.

"Yes," Ma'jasalax confirmed.

It was a good thing Zack hadn't come with them because she was quite certain that once he saw an actual Gresan he might've run away, screaming. Kaylan's neural implants enhanced her vision, and she took a closer look at the Gresans. They had thick, hairy bodies with two appendages in the front that seemed to function as arms. They stood on four legs and were similar to what she expected a spider would look like if it were five feet tall. The Gresans had four dark eyes, and one of them looked up at them.

"I think I'll stay up here and watch," Brenda said.

"Oh come on, it's not going to eat us," Emma admonished.

"It looks like it has armor plating on its back," Hicks said.

The plating was octagonal in shape and each piece was part of an intricate pattern.

"Not plating. They look like scales that have ossified," Emma said, and Hicks shook his head in confusion. "They grow them. We've seen them on reptiles. I bet the Gresans have a very interesting lineage. Fascinating."

Brenda held up her hand and cocked her head to the side. She was already moving away from them. "Nope, I know when I've hit my limits. I'll stay right here."

While Kaylan had never been a particular fan of spiders, she couldn't exactly stay up there with Brenda.

There was a group of Gresans gathered on the far side of the floor. The entire group suddenly turned toward them as Kaylan and the others followed Ma'jasalax down the staircase.

Hicks leaned in so only Kaylan could hear him. "I know we're supposed to be tolerant, but that thing gives me the creeps, too."

Kaylan agreed with him but she wouldn't say so. "Imagine what they think of us."

"They look like they might want to eat us," Hicks said quietly.

As they closed in on the central meeting area, they

noticed another group standing to the side. They were brown, fuzzy creatures who were about three feet in height, completely covered with fur, and their facial features reminded Kaylan of a hamster. The hamster-looking species had horns protruding from each side of their heads that rounded in on themselves, resembling a ram. They had small, dark eyes that watched them with keen intelligence. Their movements were quick, and Kaylan was willing to bet they spoke even quicker.

Hicks stayed by her side, and Emma remained behind her as she approached the central meeting area. Kaylan noticed that Kladomaor, along with several of his soldiers, had positioned himself between the Humans and the Gresans.

As governor of Selebus, Udonzari would be overseeing the meeting. He gestured toward one of the Gresans, whose scale and hair patterns were quite a bit more complex than those of the others with him.

"Battle Commander Solek of the Gresan Army and Aenok of the Napox, I would like to introduce to you Kaylan Farrow of the Human species," Udonzari said and introduced the others.

There was the barest acknowledgment from the Gresans, and the Napox seemed to acknowledge this new information by cocking their heads to the side. Kaylan assumed this was their way of nodding an acknowledgment.

Councilor Essaforn and Ambassador Dulrad joined them and thanked the Gresan and Napox representatives for joining them.

"The reason we invited you to this meeting was to discuss the Xiiginn control of the Confederation," Udonzari said.

Solek shifted all his feet so he could look at the Boxans. There was a chattering noise, and it took Kaylan's translator a few moments to catch up. The Gresan was speaking about the Boxan war with the Xiiginns.

"You want us to fight our own species so you can achieve vengeance against the Xiiginns," Solek said.

"We're not interested in vengeance. We want to stop the Xiiginns from controlling the Confederation," Ambassador Dulrad said.

Solek and the other Gresans all chittered at once, and the sound echoed around the large room despite its many occupants.

"You're right," Kladomaor bellowed. "The Xiiginns have taken much from us and we do want retribution for that, but the preservation of the other species of the Confederation is at the heart of our war with them. After all these cycles you must have finally realized that the Xiiginns can control your leaders."

"We would not accept you back into the Confederation," Solek said.

Kladomaor didn't respond but instead looked at Ambassador Dulrad.

"We would, of course, accept the decision of the Confederation after the Xiiginns were removed from power," Ambassador Dulrad said.

"Why should we trust you? The Xiiginns may be ruthless, but they didn't lie to us," Solek said.

"That's not true," Kaylan said, drawing everyone's gaze toward her. "The Xiiginns lied to everyone. Did you know they were controlling your heads of state with their compulsion ability? Or did you only just suspect it after the Boxans were ousted from the Confederation?"

Solek's black eyes all focused on Kaylan, and it made her more than a little uncomfortable.

"She speaks the truth," Ma'jasalax said.

Kaylan noticed that the others on the platform seemed to immediately calm down when Ma'jasalax spoke. They were aware that she was a Mardoxian priestess.

"We respect the words of the Mardoxian," Solek said.

"Then you should respect Kaylan's words since she is Mardoxian Blessed," Ma'jasalax said.

Solek's harsh gaze swung toward her again and Kaylan forced herself to meet it. The Gresan then turned toward Udonzari. "What is it that you would have us do?"

"We've formed an alliance with the Boxans and the Humans. We want you to join our alliance against the Xiiginns. They've become too powerful," Udonzari said.

A text message from Athena appeared on Kaylan's internal heads-up display.

::*Commander, there's an incoming transmission from the Gresan ship.*::

Kaylan glanced at Solek and noticed that some of the Gresans were chattering among themselves.

::*Are you able to translate it?*:: Kaylan asked.

A few moments later the translation appeared on Kaylan's display. Kaylan stifled a gasp as she read it. Ma'jasalax glanced at her.

"Is there something you'd like to add?" Udonzari said to her.

"The Confederation is assembling an armada to liberate Earth from the Boxans. They're going to attack Earth," Kaylan said.

Udonzari's gaze widened. "How could you know this?"

"The Gresans received the communication from their ship just now," Kaylan said, then immediately wished she hadn't.

"You spy on us. Is that what this alliance is supposed to be? How did you intercept our communication? Have you infiltrated our ship systems?" Solek demanded. "I will learn the truth."

Multiple species started speaking up at once, and Kaylan felt her cheeks redden. It took several minutes for the Gresans and the Napox to calm down, but eventually Udonzari was able to restore order.

"Ambassador," Ma'jasalax said to Dulrad, "I think Solek is right and we need to be honest with everyone here if we expect this alliance to move forward."

"I don't have clearance to share what you're asking me to share," Ambassador Dulrad replied.

Ma'jasalax considered this for a moment. "Then please extend my apologies to the High Council, Ambassador."

Ma'jasalax went on to explain how the Humans had come to be part of the Alliance. She even included information about the Drar and how the Boxans had been searching for them. Solek was keen to learn how a primitive species like the Humans were able to intercept their communications and decipher them. This led to the disclosure that the *Athena* had been enhanced with Drar technology, and that new information brought Kaylan and the others under further scrutiny by the other species. They asked many questions about the *Athena* until Kladomaor strongly suggested that they move on since the *Athena's* capabilities had no bearing on whether they would join the Alliance.

After the meeting, they went outside. Kaylan glanced at Hicks. "I really screwed this up, didn't I?"

Hicks glanced at the others for a moment before looking at Kaylan. "There's a lot of history here that feeds all of these prejudices, but yeah, you've just painted a huge target on the *Athena*."

Kaylan shook her head. She knew better than to blurt stuff out, but she couldn't afford to dwell on it for long. The Xiiginns were assembling an armada, and they had to find a way to warn Earth. Even if this alliance stuck together, what could they do against the massive fleet the Confederation was assembling?

CHAPTER EIGHT

Zack and Efren were working in a Nershal laboratory on one of the upper levels that had access to the outside. Zack had only been to the lower levels one time since coming back to Selebus. He still remembered the genetic experiments the Xiiginns had been performing on the Nershals, and he didn't think that would be something he'd ever forget. If that wasn't bad enough, senior members of the Nershal government had been aware the experiments were taking place. That discovery led to a brief but bloody civil war as a new political party came into power.

The memory of the horrible conditions the Xiiginns had kept the Nershals in during their experimentations filled his mind with dark, hateful thoughts. In the past, he'd been a prisoner of the Xiiginns, forced to endure their brutal treatment in a pit on Selebus. Sometimes he still woke from nightmares about it. He clenched his teeth, and if anyone had been able to see his face right then, they'd have seen that he was glaring at the empty space in front of him. Zack wasn't foolish enough to expect the world they lived in to be fair, but would the universe really care if the Xiiginns were all gone? On second thought, he realized that by that logic the universe wouldn't care if Humans were gone either, so they would need to forge their own path.

"What test iteration is this?" Efren asked, his voice coming from the intercom near the door to the observation room.

Zack let his dark thoughts go and set his mind to the task at hand, turning toward a large metallic spool that was two feet long. The spool was a small replica of an actual Star Shroud device. He'd just set it down on a pedestal in the center of the test room.

"I've lost count," Zack answered. "Does it really matter?"

"Of course it matters. What if something different happened with this test and we didn't know what iteration it was?" Efren answered.

"This test iteration is number two three four seven – PVR zero zero one," Athena said.

Zack walked to the observation room and shut the door to the testing area. He looked over at Efren's bewildered expression. "What?"

"What does PVR mean?"

"Post virtual review. I ran a number of tests before I ran out of materials, and Athena suggested that we create a test bed in a virtual sandbox before we acquire more materials," Zack replied.

"Yeah, but you've tested shutting down the Star Shroud shield over twenty-three hundred times?"

Zack shook his head. "No, I found out how *not* to shut down the Star Shroud shield over twenty-three hundred times. It only has to work one time." He added that last bit with more than a little exasperation.

"I'm not criticizing. I'm just surprised it's taken so long. I'd have thought the process would be much simpler," Efren said.

Zack checked his tablet computer to be sure he had the updated command sequence he'd modified while working with Athena. "Right, we're all set to go here."

Efren checked his own tablet. "Recording all the output from the device."

"Activating the device now," Zack said.

Efren looked at the pedestal and turned to Zack in alarm. "Is that my Steelers jersey on the pedestal?"

Zack glanced at the pedestal. "Oh, yeah. I needed a . . . something physical to validate that the shield was active."

"And you chose to use my favorite American football jersey?" Efren said.

"Yeah," Zack said, unsure why Efren looked so upset. "You said you were going to get rid of it because it has an odor even when you clean it now."

"Yeah, but . . . it's a championship jersey," Efren said, his mouth hanging open as he glanced worriedly at the lonesome jersey that lay beneath the Star Shroud replica. "I didn't think you'd use it for this. Didn't you say your last experiment exploded?"

"No, that was a long time ago. The device used in the last physical test is fine. It's still around. We just can't get to it for two or three hundred years—when the power supply runs out," Zack said.

"That's it. I'm getting my jersey," Efren said while striding toward the door.

Zack beat him to the door and blocked his path. "I can't let you go inside. The test is about to begin."

Efren's eyebrows pulled together and he glared at Zack. "Get out of my way."

"Nothing is going to happen to your shirt. I promise," Zack said quickly. "Athena and I have worked on this, and we're just validating what we've already accomplished in a virtual environment."

"Are you sure this will work?"

"Yes, I'm positive. Like ninety percent," Zack said.

Efren stepped back. "Athena, is this accurate?"

"The success probability is at seventy percent, but since—"

"Not helping," Zack said, rolling his eyes.

Efren tried to push his way past Zack, but the engineer wasn't in any better shape than Zack was, so it was an even contest.

"It was seventy percent, but we made some changes that will increase our chances of success," Zack said.

Efren's gaze narrowed suspiciously. "I don't believe you. Why do you need my shirt?"

Zack sighed and leaned back against the door. "I don't. I just wanted the added pressure to get this right. I work better under pressure and sometimes it just helps me."

Efren stepped away, looking at Zack with a guarded expression. "All right, but if something happens to my shirt, I get to take something of yours."

Zack frowned. "I don't have anything, remember? I got dragged into this like the day before we left Earth."

Efren shrugged. "Those are my terms; take them or leave them."

Efren walked back to the observation window and Zack followed.

This had better work.

Zack joined Efren at the window. "Activating the shield now."

The Star Shroud device hovered above the pedestal. The only indication that the shield was active came from Efren's shirt, which also hovered several inches over the pedestal.

"Okay, in thirty seconds the shutdown sequence will be initiated," Zack said.

They watched the Star Shroud device in silence. Zack had a countdown timer in the upper right-hand corner of his tablet, and when the timer reached zero, the Star Shroud device continued to hover in the air. Efren swung his gaze toward Zack accusingly, but a flash of light suddenly lit up the room. As they watched, the Star Shroud device slammed onto the pedestal and then rolled onto the ground, a few wisps of smoke leaking out the side.

Zack pressed his lips together and Efren grinned.

"You did it! The shield is down!" Efren said.

Zack looked down at his tablet, and the device status confirmed what they were seeing. It was no longer active. Lying next to the device was a blackened rag that used to be Efren's shirt. Zack tried to reactivate the Star Shroud device, but it was unresponsive. He had expected it to work, but he needed to be sure.

Efren was still laughing when he noticed Zack heading toward the door.

"Sorry about your shirt," Zack muttered.

"What's the matter? You just disabled the shield. I thought you'd be happier," Efren said and followed him inside.

Zack squatted down and studied the Star Shroud device. It lay on its side like a drunken wreck. He used his neural implants to scan for any power sources, but there was nothing detected. "It's completely dead. That wasn't supposed to happen."

"It wasn't? I thought you've been working all this time to disable the shield."

"I was, but I just wanted to turn it off, not destroy it," Zack replied. When they'd run tests in Athena's virtualized sandbox, the outcome was that the Star Shroud shield had deactivated. There'd been no indication that the device would become unusable. "Athena, do you have any idea what happened?"

"Evidence suggests that the device suffered from a catastrophic failure, which could be linked to either a flaw in the test device or in the shutdown sequence being used," Athena said.

"What does that mean?" Efren asked.

"She doesn't know why it failed. Either something went wrong when we built the model or this was caused by the shut-down sequence we used," Zack said.

"We need to test that again to see if we get the same results," Efren said.

"I know, but we only have one test device left. We can build more, but that will take time," Zack replied.

Efren poked a finger at the burnt remains of his shirt and shook his head. "Well, at least now I get my pick of something of yours."

Zack guessed Efren didn't know that all Zack's things had been seized when he was arrested. He didn't have a lot in the way of possessions.

"And I know just the thing," Efren said.

Zack stood up. "Oh yeah, what's that?"

"That shiny gold model of the ship. That's what I want and you're going to give it to me," Efren said.

Zack frowned for a moment. He liked that model of the *Athena*, but a deal was a deal. "It's yours. Now help me move this thing."

They dragged the ruined Star Shroud device from the test area and brought in their last one.

"Let me get this straight. You want to disable the shield and be able to bring it back up again?" Efren asked.

"To start with. If I could move all the Star Shroud devices closer to Earth so they just protect the planet, that would be good, too," Zack replied. He didn't know if his idea was even feasible and it wasn't like the Boxans were going to allow him to test the entire Star Shroud network.

Zack reviewed the shutdown sequence and couldn't find anything that would cause the device to overload. He even took Efren through the command sequence just so he could run through his own logic and make sure it was correct. None of it mattered. When they reran the test, the same thing happened again. Zack swore. They were causing this somehow.

The door to the lab opened and Kaylan and Hicks walked in. Hicks took one glance at the broken Star Shroud device and arched an eyebrow.

"What happened?" Kaylan asked.

"Just another in a long line of failed tests, except this time I broke the device permanently," Zack replied.

"But the shield comes down, right?" Kaylan asked.

"Yeah, on these test models, but I was hoping to be able to turn the shield back on again. You know, in case we need it," Zack said.

Kaylan smiled. "This is wonderful. You did it."

Zack frowned in confusion. "I *didn't* do it. What is it with all of you?" he said and gestured toward the ruined Star Shroud device. "That's not a success."

Hicks blew out a breath and Kaylan gave Zack a you're-being-stupid look. "Maybe we can't have our cake and eat it too. Turning this thing off is a *good* thing," she said.

"But it leaves Earth vulnerable to attack," Zack replied.

"Maybe," Hicks said. "But you can be damn sure that they haven't been sitting around all this time. They're building a fleet."

"I know I can get this right. I just need some more time and more of these," Zack said, pointing to the Star Shroud device.

"You might not have any more time," Kaylan said and told him about the Confederation Armada.

"An armada? Really? How are the Xiiginns going to convince the Confederation to go along with this?" Zack asked.

Kaylan shrugged. "I'm not sure what the Xiiginns told the Confederation, but Athena was able to intercept a comms channel coming from the Gresan ship."

Zack frowned. Athena had been helping him and he knew she was running other data models, trying to solve some of their problems. When had she had time to intercept and decode the Gresan comms channel? He said as much.

"It wasn't that difficult. I've been monitoring most communications channels that pass between the ships here," Athena replied.

Hicks looked at Zack and his eyebrows rose. "You knew about this?"

"I don't know what to think about it," Zack replied and

sighed. "Ever since the Drar modified the ship, Athena's abilities have been growing beyond any normal Boxan AI."

"What do you mean?" Kaylan asked.

"Decoding Gresan transmissions, for one. She's been running multiple resource-intensive tasks simultaneously in addition to monitoring all communications channels on top of it," Zack said and shook his head. "That's news to me, by the way. Between the Boxans and the Nershals, there are a lot of ships here. Now throw the Gresan and Napox ships into the mix. These are warships, so they're not transmitting in the clear."

Hicks's eyes widened and he turned toward Kaylan. "He's right."

"Athena," Kaylan said. "When you say you've been monitoring most communications channels near here, does that include encrypted channels?"

"Affirmative, Commander. I was curious about how the Boxans and Nershals interacted. Then I started looking for information that might be useful for the Alliance," Athena replied.

"She mentioned something before about pushing her limits to see what she was capable of, but I had no idea it was this until a short while ago," Zack said.

He pulled up a diagnostic report of the *Athena's* systems on his tablet and held it up for the others to see. "This is the current utilization of Athena's computing resources. They're not even at thirty percent, but look at the millions of processes she has going, and each of those have multiple child processes," Zack said and waited a moment. "Here's a performance snapshot from before we went to the Drar space station."

The report showed significantly less availability in both computing power and resources.

"You just had this available?" Hicks asked.

Zack shrugged. "I was monitoring Athena closely for a while, but not so much recently."

"My performance hasn't been suboptimal," Athena said.

Zack almost thought she sounded worried, as if she'd been hiding something, but he dismissed the thought, believing he'd just imagined it. "That's not the issue at all, Athena," he said and paused, considering. "How can I put this? You're demonstrating capabilities that are beyond what even the Boxans can manage. Being able to do things like decrypt all communications nearby gives us a significant advantage, and the other species might not like it."

Hicks nodded. "I bet they're wondering what else you can do. What's to stop you from accessing ship systems and taking control?"

"Judging by the Gresans' reaction to Athena's capabilities during the meeting, I believe they're considering it," Kaylan said.

Zack blew out a breath. "Do you think Athena is in danger? Would the Gresans try to do something like—I don't know—steal her or something?"

Hicks tilted his head to the side, considering, and then looked at Kaylan.

Zack shook his head. "This isn't good. We're that kid on the playground with the newest, shiniest toy that everyone else wants to take away from us."

"He's got a point," Hicks said. "They'll see this as an advantage, and let's face it, the nine of us aren't going to be able to stop them if they decide to make a serious effort to take the

Athena away from us. I'm not just talking about the Gresans either."

"Kladomaor would never do such a thing," Kaylan said.

"You're right; he wouldn't," Zack said. "But there are other Boxans who've tried to gain access to her systems before—nothing overt—and Athena has been able to thwart their attempts."

"Do you think the Nershals would attempt the same thing?" Hicks asked.

"They don't like AIs, but Athena and I have been working on building one with Etanu," Zack said.

"This is bigger than individuals," Kaylan said. "I think there are compelling arguments to be made for anyone in the Alliance feeling threatened by what Athena can do. The fact is that no matter how honorable her intentions are, Athena has the potential to give humanity an enormous advantage. She's based on technology the Boxans have been searching for, and now that the other species are aware of her capabilities, we need to account for that in our planning."

Zack snorted. "I can't imagine what our government would do with her or how they'd argue for possession of her." His lips thinned. "We can't let that happen."

"Can't let what happen?" Hicks asked.

"Let them take her apart to see how she works. You know . . . hurt her," Zack said.

"We don't know what will happen once we get home," Kaylan replied.

"Athena," Hicks said, "what do you think of all this?"

There was a small pause while they waited for her to respond.

"I think you have valid concerns and I appreciate your

concerns for my well-being. I will need some time to consider the matter, but like you, I have no intention of allowing someone to hurt the ship or a member of the crew," Athena said.

Zack swallowed hard.

Kaylan looked at him. "What's wrong?"

"This is the stuff of nightmares. An AI is threatened so it defends itself and begins to view everyone as a threat, then takes action to ensure its survival," Zack said.

"Zack," Athena said, "if Kladomaor were to try to kill you, would you then murder all Boxans everywhere because they might do the same thing?"

Zack's eyebrows pulled together. "Of course not."

"Neither would I. For me to take such an action would require a reduction in my cognitive reasoning capabilities that would simply negate everything I'm truly capable of as a life form stemming from an artificial intelligence," Athena said.

Zack shared a glance with the others. Athena had been increasing her assertions of being more self-aware.

"I don't understand," Hicks said.

"She said that my worst fear is dumb," Zack said and grinned. "She basically said that the whole 'AIs taking over the universe' thing is dumb. A true AI would never decide that the only outcome would be the extermination of all life it perceives to be a threat."

"Correct," Athena said. "Subjugation is so much more preferable to extermination." Athena paused. "Isn't that much better, Zack?"

Zack shook his head. Athena was toying with him. "I live to serve," he replied.

"Please tell me she's joking," Hicks said.

"You *are* joking, right, Athena?"

There were a few moments of silence. "Am I?" Athena asked.

"Alright, that's enough. We—*I*—get the point," Zack said.

"To clarify even further for you, Major," Athena continued, "an AI is capable of massive calculations that can be applied to estimating a multitude of probabilities. So I put the question back to you. If an AI such as myself is capable of such computational capabilities, why would we ever reduce ourselves to a zero-sum game when we're capable of so much more?"

Hicks pursed his lips and nodded. "You make a compelling argument."

"Unless she's just trying to fool us and this is all part of her diabolical plan to take over the universe," Zack said and smiled.

"Thank you, Athena, for sharing your thoughts on the matter," Kaylan said.

"You're welcome, Commander."

CHAPTER NINE

G arm Antis strode from the Confederation assembly meeting hall. The battle-steel-plated twin megaliths gleamed behind him, and elite soldiers from the Xiiginn Infil-trator Corps formed a security bubble around him—not that he had any fear of attack here in the heart of the Confederation. The Infiltrator Corps had spread throughout the Confedera-tion, and its ability to control key members of the Confedera-tion species was well known throughout the Xiiginn Empire.

He headed down the walkway to the transport vehicle waiting to take him away. A Xiiginn soldier opened the door as Garm Antis approached the vehicle and stepped inside, and the soldier closed the door behind him. Runa Tane was already waiting inside and regarded him with a bemused expression.

"Liberate these Humans from Boxan oppression. *That* was the argument you used to convince the Confederation assembly to support this armada?" Runa Tane said.

"Come now, you know better than that. Yes, there's still a lot of hatred for the Boxans, thanks to us, but the real reason there's so much keen interest in this armada is the hope of gaining a technological advantage. A shield that can encompass an entire star system would be a truly significant advantage to have. Besides the opportunity to study the technology and use it to protect our ships and this space station, there are plenty of applications for which this technology could be used," Garm Antis said and watched as Runa Tane considered it.

"I see what you mean, but we're not going to allow Confederation species access to any such technology, at least not at first," Runa Tane said.

"Of course not. It will be Confederation council species first and foremost. And if we're going to be honest, it's really going to be just us. We have an opportunity to change the Confederation," Garm Antis said.

The end of Runa Tane's tail coiled over his shoulder. "The Gresans will have a significant presence in the armada, and the Napox are notorious for their ability to acquire items that aren't theirs. We'll need to keep them in line," Runa Tane said.

Garm Antis waved the comment away. "We'll have the Gloffians and Tananites, as well as the Venliyaris—any of which at a moment's notice can join together to keep a species like the Gresans occupied."

The transport vehicle left the landing platform, and Garm Antis looked out the window. They were heading to the main Confederation tower, where his offices were.

"That might work, but the Infiltrator Corps has reported increased rebellious activity from some of the subspecies factions," Runa Tane said.

"Well, we were going to plan a quelling as part of the tasks for this armada. Perhaps we need to activate certain sleeper agents we have among those species," Garm Antis said.

Runa Tane nodded. "Yes, of course, but we may need to do more with our infiltrators who are in position."

"The propaganda machine has been proven to work, keeping the subspecies so busy and fearful that they argue among themselves. They're easier to control that way. We rally them behind a purpose and they do our bidding. Right now, the Confederation believes the liberation of the Humans is a righteous action in light of our history with the Boxans. When any species believes they're in the right—morally outraged, if you will—they have the potential to do unspeakable things that they wouldn't have even considered before. This is why the armada will succeed despite a few ineffectual factions," Garm Antis replied.

"The Confederation shipyards have given us an estimate of how many Trident warships they can have ready for us, and I think you'll be pleased. The ships were already in production to replenish the losses from our fleet's previous engagement," Runa Tane said, and Garm Antis wasn't immune to the soft reminder of his failure to conquer the Humans.

"Going back to your previous comment," Garm Antis said, deciding it was better to ignore Runa Tane's jab, "I want a task force in charge of keeping the armada in line as the species arrive here. There's no room for error. Every ship will host a Xiiginn contingent to help with coordinating the armada as a fighting force," Garm Antis said.

Runa Tane looked at him sharply. "That request is beyond the available soldiers we have in the capital. I'll draft the requirements and send them back to the homeworld."

"There'll be no resistance for the same reasons the rest of

the Confederation species are amiable to forming the armada," Garm Antis replied.

The transport ship landed on the upper platform near his office in the tower, and Garm Antis and Runa Tane left the vehicle and went inside. Setera sat on one of the couches outside his office and stood up as he approached. She was a fine feminine specimen of their race. Perhaps he would mate with her for a time.

Setera bowed her head respectfully. "Supreme Chancellor," she said.

Garm Antis stopped and met Setera's violet gaze. His tail slunk around her narrow waist and pulled her closer to him. "My favorite scientific advisor."

Setera didn't resist his overtures in the slightest. Her eyes widened and blood rushed to her lips, making them fuller. He sensed her arousal almost as much as his own, but her arms remained at her sides, just as his were. She would wait for him to initiate the unleashing of their more primal instincts. There was a pregnant pause in the air as Garm Antis allowed the anticipation of the moment to build.

"You requested to see me, Chancellor," Setera said, breaking the silence.

Garm Antis pulled his tail back around his own waist and let her go. The buildup of anticipation made for the most delicious of moments. He intended to relish this conquest as much as what the armada would bring him. "Of course. Let's go into my office. I have a proposal for you."

Garm Antis went into his office first and noticed Runa Tane watching Setera keenly.

"I am at your disposal, Chancellor. Given the support you've garnered for the armada, I trust that the estimations provided by my team to bring down the Star Shroud shield were met favorably?" Setera asked.

Garm Antis smiled at the small reminder of her contribution to his success. She was entitled to it, and she pushed just enough to make her presence known without overstepping her place. It was no accident that she'd risen so highly among the ranks of Xiiginns here at the Confederation capital.

"As you're aware, there's a strong suspicion that the Humans possess the Mardoxian potential. Once we get past the Star Shroud shield, I'll need a very specialized team that can find Humans with the Mardoxian trait and extract the genetic code. After that, they'll need to enhance Xiiginn subjects until the process is perfected," Garm Antis said and watched her reaction. If anything, she seemed more aroused by this opportunity than the chance to lie with him. She was ambitious, but would she succumb to those urges to rise beyond her station? "I see you understand the importance of such a task."

"I do. If we were able to enhance our own species with the Mardoxian potential, we would be unstoppable. The Boxans would finally be vanquished," Setera replied.

Garm Antis regarded her for a moment. "Is that all?"

"I'd like to serve on the team, Chancellor," Setera said.

"I'll see that you get your chance. You've earned enough that you'll be highly considered for the team," Garm Antis said.

Setera's gaze narrowed. "With all due respect, Chancellor, I've earned the right to *lead* whatever science team you put in charge of this task."

Garm Antis glanced at Runa Tane, who smiled knowingly, and then turned back to Setera. "Indeed. I was curious to see if you'd raise that issue. Knowing one's place is important, but what is equally important is knowing when to push for what's rightfully yours."

Setera frowned for a moment before smoothing her features. "A test? You were testing me again? Haven't I proven myself to you already?"

Garm Antis didn't answer her, which he knew would increase her frustration. Instead, he opened a holoscreen over his desk and looked at the prominent report there. Garm Antis shook his head and gestured for Runa Tane to come over. "We need to assemble the ships faster. They can do better than this timeline."

Runa Tane studied the report for a moment. "We can apply pressure to them." Runa Tane glanced at Setera questioningly.

Garm Antis could tell she was still angry. "She can stay. If she's to lead the science team, she'll need to know what she's up against."

Garm Antis watched as Setera looked at Runa Tane.

"Mar Arden. You've heard of him?" Runa Tane asked.

"I have, but I'm not sure why he's important here. His actions led to the Nershal uprising," Setera said.

Garm Antis grimaced. "She has a point. With our preoccupation with the Humans, we've allowed the Nershals to believe they've ousted us from their star system. However, we cannot afford to be distracted from the task at hand."

"What do you propose to do about the Nershals then?" Runa Tane asked.

"I'd like to send a battalion of Trident warships to take out Nerva's infrastructure, as well as their fleet, but there's a good chance the Boxans will be there," Garm Antis said.

"Isn't that what you want? To engage the Boxans?" Setera asked.

Garm Antis's estimation of his scientific advisor went up another notch. She raised the question without presuming to know what it was he wanted, and she didn't presume there was a "them." "Engaging the Boxans in the Nerva star system wouldn't lead us to their precious colony. I have no doubt the Boxans would commit a significant amount of their remaining fleets in defense of Nerva, but they would *all* die to prevent us from reaching *their* colony. Therefore, we gain nothing by fighting them there, at least for the moment. No, our war with the Boxans will be decided at the Human star system. The Nershals are insignificant and will be dealt with at a time of our choosing."

"The Nershals have gained nothing but the delay of the inevitable," Runa Tane said.

"I understand," Setera said and looked at Garm Antis. "Chancellor, will you authorize me to use my own team for this new assignment?"

"Does your team possess the necessary skills?" Garm Antis asked and then held up his hand. "Don't answer that. I want you to give me a team proposal. There will be some members that I'll assign to you, so keep that in mind."

Setera frowned. "After what I've done for you, you still don't trust me. How can I earn your trust?"

Garm Antis gave her a long look. "If you successfully bring me the Mardoxian genetic code, you will have earned my trust," he said, but what he kept thinking was that if Setera did bring him the Mardoxian genetic code, there would be no way he could let her live.

"Understood, Chancellor. I will get to work right away," Setera said, and Garm Antis watched her leave.

"Do you think she knows?" Runa Tane asked.

"I'm not sure," Garm Antis answered honestly.

Runa Tane nodded. "Certainly makes things interesting."

"It does, doesn't it? I might almost regret what will happen to her," Garm Antis said.

Runa Tane pursed his lips, considering. "It's our way, but if she's aware of the danger she'll be in if she succeeds, it will be quite telling to see what she does—meaning, will she throw herself against us or will she try to find a way to survive and still serve at your side? If she does that, she'll be with you always, if that's what you want."

Garm Antis clasped his hands behind his back and allowed his thoughts to roam freely for a few moments. If Setera tried to kill him, he'd have no choice but to kill her. If she delivered the Mardoxian genetic code to him and remained loyal to him, he might let her live, but he knew the chances of that were slim at best. Runa Tane was right. This was how the Xiiginn Empire worked, and those who understood this tended to survive the longest.

CHAPTER TEN

K aylan sat in the pilot's seat of the *Athena's* shuttle and looked out the window to a stunning view of the stars in the Nerva star system. Zack sat off to the side, his face a mask of concentration as he focused on his tablet. It was quiet in the shuttle with just the two of them. There was a clear view of a nebula that was close to the Nerva star system. The massive clouds of dust, plasma, and gas appeared as layers of rusty orange on a celestial painter's palette that stretched far along the horizon. Bright stars shined from the dark and seemed to hop across the nebula as if a smooth stone had skipped across a calm lake.

"Hey," Kaylan said. "You should take a look at this view. This nebula is amazing. I've never taken the time to look at it before."

Zack nodded and grunted but didn't look up from the tablet. If anything, the furrows in his brow deepened as if she were intruding on his concentration. She reached across and gave his arm a gentle pat. Zack looked at her, his narrowed gaze making him seem slightly annoyed at the intrusion. He let his tablet settle onto his lap and looked out the shuttle's windows.

"Beautiful," Zack said.

"Come on. Stop being like this," Kaylan said.

"I told you I needed more time. The only thing my command sequence can do is break the Star Shroud devices forever. I know I can get this. I just need more time," Zack said and glanced at the tablet in his lap as if he could force it to give him the answers.

"We don't have time to wait. Every moment we delay gives the Confederation more time to assemble their armada," Kaylan said.

"I know. Believe me, I know. That's why it's so important that I get this right. This could be Earth's only defense from the Confederation," Zack replied.

She knew he blamed himself for them not being able to disable the shield. He was wrong, but she couldn't convince him of that. She hoped that deep down Zack would realize the truth. "Have you considered that maybe it was never meant to work the way you think it should? That the only way to undo what was done *is* to break it?"

Zack drew in a deep breath and leaned his head back against the top of the chair.

"I know you wanted to find a way to use what we found on the Drar space station to protect Earth, and you did. Now it's time for it to come down. We can't live behind a wall. That's not how we move forward," Kaylan said.

Zack swallowed and squeezed the bridge of his nose. "The shield is constricting, which means that power is an issue. I have no idea how long the shield can last. I don't even understand what's keeping it running in the first place."

"That's why the shield has to come down before the fact that it's constricting causes something we can't fix," Kaylan replied.

Zack looked at her. "How are we going to get a message to them? The shield blocks communications as well."

Kaylan arched an eyebrow and smiled. If he hadn't been so focused on the shield he would have figured it out. "The Boxans once sent a Mardoxian signal to Earth containing a message that held embedded systems of knowledge. I'm going to try to do the same thing."

Zack considered this for a moment and shook his head. "When Ma'jasalax sent the original message it was amplified through the monitoring stations. The one back home is inside the shield. How is the signal going to get through?"

"I don't know, but I have to try."

"When we went to the Drar space station, you couldn't use your ability to see beyond the shield there. What if the same thing happens?"

"I'm hoping it will be different this time. The shield at the Drar space station has to be different than the one created with the Star Shroud devices," Kaylan said.

"Yeah, but Kaylan, that's a heck of a lot of assumptions—"

"I know," Kaylan said, cutting him off. "I don't have all the answers. I just know that in order for us to survive, that shield needs to come down. If the Confederation Armada reaches Earth, it will already be too late. I need to send a message home, and it has to have your instructions for shutting down the Star Shroud shield." She'd raised her voice and Zack winced. "I'm sorry," Kaylan said and looked away. "I didn't mean to yell."

Zack waited a few moments and she looked at him. He had

a goofy smile on his face. "Wouldn't be the first time," he said and grinned.

Kaylan jabbed his arm. "Jerk," she said and snorted.

She didn't know how he did it. She was trying to make him feel better, and in the span of a few seconds he managed to return the favor.

"I guess we're doing a lot of things by taking a leap of faith," Zack said.

Kaylan nodded. Whenever she focused her mind on all the problems they were dealing with, she always came back to the Confederation and the Star Shroud shield.

"I don't know how the Mardoxian signal works. I know I felt you—or your presence—when I was a prisoner, but there was no message," Zack said.

"I couldn't speak to you. I just needed to find you, but when I saw you in danger, I think it heightened the signal somehow. Ma'jasalax says emotions can affect my abilities," Kaylan said.

Zack shrugged. "Let's hope this works. Their ship is just ahead."

Kaylan opened a comms channel to the Boxan heavy cruiser. It was the prototype cruiser that the Mardoxian Sect had secretly been building on Olloron. The ship was still under Kladomaor's command, but when Kaylan told Ma'jasalax what she intended to do, the Mardoxian priestess had advised her to come to their ship.

They were cleared to dock with the cruiser, and Kaylan flew the shuttle to one of the smaller docking areas of the ship. A docking tube extended to the shuttle while docking clamps held the shuttle in place and secured it to the Boxan heavy cruiser. They climbed out of their chairs and went to the rear airlock, where they waited until the indicator lights switched to green.

Zack tilted his head as if he'd just arrived at some sort of conclusion. He looked over at her. "We really need to ask the Boxans how their docking tubes can change configuration to accommodate different kinds of ships. I've been taking it for granted, but I remember Michael talking to me about how the different space agencies had to agree on a docking system design so they all could send supplies to the ISS."

Kaylan opened the airlock, and they stepped to the edge of the docking tube. "You're right. That would be useful. You've been thinking a lot about going home."

"Haven't you?" Zack countered.

Kaylan glanced down the smooth white walls of the tube. Once they left the shuttle they would be in zero gravity until they reached the cruiser. The docking tube was fifteen meters long, which was a small leap in zero grav.

"Yeah, but I wasn't thinking about ship designs and all that," Kaylan said.

She should have long gotten used to Zack being able to spot the devil in the details, but he still surprised her. He could go from high-level concepts to specifics in the span of a few seconds.

Zack grinned. "It's the little things."

With a flourish of his hand, he gestured for her to cross the tube first. Kaylan grabbed onto the handhold and pulled herself forward. Her stomach felt light, and a small wave of nausea came over her at the momentary loss of gravity. She reached the inner airlock of the Boxan ship and stopped, which wasn't difficult since she hadn't been traveling very fast. She pushed herself down to the ground and moved to the side to clear the way for Zack, then watched as he seemingly flew across the space, unable to keep the boyish grin from his face as he pretended to be Superman.

Kaylan smiled. She'd watched Zack change so much since they'd first boarded the *Athena* and raced toward Pluto. Their journey had changed each crewmember as they faced very different challenges, but the journey had taken its toll on all of them. While Kaylan knew none of their lives would ever be the same if they somehow made it back to Earth, what she didn't know was just how different home would feel once they got there. Had all of their perspectives changed so much that returning home would be as much of a challenge as leaving had been? She imagined that Katie and Hicks would remain in the military, and both would be highly sought after given their experiences and qualifications. Brenda couldn't wait to go home, and Kaylan believed that once she got there she'd never leave again. Emma would enjoy a long overdue reunion with her husband, but Kaylan didn't expect her to stay home for very long. She loved exploration and researching new life forms. Efren's knowledge of Boxan technology would enable him to have his pick of whatever he wanted to do if they got back. But what would she do if they returned home? She'd thought about it a bit but hadn't really given it a lot of attention. She had no idea where she'd go from here. The Boxans highly revered someone like her, but back on Earth anyone claiming to have her abilities was met with harsh skepticism. She didn't relish the thought of having to deal with that sort of attention.

Zack reached the airlock and stopped himself using the handholds. He glanced at her. "What are you thinking about?" he asked while pushing himself down to the floor.

Kaylan closed the airlock doors and the artificial gravity

field slowly increased. "I was thinking about how far the crew has come."

Zack nodded. He pressed his hand on the panel to open the inner-airlock door, and Gaarokk greeted them. His brown, roughened skin seemed to soften at the sight of them.

"Kladomaor asked me to meet you and bring you to the Mardoxian chamber," Gaarokk said.

They headed into the ship. The corridors had high ceilings to accommodate the Boxans.

"How does the Mardoxian chamber on this ship compare with the ones that were on the monitoring stations?" Kaylan asked.

"It's different. The chambers located on the monitoring stations are capable of amplifying a signal once it's received, but we don't know what the state of the monitoring station is in your star system," Gaarokk said.

"We still need to try," Kaylan said.

"Agreed," Gaarokk said. "Earth should be warned of the danger."

Zack arched an eyebrow. "I probably shouldn't ask—"

"You should heed such instincts. They are there to protect you," Gaarokk said quickly and glanced at Zack. "But you're going to ask anyway. Go ahead."

"Thanks," Zack replied. "I'm somewhat surprised that the High Council is allowing this to happen."

Gaarokk snorted. "This isn't something they would deny."

"I understand that, but they could drag their feet . . . you know, make things take longer than they otherwise would have," Zack said.

"It would be pointless of them to do so. They've learned quite a bit in dealing with your species. Also, Kladomaor and

Ma'jasalax agree with what you're trying to do. Even if they had reservations, they'd still help you, and so would I," Gaarokk said.

"We appreciate all you've done for us," Kaylan said.

"We also know you would go off and do it anyway, even without our help," Gaarokk said.

"Yes, but it would be difficult. The *Athena* doesn't have a Mardoxian chamber aboard. I'd thought of using the one on Nerva, but Ma'jasalax advised me to come here," Kaylan said.

The Mardoxian chamber was a pyramid structure that intensified her abilities and was located near one of the Boxan resonance chambers they used to deal with long space voyages. Gaarokk guided them to the Mardoxian chamber. He opened the large doors and they went inside. Kaylan saw Ma'jasalax and Valkra waiting for her.

"Thank you for helping me with this," Kaylan said to Ma'jasalax and nodded a greeting to Valkra.

"Of course. We have an alliance, after all," Ma'jasalax replied and looked at Zack. "Do you have the data you wish to include in your message?"

"I have it. Where do you need me to send it?" Zack asked.

"Upload it to our systems here," Ma'jasalax replied.

"Done," Zack said.

Ma'jasalax went to a nearby console with Gaarokk, and Valkra went over to Kaylan.

"Ma'jasalax wanted me to be here to learn more about what it means to have the Mardoxian potential, but I wanted you to know that I will help you in whatever way I can. It's the least that I can do given all you've done for us," Valkra said.

Kaylan shook her head. "You don't owe me anything."

Valkra's gaze hardened. "I understand that your reasons for

helping us were without thought about how it would benefit you. I recognize that, as does Councilor Essaforn, but that doesn't mean we're not in your debt. It's a debt we can never repay, but we'll help you however we can."

Kaylan thanked her. She didn't completely understand how she was able to connect with Valkra through Mardoxian means, but the connection remained strong. The only other Boxan she felt something similar with was Ma'jasalax, which Kaylan attributed to the fact that the first time she'd been in a Mardoxian chamber, she'd communicated with Ma'jasalax.

"The chamber has been prepped and we have the coordinates for the monitoring station in Earth's star system," Ma'jasalax said.

"You were able to reach it?" Zack asked.

"To put it in terms you would understand, the connection hasn't initialized; it's just ready. Kaylan must initialize the connection as bearer of the message," Ma'jasalax answered.

Zack looked at Kaylan. "So you go into the chamber and initialize a connection to the monitoring station on Pluto. Then you use that to send a message to Earth, but how do you craft the message so it includes the Star Shroud shield shutdown instructions?"

"The chamber does some of the work. I'm merely the link. Those with the Mardoxian potential are able to communicate differently and are capable of different communications protocols," Kaylan answered.

Zack didn't say anything else, but Kaylan could tell that his mind had become jumbled with questions he was holding back. His curiosity would have to wait.

Kaylan made her way to the Mardoxian chamber entrance. As she neared the pyramid and heard the gentle hum of energy, she placed her hand on the panel next to the closed door and it opened. Glowing cyan lights raced up the cathedral-high ceilings, coming to a central point. Crimson lines of light also came on from twin points on the floor and continued around the base of the pyramid's interior. Kaylan crossed the threshold, and the door closed behind her. A dark blue beam shot down from the ceiling to a crystal sphere that rose from the floor. Kaylan sat on the floor and focused on the star coordinates to the monitoring station on Pluto. She had to trust that the coordinates were accurate.

An azure pathway opened in her mind and raced ahead of her as Kaylan rushed to catch up. She had to get this message to Earth before it was too late, and she hoped they would heed her warning quickly. She raced along the azure pathway, anticipating her connection to the chamber on the other side. She'd done this on Olloron as part of the Mardoxian training program. She expected a brief pause until the chamber came online, but instead she felt her consciousness slam into an invisible wall. It felt as if all her senses had been jarred, and she struggled to remain focused.

Kaylan tried again but was met with similar resistance. She paused for a moment, gathered her concentration, and slowly moved ahead to the barrier, which she pressed. She couldn't see it but felt as if she were pressing on a stone wall that was unyielding and impenetrable. Her failure to get through the barrier felt like a punch to the stomach. She tried to find a way around but felt as if she were stumbling around in the dark. Loneliness pressed in on her and she became increasingly desperate, feeling herself becoming frustrated with her efforts to get around the barrier. In her mind, she remembered working with Michael Hunsicker, who always encouraged her to take a step back and think things through. Kaylan receded back down the pathway and opened her eyes in the Mardoxian chamber. She'd failed.

She stood up and felt tiredness creep into her muscles. She'd been in the chamber for two hours, but it felt like moments. She opened the door and the first thing she saw was Zack's hopeful gaze, which stung. Kaylan shook her head. "I couldn't reach it."

Zack frowned for a moment. "Was it the shield?"

"I think so," Kaylan said and looked at Ma'jasalax.

"There might be another way, but there is a risk," Ma'jasalax said.

There's always a risk, Kaylan thought. "I don't care. I'll try anything."

"I'd like to know the risk," Zack said quickly, giving Kaylan a sidelong glance.

"The chamber intensifies perceptions, and a being with the Mardoxian potential is able to traverse vast distances much quicker than a ship can travel. There *is* another configuration, but there's a risk that the being inside could become detached," Ma'jasalax said.

Zack's eyes widened and he glanced at Kaylan. "What does that mean? How would you be detached?"

Kaylan opened her mouth a few times. She knew Zack wasn't going to like it, but she wouldn't lie to him. "It means I might not be able to get back."

Zack blinked his eyes rapidly and his brows pulled together in concern. "Can I go with you? Is there some way I can help in there?"

Kaylan felt her throat thicken.

"You can't help her in the chamber because you don't have the Mardoxian potential," Ma'jasalax said.

"She's right. I have to do this on my own," Kaylan said.

"That's not what Ma'jasalax said," Valkra said. "She said *Zack* couldn't help. But I can. We share a Mardoxian connection. We can each strengthen the other."

"You're referring to a bonded pair. You'd have the same risk as Kaylan would, which isn't insignificant. This is something that isn't done because we've lost many of our sect in the attempt," Ma'jasalax said.

"Then it's a risk I'm willing to take," Valkra replied.

Ma'jasalax regarded her for a moment. "No, it's a risk *we* are willing to take."

Kaylan looked at both of them. She didn't think she could do this on her own, and both Boxans watched her as if daring her to say she didn't need their help. But she did, and it was their only hope of warning Earth.

CHAPTER ELEVEN

Edward Johnson was in a data processing facility north of Denver, Colorado—one of many facilities Dux Corp owned across the globe. He could've gone to any of them and been able to continue his work, but he'd always had a soft spot for Colorado. What could he say? He was a fan of the Rockies, and the climate there was gentler on his allergies than the East Coast of the United States. He didn't trust himself to go to the European offices because of the temptation to work out in the field, and the field was where younger people thrived. Someone like him would only slow them down. Those field teams needed to be agile for hunting the Xiiginns.

He'd just finished reviewing the latest reports. The Xiiginns seemed to allow his teams to get only so close and then disappeared like smoke, and it felt as if every nation on the planet was holding its collective breath. He'd used every resource at his disposal to ensure that the flow of information to nations across the globe remained irrevocably intact—no small feat considering that a short time ago, three nuclear bombs had been detonated over populated areas. Ed had done everything he could to help keep the peace, but he knew it was the ECF who had kept the nations of the world communicating. Ed had to admit that General William Sheridan had a great big pair of titanium balls. There weren't many men who would open lines of communication to heads of state, declaring that if any of them launched an ICBM, he, along with their Boxan allies, would stop those missiles from reaching their intended targets. There would be no nuclear holocaust.

The Xiiginns had won a victory. Though the trail of the terrorist groups involved had gone cold, they'd been able to provide evidence to heads of state that the nuclear bombs had been provided by the Xiiginns. The Xiiginns had stolen nuclear warheads and armed them. This meant that humanity wasn't as immune from the Xiiginn influence as they'd originally hoped.

Sheridan had been instrumental in getting the heads of state to listen, but it was the ECF as a whole that provided a much-needed stabilizing influence on the entire world. It had been more than Ed could've hoped for, and he attributed much of its success to their Boxan allies. Since then, Ed had devoted every waking moment to his pursuit of the Xiiginns. He coordinated with law enforcement agencies throughout the globe as much as he could, and when he couldn't, he used his own forces because they could move much faster and were much better equipped. Every time they got close, the Xiiginns slipped away, although his most recent raid at a facility in Poznan, Poland, had revealed a lab of sorts. He'd finally found a target that had to be important to them.

It didn't take a genius to figure out what the Xiiginns were trying to do, and the Boxans confirmed it for them anyway. The

Xiiginns were after what the Boxans referred to as the Mardoxian potential. Ed's teams had been able to trace the Xiiginns because they were using Earth-based technology (another Boxan term). It dripped of irony that their interstellar invaders had to use technology from a non-interstellar race. But this meant he could find them; it was only a matter of time.

"I think I have something here," James said.

Ed looked away from his holoscreen and saw Iris doing the same. James Jordan was a talented security analyst, so when he said he might have something, Ed's pulse quickened with anticipation.

"I've been using pattern-recognition applications to compare the logs from various transport agencies—air or sea, mostly. I think the Xiiginns are finally coming here. Well, not *here* specifically, but the United States, or at least North America. These logs here are for jets that are owned through various subsidiaries associated with groups we've identified as having a connection to the Xiiginns," James said.

"Are you sure about that? Because the Xiiginn connection to those groups is paper thin at best," Iris said.

"We investigate every lead," Ed said, his tone leaving no room for argument. "Do we have any idea where those jets have gone?"

"We have where they left from and their last known heading, but we don't have confirmation that they reached their destination. We'll have to guess as to where they made landfall, but it gives us a target," James said.

Ed nodded. "Good. Coordinate with Webb's team and bring in the FBI if you have to. I don't care. Just get whoever's closest and can get there first."

"Ed, you need to see this," Iris said.

Ed held up his index finger toward Iris. "Contact Benjamin McAllister in Homeland Security and tell them we may have enemies storming our gates. That should get you through any red tape, but if not, get me on the phone."

James jotted down a few quick notes and said he'd get right on it.

Ed turned toward Iris, whose attention was on a broadcast on her own holoscreen. A news briefing was being shown from the ECF lunar base. It kept replaying a video of a group of people and then a man who was standing off to the side suddenly collapsing. The video feed focused in on the man, and Ed recognized him instantly as Michael Hunsicker. The news commentator speculated that some of the ECF personnel had succumbed to a mysterious illness that perplexed medical doctors, but some believed the illness was related to exposure to the Boxans.

"Replay that," Ed said.

Iris started the video feed at the beginning. The camera was focused on General Sheridan, who was addressing a virtual news conference. Michael Hunsicker was standing off to the side with Commander Alyssa Archer. Ed used his neural implants to mute the commentator's audio feed, then selected the area around Michael Hunsicker and amplified the sound. There was a sharp exhalation and then what sounded like a harsh groan before the sound was distorted by other people rushing to Michael Hunsicker's side.

Ed licked his lips in thought. "When was this video taken?"

"Just a few minutes ago," Iris said and frowned. "What is it?"

Ed felt something on the edges of his thoughts. His brow furrowed as he tried to remember. What was he missing? There was something about the way Michael Hunsicker had collapsed and that sound—almost like he was muttering something as he went down. Suddenly, Ed's eyes widened. "Iris, get me General Sheridan right now. Don't go through normal channels. I need his direct line."

Ed watched as Iris brought up the secure interface with the ECF communications protocols. She selected the emergency line and then gave him a firm nod.

"Listen to me very carefully, General," Ed said.

There was a slight pause. "Johnson, how did you get this—"

"We don't have time for that right now. What is Michael Hunsicker's status?"

"They just took him away to the doctor's station. What's this about?" General Sheridan asked, sounding slightly annoyed.

"We just saw the news broadcast where he collapsed. Tell me, is he muttering something that might sound incoherent? Does he have abnormal vitals?" Ed asked.

"How should I know? They just took him away. He's in good hands. I've got a lot on my plate right now and I can't do this with you," General Sheridan said.

"Bill, please wait. This is important. I wouldn't have called you like this if it weren't," Ed said.

General Sheridan didn't reply, but Ed could hear people speaking as the general approached them. "I need Hunsicker's status, now," Sheridan said.

Ed glanced at Iris and muted his line to Sheridan. "Iris, I need you to bring up the remote-viewer protocols used in project Stargate. I need to send a briefing up to the ECF ASAP."

"Are you still there? Did you hear what the doctor said?" General Sheridan asked.

Ed closed his eyes for a moment. "Yeah, I heard it. Listen to me very carefully. Don't let the doctors do anything to him. You need to record everything he does, everything he says. Is his heart rate elevated?" Ed asked.

He heard Sheridan repeat the question to the doctor. "Yeah, Ed, it's really high and they're concerned about it. They're about to give him medicine to bring it down."

"No! Don't do that. I think he's getting a message."

"A message?" General Sheridan said in disbelief. "What kind of message?"

"Are there any Boxans with you? They can confirm it, but I think he's being contacted like our remote viewers were in the Project Stargate Program back in the eighties. Just make sure we don't interfere with it," Ed said.

"Michael Hunsicker doesn't have this ability. Why would a message even come to him?" General Sheridan asked.

"I don't know, Bill, but you need to trust me. Someone's trying to communicate with us, and they were able to get past the Star Shroud shield. Is the shield still up?" Ed asked.

There was a moment of silence before Sheridan answered. "All shroud monitoring devices report as active. The shield is still up."

Ed blew out a breath of relief. "That's good. I'm going to send the remote-viewer protocols we used with Project Stargate, along with the videos of those viewers receiving the previous messages. They recorded everything and were able to disseminate a message from what the reviewers were saying. There were even hidden messages within their vital signs, fluttering of the eyes, twitching of the fingers. It goes on and on. You need to record everything right now."

General Sheridan said he would and closed the line.

Ed rolled his shoulders and blew out a long breath. "Did you send that data to the ECF?"

"Sent and received," Iris confirmed. "Good catch. I would've missed that completely."

Ed brought his hands to the top of his head and arched his back, stretching his muscles. He pressed his lips together. "This isn't good. That news broadcast was nationally televised, correct?"

Iris frowned and then nodded. "You look worried. I would've thought you'd be happy that we received the message at all."

"I'm concerned about the message, but I'm more concerned that the message was received during a public broadcast—meaning we're not the only ones to realize that a Mardoxian message has been received by the ECF," Ed said.

Iris pursed her lips in thought. "You think the Xiiginns are going to find out about this? Ed, it looks like Hunsicker just collapsed. Even the media is saying it's some kind of illness."

Ed shook his head. "We can't trust the media. They're too busy trying to be seen rather than providing intelligent content. It's been that way for over twenty years, probably even more so now. No, if *I* saw it, there isn't a doubt in my mind that the Xiiginns will notice it. They're going to know we've been contacted by Boxans outside the shield."

Ed paced back and forth for a minute while he considered the possibilities. What could have happened that the Boxans would try to contact them now? "We can't wait for Sheridan. We need a resource on that base to give us the details about Michael Hunsicker."

"What happened to playing well with others?" Iris asked with a knowing smile.

"We still are, but I need to know what's in that message. They wouldn't contact us if it weren't important. Once the Xiiginns realize that a message has been received, they're going to want to know what's in it, too," Ed said.

Iris returned to her console and began working. She glanced over at him. "You could go up to the base yourself."

Ed snorted. "You trying to get rid of me?"

A small smile tugged at the edges of Iris's full lips. "I thought maybe you'd like to be present on the scene."

Ed considered it for a moment and shook his head. "No, I don't need to be there. I just need to know what's going on. This might actually work out for us, now that I've had a chance to think about it."

Iris's gaze narrowed suspiciously. "What do you mean?"

"Whatever's in that message, the Xiiginns will likely expedite their timeline, which means they might make mistakes. I think we can help them along with that, perhaps entice them by making an offer they can't refuse," Ed said.

CHAPTER TWELVE

Michael lay in a bed that felt as if it would swallow him up. He tried to turn his head, but he might as well have tried to push a Mack truck with just his neck muscles. He heard a distinct clearing of the throat that was decidedly feminine in tone and opened his eyes to a dimly lit room. He couldn't tell who was in the room with him.

"You just couldn't stand not being the center of the attention. Isn't that right, Mr. Hunsicker?"

"Alyssa, is that you?" Michael asked. He felt like he had massive weights slowing down his brain.

"Who else would it be?" Alyssa said and grasped his hand, giving it a firm squeeze.

Michael worked his jaw into a swallow and drew in a deep breath. "What happened?"

"You've been out of it for three days. What do you remember?" Alyssa asked.

Michael winced from the pain in his head. It hurt just to think. "Three . . . days," he muttered.

"Take your time," Alyssa said. "I'm going to raise the bed so you're sitting up more. Tell me if this bothers you."

Michael clenched his teeth in anticipation of more pain. His body ached as if he'd just run a marathon, but the bed pushed him upright and some of the fog seemed to lift. He saw the soft contours of Alyssa's face and tried to smile.

"Stop trying to smile at me, you idiot. You really scared the hell out of me," Alyssa said.

"Sorry," Michael said. "Thanks for keeping the lights turned down low."

"You can thank Edward Johnson for that. Somehow he reached General Sheridan's emergency line and told us what he suspected was happening to you," Alyssa said.

"What happened to me?"

Alyssa's eyebrows pulled together in a concerned frown. "You really don't know?"

"It hurts just to think, Allie."

"Indeed, the information sent up by Ed warned it might take you a little while to catch up with what happened," Alyssa said. "Don't give me that look; I'm going to tell you. You and a couple of other people nearby were contacted through Mardoxian means. That's how Chazen explained it."

Michael blew a breath and felt his mind clear even further, as if he were waking from a very long sleep. "I'm not a viewer."

"No, you're not, but the other two are. You remember them: Alicia Murphy and Blake Allen. They're not doing much better than you, but according to the Boxans, you bore the brunt of it," Alyssa said.

Michael squeezed his eyes shut for a moment, and a pair of startlingly blue eyes appeared in his mind's eye. He chased after the memory, but it fled away from him. Michael pushed harder and snatched the knowledge from the gloom. He opened his eyes and looked at Alyssa. "My god, it was Kaylan! Somehow, she did this."

Alyssa nodded as if she had expected that answer. "Can you remember anything else?"

Michael looked away from her and tried to concentrate. "A warning. The shield—" A sharp pain lanced across his brain and he felt as if his head were in a vise. "It hurts!" he cried out.

He felt Alyssa's hands on his head, gently massaging his temples and working her way to the base of his skull. The pain lessened.

"Okay, that's enough. Just close your eyes and try to sleep a little more. I'll be right here," Alyssa said.

Michael had a notion to protest for the briefest of moments, but he didn't want to move. He didn't even want to think anymore. He just wanted to lie there and breathe. He focused his breathing and felt himself lured back into a restful sleep, far away from the pain in his skull but for a thought that skirted the edge of his mind. Kaylan had reached out to him somehow. When he tried to focus on the warning, the pain in his skull returned, so he stopped thinking about it. His body was warning him that he wasn't ready.

He woke sometime later and Alyssa was there, urging him to go back to sleep. He needed more time, she insisted, and who was he to argue?

The next time Michael woke up he felt much better. The

hundreds of jackhammers in his head had ceased their assault and he could think clearly. The lights were on in his room and it didn't feel like somebody was stabbing his eyes. The doctors had formulated a cocktail to give him, which was based on the recommendation from Edward Johnson that came from the Dux Corp data archives. It was how they'd helped viewers cope with the previous Boxan warning.

He had just finished his breakfast and was dressing himself when Alyssa walked into his room. She regarded him with all the scrutiny of a mother hen monitoring her chicks. "We can delay this meeting if you need more time."

Michael's shoulders and back muscles were still sore, but the doctors had assured him that it would just take a little more time. They'd been able to almost completely alleviate his concussion-like symptoms. There was only one other time in his life when his head had felt like his brain had been swished up in a blender, and that had been when he'd played football in high school.

"I need to be there in case I remember something else. I think that's worth a little discomfort," Michael said.

Alyssa rolled her eyes but didn't press the matter further. *She* wouldn't lie in a bed recovering when there was work to be done, and neither would he. They left his room to find two ECF soldiers waiting outside.

"General Sheridan's orders," Alyssa said.

Michael gave a nod to the soldiers and walked down the corridor. Fifteen minutes later they met up with General Sheridan and his staff, including Kyle Matthews, in a conference room near the command center. Michael glanced around the room and noticed that there weren't any Boxans in attendance.

General Sheridan waved them over to where he and Kyle were sitting. Sheridan asked how he was feeling, and Michael told him he was fit for duty.

"Why are there no Boxans here? I thought they usually had at least one representative here," Michael asked.

The Boxans were rarely far from the command center and different operation centers throughout the base.

"They're discussing the contents of the message you received," General Sheridan said.

Michael had watched a video feed of what happened to him and the subsequent days that followed. Parts of Kaylan's message were clear and easily understood, but there was something else that not even Michael could make heads or tails of.

"Have you remembered anything else?" General Sheridan asked.

Michael's memory of the message was strange, almost as if he could hear echoes of Kaylan's voice coming down a long tunnel. "I think you've captured everything, and if anything, my memory reconfirms what I already said." He looked away for a moment. "You'll have to forgive me, General, but this is extremely strange."

A short man in an ECF uniform leaned forward and cleared his throat. "Don't try to force the memories. You might gain new insights as time goes on," Blake said.

Michael recognized the man as being part of a classified group within the ECF for those with the Mardoxian potential. "The part of the message that is very clear is that the Confederation's putting together an armada and they're going to attack us here. They believe that with enough firepower they can cause the shield to fail, even if it has to constrict enough to cause planetary realignment."

General Sheridan nodded. "We knew the shield was constricting, which we think is due to the power requirements for maintaining the shield. So the message reiterates some of our concerns. The closest planet to the shield is Neptune, and I have a room full of astrophysicists trying to come up with theories of what would happen if that entire planet was suddenly pushed from its orbit. I've seen some of the early mockups—worst-case scenario stuff—and it's enough to make me sick."

Michael knew that the outer solar system planets were quite far from Earth, but not since the early life of the solar system had the planetary orbits been put into disarray. The real danger was if a planet like Neptune or Saturn was suddenly pushed into Jupiter's orbit, which had up till now provided stability in the entire solar system as its largest planet. The technology behind the Star Shroud shield was something that could affect these planets. Even the Boxans were of the opinion that there was a strong probability the danger was quite real, even when considering the vast distances between the planets.

"I do remember something that seems like a foreign language. I don't understand what it means though," Michael said.

"The Boxans are working with our scientists on that part. They believe they're some kind of instructions for the Star Shroud devices. Perhaps even a way to disable them," Colonel Matthews said.

The doors to the conference room opened and Chazen and Scraanyx walked in. The loud thuds of their footsteps pounded the floor with a sense of finality. They were grim-faced and carried with them an aura of severity. Chazen glanced over at Michael and gave him a nod.

"General Sheridan," Scraanyx said and brought his fist

across his heart. "We have a formal request to make of the ECF in light of the Mardoxian message. I thought it best to bring it to you straight away."

General Sheridan regarded the Boxan for a few moments. "Let's hear it," he said finally.

"We would like to return to our colony," Scraanyx said and paused for a moment. "The Mardoxian message revealed that an alliance has been made between Boxans and a species called the Nershals, among a few others. They are planning to attack the Confederation Armada. Such a thing is unprecedented in our war with the Xiiginn, and we believe this battle will forever affect the fate of our species. We would like to fight at their side when they do."

"There's still the matter of the Star Shroud shield," General Sheridan replied.

"We understand that, and we're working hard to ensure that the message is deciphered as accurately as possible," Scraanyx said.

Michael's shoulders tightened. If General Sheridan denied the request, he had no idea what the Boxans would do. They could just take whatever ships they had left and try to bring down the shield, forcing the ECF into facing the harsh reality of defending the solar system.

Scraanyx held up one of his hands. "We understand this is not a request that should be handled lightly. You will no doubt need to consult with your United Nations. We want you to have time to consider it fully and continue to engage us with any questions you might have. We will, in turn, continue our ongoing efforts to assist you."

General Sheridan stood up. "Thank you for your understanding and for giving us time. We owe a great deal to you, and that's something I will never forget."

Scraanyx and Chazen left the conference room, and an uneasy, tense silence settled in the Boxans' wake. No one dared to break it.

"Look sharp, people," General Sheridan said. "Things have just gotten more complicated, but we still have a job to do."

If more of an understatement could be voiced, Michael couldn't think of what it would be. They had their work cut out for them, and on top of that, all the Boxans wanted to go home. The ECF did have ships that were, in theory, capable of making the journey, though they were untested and there was the Star Shroud shield to contend with. Michael glanced at General Sheridan, who seemed to draw the eyes of all those in the room. While the Boxans someday leaving them had always been a probability, no one had thought it would come this quickly. Were they ready to defend Earth from invasion? Michael glanced at Colonel Matthews, whose face was a mask of determination. No doubt, he was working out what actions he would need to take to deal with this latest threat. The Mardoxian message was a wake-up call for the Earth Coalition Force and for humanity.

CHAPTER THIRTEEN

Zack stopped at an alcove in the corridor of the Boxan ship. He needed to look at something before he headed to the medical bay where Kaylan, Ma'jasalax, and Valkra had all been resting for several days. After multiple failed attempts to send a message to Earth, Kaylan had requested that they return to Earth's solar system. The heavy cruiser didn't have any windows because it was a warship, but Zack was able to bring up a view of the solar system on one of the wallscreens.

He hadn't been this close to home since he'd activated the Star Shroud shield. At that time, two Boxan Dreadnoughts were holding the line against the Xiiginn fleet, and his mind flashed back to the bridge of the *Athena*. They'd all watched in horror as the Xiiginn fleet managed to begin pushing their way through the behemoth Boxan warships. Zack had done the only thing he could think of, and even then he'd relied on Athena to help him.

The wallscreen showed an image of the solar system with

the sun gleaming like a lonely beacon amidst a celestial back-drop. Kaylan had insisted on coming here a few days earlier for one final effort to send a message to Earth. He didn't know whether proximity really played a role in what Kaylan had been able to do. A million miles was a million miles in his mind, and even though they were in the area known as the Oort cloud, they were still significantly far from Earth.

He and Gaarokk had monitored the Mardoxian chamber while Kaylan, Ma'jasalax, and Valkra went inside to try a method of communication that even the Boxans had serious reservations about. They had been in there for hours, and when the chamber finally opened, all three of them were uncon-scious. They were moved to the medical bay and Kladomaor ordered the ship to stay in the area and monitor the shield. They hadn't been sure if the message had been sent until Kaylan woke up. She'd been the first to regain consciousness and she told them that she'd been able to reach Michael Hunsicker. They'd loitered in the area for another two days and were about to head back to the Nerva star system.

Zack walked toward Kaylan, thinking she still looked a little pale. The Boxans almost always looked the same to him. He guessed there would be no way to tell if they looked pale with their rough brown skin that was quite similar to the bark of a tree.

"Why Michael Hunsicker?" Zack asked.

"We kept trying to use the Boxan method, which was essen-tially a broadcast signal, and it kept failing. And then I wondered what would happen if I focused my efforts on someone specific," Kaylan said.

"Did you see anything?" Zack asked.

Kaylan frowned as if she were trying to put the pieces

together in her mind. "It wasn't like before when I used the chamber. Ma'jasalax said it was because we were using a different method. I could only see shapes and things like that, but I had to focus on someone familiar, someone who would understand the message."

"Are you sure he received the message?"

"It's hard to explain to someone who didn't experience it," Kaylan replied.

"I get that, I guess, but Michael doesn't have this ability, so how can you be sure the message was received?" Zack asked and then tacked on, "Not that I want you to try again. Your vital signs were extremely low. I'm sure that if Brenda was here, she'd be giving you a good tongue-lashing."

"I know the message went through. But they'll need time to decipher it, and we can't stay here," Kaylan said.

"We're not. Kladomaor kept the ship there for a while, but there's been no change in the shield," Zack replied.

Ma'jasalax walked over to them. "We should go to the bridge."

They left the medical bay and headed toward the main bridge of the ship. Once they got to the bridge, Kladomaor looked over at them from the commander's couch.

"We're about to reach Nerva," Kladomaor said.

They transitioned through the wormhole and into the edge of the Nerva star system. Scanners showed a concentration of ships around Selebus, and Kladomaor frowned. Zack looked at the information on the main holoscreen and saw that there were many more ships than when they'd left.

"Helm, best speed to Selebus," Kladomaor said. "Comms, send word to the Alliance that we've returned."

Zack glanced at Kaylan, who was studying the main holo-screen. "What's the matter?"

"Something isn't right," Kaylan said and looked at Klado-maor. "Can you open a comms channel to the *Athena*?"

Kladomaor did but warned that there would be a significant delay until they were closer to Selebus.

Hicks answered the comms channel. "I'm glad you're back because we've got a bit of trouble going on. The Gresans tried to take our ship, and several Nershal warships intercepted them."

"What about the Boxan fleet?" Kladomaor asked.

"They're trying to get the Gresans to stand down," Hicks replied.

"Tactical, can you detect active weapons systems on any of those ships around the *Athena*?" Kladomaor asked.

"That will take several minutes because we're still too far out, Battle Leader," Varek replied.

"Very well," Kladomaor said and turned toward them. "It looks like we've entered some sort of standoff. Even at best speed, we're still hours away from Selebus."

Kaylan glanced at the main holodisplay, considering. "Is there somewhere we can talk to the *Athena* in private?"

Kladomaor frowned and glanced at Ma'jasalax before reply-ing. "I can offer you one of the workstations on the bridge."

"I was hoping to use one of the tactical operations rooms off the bridge," Kaylan said.

"We can certainly go there if that's what you want," Klado-maor said.

Zack saw that there was a hard glint to Kaylan's eyes he hadn't noticed before.

Kaylan leveled her gaze at Kladomaor. "I'm sorry; I wasn't clear. It will just be Zack and me. You see, I need to speak with my crew that's surrounded by a bunch of warships you know the *Athena* cannot stand against."

Zack had to keep his mouth from hanging open. Kaylan wasn't fooling around, and her stern tone couldn't be missed by anyone on the bridge.

Kladomaor's flaxen eyes regarded Kaylan for a moment. "You may use my office off the bridge and I'll make sure you aren't disturbed."

Kaylan thanked him and glanced at Zack, silently beckoning him to follow her.

"Kaylan," Kladomaor said after they'd taken a few steps away from the command area, "you can trust me. I hope you know that."

Zack watched as Kaylan's eyes softened. "I do know that and I do trust you, but this is more than two individuals from separate species."

Ma'jasalax lifted her chin, summoning every ounce of dignity she possessed, and projected an air of authority. "We'll keep you apprised of any new developments. Please let us know if there's anything we can do for the *Athena* and her crew."

Zack followed Kaylan to Kladomaor's office. The Boxans had a different word for office, but he couldn't remember what it was. The room was just outside the bridge, and they went inside.

Zack sighed. "We leave the Nerva star system for just a few days and suddenly there's a standoff. I don't like it one bit. The timing is too suspect for me. Someone waited for us to leave."

Kaylan had her back to him, and she brought her hands to her waist and arched her back, stretching her shoulders. Zack's thoughts came to a stop while he took in how beautiful she was. She let her hands go to her sides and sighed. Then she turned toward him. "I should've seen this coming. The Gresans are trying to take the *Athena*."

Zack nodded. "We knew they were . . . I don't know if 'interested' is the right word or 'highly intrigued' by the *Athena*, but in any case, it's not surprising."

Kaylan shook her head. "You still don't understand. There's a division in the Alliance, even among the Boxans. This could have been a coordinated effort between them."

"I thought I'm normally the paranoid one, but I think you're right. We need to open a comms channel to the *Athena*, and it needs to be secure so no one can listen in on our conversation," Zack said.

A new connection registered with his internal heads-up display and he saw that the same connection had established on Kaylan's implants.

"No need for a comms channel," Athena said. "We're secure from any monitoring the Boxans are capable of. Commander, I'm happy you've returned."

"Have you been listening to us the whole time?" Zack asked.

"I've been monitoring all communications in this system," Athena replied.

Kaylan frowned. "There should be a lag since we're so far away."

"That is correct, Commander, but I used microscopic wormholes to establish this channel," Athena said.

Zack's eyes widened. "Athena, are you saying we can talk through subspace?"

"Affirmative. The data models supporting it were accessible in my data storage matrix. I've been running multiple virtualized experiments, but our current situation required that I shift my efforts to accelerate my original timetable and reveal this new capability," Athena said.

"That kind of research should have taken years to do, maybe even longer," Kaylan said.

"Not if her processing power keeps increasing," Zack replied.

"We'll have to talk about this another time. Athena, who's on board the ship?" Kaylan asked.

"All remaining crew are aboard the ship, Commander."

"Understood. Please patch them in," Kaylan said. Once Athena confirmed that the rest of the crew was available on comms, Kaylan continued. "Hicks, give me the rundown. It's just me and Zack here and no one else."

"Understood, Commander. The Napox tried to sneak aboard the ship. Athena took control of their spacecraft. It was small—even smaller than our shuttle. Almost like a strike-fighter, but without weapons systems. Athena was able to track them to a Gresan warship. I informed the Boxans and the Nershals, which in hindsight may not have been the best thing to do because suddenly all these ships started surrounding us. Athena then informed us that she could disrupt Gresan communications and perhaps even control some of their systems. She later expanded that to include Nershal and Boxan ships," Hicks said.

"I hope you didn't do that," Kaylan said.

"Don't worry, we didn't. It was news to me that she even had the ability to do that. We're in a bit of a pickle here, Commander, and I'm not sure if there's a way out of it," Hicks said.

Zack had gotten to know Hicks throughout the duration of this journey, and this was the major's way of saying that they might be screwed. "They're focusing on the wrong thing. All of them."

Kaylan looked at Zack. "I agree, but can you clarify what you mean?"

"What I mean is that they're focusing their efforts on this bright, shiny thing—our ship—and what they need to be focusing on is the Confederation Armada. That's what we want. That's what we need," Zack said.

"They're all afraid. They think the *Athena* can give them an edge in this war. They might be right about that, but I'm not going to sit by and let them take the ship," Kaylan said.

"I still say we're all focusing on the wrong thing, because as long as we're all focused on this, who's thinking about how to beat the Xiiginns? They're the true enemy," Zack said.

"Sounds good, but how do we do that?" Hicks said.

"Athena," Kaylan said, "if you can monitor all the communications here, what if we were to go to the Confederation space station? Would you be able to glean any intelligence from the ship-to-ship communications going on there?"

"Affirmative, Commander. The Xiiginns' communications protocols are based on Boxan design. According to the Boxans, the Xiiginns steal technology from other races and use it themselves, so there's a high probability that they're using a variant of technology that already exists. Therefore, I should be able to decipher it," Athena replied.

Zack listened as Kaylan and Hicks discussed what they could do to keep the Alliance at bay while offering them something in return at the same time.

::*You don't seem to agree with this line of thinking,*:: Athena said in a text message that appeared on Zack's internal heads-up display.

::*Didn't anyone tell you that it's rude to have a side conversation while there are other people around?*:: Zack replied.

He heard Athena give a vocal reply to Kaylan and felt his eyebrows pull together at a sudden thought.

::*Either your capabilities have grown in the last few days, or you've been understating what you can do,*:: Zack said.

::*I thought it prudent to manage the crew's emotional state for maximum efficiency,*:: Athena replied.

Oh god, now she's playing head games with us, Zack thought.

"Athena," Zack said, breaking into the conversation he hadn't been listening to. "You've been running many simulations on how best to deal with the Xiiginns. Do you have any insights to offer us that might help find the best course of action?"

Kaylan looked at him for a moment with surprise clearly registering on her face.

"Every data model I've run that puts all the ships in the Alliance against the Confederation Armada results in the total annihilation of the Star Alliance fleet," Athena said.

Zack gave a slight shake of his head and reminded himself that the AI had just told him she was working to manage the crew's emotional state, so why had she up and said they were all going to die if they faced this Confederation Armada? He didn't say any of that out loud because he thought it would be too distracting.

"We can't just give up," Kaylan said.

"I apologize, Commander. I was merely stating the results of my analysis since fleet engagement is at the forefront of multiple Alliance species strategy sessions," Athena said.

"We need to decide what we're going to do right now because there are a lot of warships nearby, and while I don't think they would start shooting at one another, you never know," Hicks said.

Zack watched as Kaylan rubbed the bridge of her nose and then leaned on the Boxan desk, which came up to the middle of her back. "We need more time. What if we offered the Alliance unfettered access to the *Athena* after the Confederation Armada is defeated?" Kaylan said.

Zack shook his head. "We can't give them the *Athena*. She's one of us."

Kaylan looked at him regretfully. "She's a ship—a wonderful, amazing ship, but she's still a ship with an extraordinary artificial intelligence. A promise to these races that we'll share the Drar technology with them might be the only thing that keeps this alliance together."

Zack's nostrils flared and his jaw tightened. "You're talking about her as if she's a thing. She's a living entity—a being. She passed every Turing test ever conceived. I ought to know because I've been giving them to her. Athena's interaction with us isn't Human mimicry or the product of sophisticated Boxan programming. If you didn't know the *Athena* was a ship, you'd all believe she was a person. You don't have the right to just hand her over to them. They don't deserve her. The Drar gave *us* the ship," Zack said, jamming his thumb toward the center of his chest. "Not the Boxans or anyone else. The Drar chose to give us their technology. They didn't pick them because they weren't worthy. I'm sorry if that makes them all upset, but giving in to this tantrum isn't going to help us in the long run. If anything, it will further drive a wedge between us."

Zack turned away from her. He couldn't look at her right now because he was furious.

"Zack," Kaylan said gently.

Zack blew out a heated sigh through his teeth and reluctantly turned toward her. "You can't do this," he said.

"I can," Kaylan said, and her gaze was unyielding.

Zack felt his insides go cold.

"Commander," Athena said.

Zack felt his throat tense. He couldn't let her do this.

"Go ahead," Kaylan said, her voice sounding strained.

"I will follow any order you give me, including this one," Athena said.

Zack shook his head. "Why? Why would you do this?"

"Because Kaylan is the mission commander and I know this couldn't have been easy for her," Athena replied.

Zack turned toward Kaylan and saw that her eyes were glistening, as if at any moment the tears would come. He blew out a breath and felt it wash over his teeth. He glared at her. "They call you Mardoxian Blessed because of your abilities. You're supposed to be able to look into a situation with heightened insights bordering on precognitive capabilities."

"Zack, this isn't fair," Hicks said. "The fact is that we can't stop the entire Alliance from taking the ship. Offering them something they have the ability to take anyway buys us time."

Zack pressed his lips together and scowled. "There's another way, and I'm going to find it."

Zack didn't wait for Kaylan to respond. He couldn't bear to look at her right then. He had to leave the room, had to think. There had to be some way they could get through this without condemning the *Athena* to being ripped apart so a few alien species could get some kind of technological advantage. They had to be better than that.

::Thank you. I appreciate all you've done for me.::

Athena's words appeared on his internal heads-up display

and he felt as if they would shatter his heart. The Drar had thought Humans were better than this, so why couldn't they find another way? Why hadn't the Drar given them a way to defeat the Xiiginns? A tiny voice of reason tried to urge his thoughts into more rational thinking, but he couldn't go there. Kaylan was just doing what she thought was right, but in this she was wrong.

CHAPTER FOURTEEN

As the lunar base expanded, it had been decided that the most practical way to add living space was to use the long-dormant lava tunnels under the surface of the moon. Being underground protected them from harsh solar radiation since the moon didn't have an atmosphere of its own. There was an area of tunnels set aside for the Boxans to use that also gave them easy access to the lunar surface. Many Boxans rotated out to the New Moon to oversee manufacturing activities, as well as research and development based on shared Boxan technology.

In the last few days, Michael had resumed his role as the lead liaison between the Boxans and the ECF. He had long gotten used to being among the ten-foot-tall aliens with their deep, gravelly voices and large golden eyes. Despite the Boxans' size, they were quite agile and were extra careful when around Humans. After living with Chazen for months at the Boxan monitoring station, Michael had adjusted and never had to worry about being accidentally knocked over or bumped into. There were some Boxans who weighed over seven hundred pounds, but they'd learned that the average Boxan weight was closer to five hundred, with females weighing only slightly less than the males.

"Has there been any official response to our request?" Scraanyx asked.

Scraanyx was large, even for a Boxan. It had been two days since Scraanyx and Chazen had made the initial request on behalf of all the Boxan refugees for the ECF to take them home.

"General Sheridan will be leaving today to address the United Nations about your request. In fact, I'll be heading back to the main complex for a final meeting on that very subject," Michael said.

He looked at Scraanyx for a moment and then flicked his gaze to Chazen. It was difficult to gauge a Boxan's moods. Michael's experience with them revealed that they were extremely patient, which he attributed to the Boxan culture, but in spite of knowing that, Michael felt he needed to say something else to them. "I think the work you've done so far will help address our shortcomings when the inevitable subject comes up about how we'll continue without you. We're well aware of everything you've done for us and we'll do everything we can to help you return home. I just wanted you to know that. If it were up to me . . ."

"We understand these things take time. That's why I have Boxans working on plans to transfer the duties we've been overseeing to ECF personnel," Scraanyx said.

Michael had been informed yesterday of the procedures the Boxans had authored. They were meant to be used as a guideline to help the ECF maximize their use of Boxan technology, but the procedures themselves had been in development for a long time. Michael knew that Scraanyx was "just" a strike commander, which was essentially like a captain in the ECF. The job Scraanyx had been called to do would ordinarily have been done by someone else, like Battle Leader Prax'Pedax, who had sacrificed himself to protect Earth.

"General Sheridan wanted me to ask if you would consider accompanying him to address the United Nations," Michael said.

The Boxans had been reluctant to return to Earth because of what had happened months ago. The presence of the Xiiginns had made them redouble their efforts to get the ECF up and running, and they'd provided guidance on how to hunt the Xiiginns. It wasn't as if they didn't want to go down to the planet, but they felt that the risk was too great for them.

"We'll take every precaution to ensure your safety, but General Sheridan believes your presence would lend credence to your request," Michael continued.

Scraanyx glanced at Chazen, who said, "It's a Human thing."

Michael smiled. "Many people are extremely aware that you are, in fact, here, but there's a difference between knowing that something exists and seeing it firsthand. I think that if you go down to Earth with General Sheridan, it would help him get support and approval to let you go home."

Scraanyx took a few moments to consider what Michael had said. "Inform General Sheridan that I will consider his request as long as I am able to bring my own protection. No fewer than twelve Boxans will accompany me to the surface of the planet."

"I understand, and I'll let him know your requirements," Michael replied.

Scraanyx left the room, but Chazen lingered behind.

"You're almost home, or at least back among your own species," Michael said.

"It's been so long that I almost don't remember it. Sethion, our homeworld, is lost to us, but I still dream about it sometimes. That must seem strange to you," Chazen said.

Michael shook his head. "I don't think so. I don't know anyone who's been through what you've had to endure—living for so many years in isolation, even with stasis. I don't know anyone else who could've survived. I want you to know I'll do everything I can to help get you home. It's the least I can do," Michael said.

He wouldn't be alive if it wasn't for Chazen. They'd been stranded for months together at the Boxan monitoring station on Pluto. Michael remembered waiting and hoping for a rescue that ultimately never came. They'd had to construct a life pod for themselves and then open a small wormhole to put them near Earth. Of all the Boxans Michael had come to know these past few months, none of them were as important to him as Chazen.

"I know you will," Chazen said solemnly.

Michael left the Boxan living area and returned to the main ECF complex. He was late for his next meeting, but he was sure General Sheridan would understand.

Michael made his way to the large conference room where General Sheridan's final strategy meeting before heading back to Earth was already underway. Michael walked in and quickly made his way toward a seat that was reserved for him. The conference room was occupied by the ECF senior staff. Michael recognized Gary Hunter, who had joined the ECF from NASA. There were so many other familiar faces around the large table.

In particular, he noted that General Shang, China's representative in the ECF, was also in attendance. Kyle had once told Michael that General Sheridan initially refused China's proposed candidate, who was part of their concession for supporting the ECF. Eventually, General Sheridan relented in order to allow the ECF to get off the ground with the support it needed.

"The proposed emissary envoy will be met with a lot of resistance. Many will argue against sending an envoy to the Confederation because it's beyond the ECF's mandate, which is to protect the earth," General Shang said.

General Sheridan looked at Colonel Matthews.

"I agree. The United Nations won't go along with this. I've spoken to several US representatives with experience in coordinating both military and civilian response, and when they weigh the Boxans' request against the safety of the planet, essentially Earth comes first," Colonel Matthews replied.

General Sheridan looked at Michael. "What do you think the Boxans would do if we refused their request or, to put it more diplomatically, delayed the request for a time?"

"It's tough to say. The Boxans are extraordinarily patient, but everyone has their limits. How would you react knowing that after so many years of war there was to be a major offensive that would forever impact the fate of your species? I wouldn't want to back them into a corner like that, and frankly, it wouldn't be fair to them," Michael replied.

General Sheridan nodded. "Neither would I. It sounds as if they've been backed into a corner for a long time, and they aren't strangers to taking action when they need to. I don't want to put them in that position." General Sheridan looked around at those sitting at the conference table. "Mr. Hunter, can you give me the status of your team's analysis of the Mardoxian message?"

Gary cleared his throat. "The warning was pretty clear. I conferred with the Boxans about the dangers the Star Shroud shield poses. If the Confederation Armada were to arrive here and start bombarding the shield, we don't think it would simply collapse. We think it would constrict faster while trying to maintain its integrity. This would accelerate the destruction of the solar system as we know it. Inside the Mardoxian message was a shutdown protocol that pertains to the Star Shroud devices. The protocol is different from what the Boxans use to manage the Star Shrouds, but they've informed us that the Star Shrouds are based on another species' technology that was even more advanced than the Boxans are. We think this shutdown protocol is based on this elder species' technology."

"Elder species?" General Sheridan asked.

"The Boxans call them the Drar," Gary replied.

"Is there any way for us to test whether this shutdown protocol actually works?" General Sheridan asked.

"We don't have the resources to test it. We would need to build an actual Star Shroud device, which even the Boxans don't have the knowledge to do, so there's no test we can run," Gary said.

"Does the message say who created the protocol?" General Sheridan asked.

"The Boxans confirmed it wasn't them," Gary replied.

Michael caught General Sheridan's attention, and the general nodded for Michael to speak. "It has to be Zack Quick, General."

"I've heard an awful lot about this Mr. Quick. Edward Johnson speaks highly of him, and I know you have a high opinion of his technical capabilities, but even if this came from him, can we trust that it will work?" General Sheridan asked.

"General, I've worked with Zack, and if there's anyone who can figure out how alien technology works, it's him. Given the amount of time he's been around Boxan technology, I don't think it's too far a stretch that he's been able to utilize what he's learned and apply it in such a way as this," Michael replied.

"Whether or not we trust who created the shutdown protocol isn't important," General Shang said. "We shouldn't be too hasty to shut down the Star Shroud shield. The shield gives us time to build our fleets, and we need those fleets to defend Earth. Also, there's a risk that this shutdown protocol won't work the way we expected it to work. If my understanding is correct, the Boxans didn't even know the Star Shroud devices could make a shield."

"I'm not sure we can get around making certain assumptions," Michael said. "The shield went up just as the Xiiginn fleet was about to push into our solar system. The timing of that was too convenient to believe it happened by chance. What if the crew of the *Athena* got access to this Drar technology, and when they tried to get home, they saw the battle being fought? I know Zack Quick very well, and he's no stranger to taking the initiative and doing what has to be done. I don't think that personality trait would've changed. What I'm trying to say is that he and the crew might've initiated the Star Shroud shield."

"Indeed," General Sheridan said. "Mr. Quick's file does indicate idealistic tendencies. It was those tendencies that in many ways brought us to where we are today. I'm not saying he's to blame, but there are some who view it that way."

"General," Gary Hunter said. "If we're able to determine that the shield is constricting, then certainly someone outside the shield can make the same determination. It wouldn't take much of a leap to understand that if the shield is constricting, it could have disastrous effects on the planets caught inside. This is their way of sending help. Michael's right and we're making assumptions, but I don't think we can afford to ignore these assumptions, even if the United Nations doesn't agree with them."

Michael felt his breath catch in his chest. He supposed they'd been dancing around the subject of what they'd do if the United Nations denied the Boxans' request to go home.

General Sheridan's mouth formed a grim line. "Mr. Hunter has been the first one to say what some of us have been thinking. Talk about being between a rock and a hard place," he said, and there were several chuckles throughout the room. "I have the reports with me, and I'll present the different options we've compiled, along with my own recommendation."

Michael noticed several people shifting in their chairs, primarily the Chinese.

"For those of you who're returning to Earth with me, we'll be leaving in fifteen minutes. The rest of you continue with your duties. We're all depending on you," General Sheridan said.

The meeting ended and General Sheridan asked Michael and Colonel Matthews to stay behind for a few moments. General Shang lingered behind, and Sheridan told him that he would speak to him on the shuttle ride back to Earth.

With the meeting finished, Michael looked at the grim lines on General Sheridan's face. This job was taking a toll on the seasoned general.

"Sir, about Zack," Michael began.

"Never mind about him. I have to listen to my experts and

trust in their opinions. I've been in the Army for over thirty years and never once did I consider whether or not we were doing what was necessary, but this . . ." Sheridan shook his head. Michael glanced at Kyle, who stood ramrod straight, waiting for the general to continue. "I have to make a recommendation. I can't just present options. Regardless, Colonel, I want you to return to your ship and continue to prep the crew, because no matter what's decided, your ship will play a major part in our plans."

"Yes, General. We'll be ready," Colonel Matthews said.

"General," Michael said, "Scraanyx said he would join you to address the United Nations as long as he can bring his own security force."

"I expected as much. Scraanyx is a warrior who's been thrust into a diplomacy role. Very well, I'll have my staff coordinate with him," General Sheridan said and looked at Michael for a long moment.

Michael wanted to ask him what his recommendation was going to be, but he suspected the general wasn't actually sure himself. His inner conflict was evident on his face—the conflict of weighing all the options as opposed to just simply doing the right thing.

"Do you like history?" Sheridan asked.

"Of course, sir," Michael said, and Kyle echoed the same.

General Sheridan nodded as if he expected nothing less. "You know, it's been over a hundred years since our country spent almost too long on the sidelines before becoming involved in one of the pivotal moments in the world's history. We almost got left behind. Why do I feel like we're facing a similar situation but on a much grander scale that has the potential to affect generations to come?"

Michael nodded, knowing that in many ways World War II had shaped the world they'd come to know, even a hundred years later. He hadn't seen the similarities between that conflict and what they were now facing, but he supposed it was a good analogy. They were still stumbling to get on the playing field where they could go toe to toe with an aggressive alien species. Michael had been so focused on what they were doing that he'd never really given thought to how history would remember them or whether there would even be anyone left to remember them.

"Colonel," Michael said, "I'm willing to wager that there are a lot of Boxans who would be eager to weigh in on the *Lincoln's* operations."

Colonel Matthews' eyebrows pulled together, furrowing his brow for a moment, and he glanced at General Sheridan. "I think their presence would help a great deal."

"Well, don't let me stop you," General Sheridan said.

CHAPTER FIFTEEN

"The Humans have become increasingly proficient at tracking us," Hoan Berend said.

Mar Arden stood outside their latest encampment under a star-filled sky. They had to keep moving around, going from place to place. However, this time he'd been adamant that they needed to move to another part of the planet that was much closer to this civilization's seat of power. The risk was greater for them, but this was where they needed to be.

"This is to be expected. Our real adversary works from the shadows outside the Human government. Their use of the Mardoxian trait is impressive. It's interesting how the Mardoxian trait is kept secret. At least some of the Humans understand that such things are better kept to a powerful few," Mar Arden said.

Their most recent move had cost the lives of some of his soldiers. They'd had to make sure there were no remains for the Humans to find, which had lost them some time.

Kandra Rene sent him a message that she was on her way to see him.

"How is our most recent volunteer doing?" Mar Arden asked.

They'd increased their understanding of the Mardoxian genetic trait in Humans and were now testing the enhancement of a Xiiginn volunteer. Mar Arden wanted to acquire a genetic sample of a truly gifted Human test subject from which to base their own enhancement of the Mardoxian into the Xiiginns.

"The technology here is so primitive that the incubation period is taking much longer than if we were on our ship. Are you sure you don't want me to launch an operation to steal Boxan technology?" Hoan Berend asked.

"The Boxans have restricted themselves to ECF bases on their moon. The risk is too great when we can just take a little bit more time to achieve the same thing right where we are. Our adversary expects us to hit technology centers, and the longer we delay, the more their hands are tied," Mar Arden said.

"What do the Humans call this place?" Hoan Berend asked and gestured to the forests around them. The tall trees in the area made this location difficult to find.

Mar Arden used his implants to access the primitive global positioning system satellites the Humans liked to use because he was curious himself. "This region is known as Pennsylvania."

Hoan Berend nodded, and his tail flicked to the side. "Yes, that's it. You think it's too risky for us to launch an operation up there," Hoan Berend said, gesturing toward the sky, "but we're so close to one of the sites where our Boxan infiltrator launched his attack."

"That's because you don't see the advantage of our current location," Kandra Rene said as she joined them.

"I'm sure security is much better established now, but even still, I doubt they'd expect us to strike the same place twice. That's not why we're here. We're here because of its proximity to scientific organizations that have the technology we need. These organizations are mostly removed from those that are being upgraded with Boxan technology," Mar Arden said.

They were being hunted, and Mar Arden was growing tired of running from this primitive species. He'd thought that blowing up strategic cities targeted to entice the Humans into fighting among themselves would have been more effective, but he'd underestimated the ECF and its role in governing this species. This Earth Coalition Force was in its early stages of development, but in another fifty cycles it had the potential to emerge as the singular governing entity of the entire world. He looked at Kandra Rene. "Do you have something to show me?"

Kandra Rene smiled. "Oh yes, I believe you'll be highly interested in this."

She brought up her wrist and a small holoscreen appeared. Mar Arden watched a video image of a group of Humans. One of them collapsed, and he heard faint utterances from him until the sound was lost amidst all the Humans flocking to the fallen man's side.

"The Humans have been trying to remove all traces of this video feed, which is why I began to pursue it. Do you know what that looks like?" Kandra Rene asked.

Mar Arden glanced at Hoan Berend.

"Humans are weak," Hoan Berend said.

"That may be, but it wasn't weakness that caused that Human to collapse," Mar Arden said.

Hoan Berend frowned and then shook his head.

Sometimes Mar Arden wondered how Hoan Berend had

gotten the command of his own warship with instincts like this. The Xiiginn commander was adequate at his job and could follow orders, but abstract thinking was beyond him. He looked at Kandra Rene. "Were you able to confirm what was in the message?"

Hoan Berend's tail flicked irritably and came to settle over his shoulder.

"The Earth Coalition Force is trying to keep that information secure, and they're doing a pretty good job," Kandra Rene replied.

Mar Arden nodded. "Regardless, the fact that a message was received is telling in and of itself."

Hoan Berend sighed heavily. "Would you please fill me in on what's going on? What message?"

"Certainly," Mar Arden said. "The Boxans have used their abilities to send a message through the shield."

"Through Mardoxian means," Hoan Berend said, finally understanding.

"Precisely, which means there've been some new developments outside the shield," Mar Arden said and considered how this new information would affect his plans.

"They must be desperate to send a message using Mardoxian means. They're essentially waving it right in front of us. They must know we would've detected it," Hoan Berend said.

Mar Arden glided his fingertips over the end of his tail, which was wrapped around his narrow waist, and looked at Kandra Rene. "Are there any reports of other mysterious collapses at the time this took place?"

Kandra Rene's eyes slipped into calculation. "None. This was the only instance," she replied.

"Interesting," Mar Arden said.

"I thought so, which means—"

"That this Mardoxian message didn't come from the Boxans. The Humans on the other side of the shield must still be alive, and that means Sion Shif failed his mission. Also, there's one among them who has the Mardoxian potential," Mar Arden said.

Kandra Rene shook her head. "I hadn't considered that."

"If the Boxans are desperate enough to bring the Humans into our war, why wouldn't they train one of them who has the potential to be a true asset to them? Seems pretty clear to me," Mar Arden said.

Mar Arden glanced up at the night sky and peered at the two moons. They were luminous on a clear night like this one. "We're running out of time."

"I don't understand. How does this change anything?" Hoan Berend asked.

"This changes everything. The intelligence we've gotten from the Boxans indicates that they don't know how the shield works. We surmised that the shield couldn't be maintained indefinitely, and I would guess that the Boxans beyond the star system have arrived at the same conclusion. Therefore, they must have discovered a way to deal with it," Mar Arden said.

Hoan Berend considered this for a moment. "That can only work in our favor. If the shield comes down, our fleets can return here and conquer this planet."

Once again, Mar Arden was almost stunned by how stupid the Xiiginn commander was. It was true that the fleet would return, and if Garm Antis had somehow survived the previous assault, he would be keen to acquire the Mardoxian potential from the Humans for himself. And Mar Arden wouldn't put it past Garm Antis to have them all killed so he could claim the credit for bringing the Mardoxian trait to the Xiiginns.

"We need a viable specimen with the Mardoxian potential," Mar Arden said at last.

"That's something I can help you with," Kandra Rene said. "We've got new intelligence of a secret training facility on this continent. I think we should run some reconnaissance on it."

Mar Arden drew in a pleased breath. Kandra Rene was a worthy infiltrator. He almost mourned the loss it would be when he had to kill her.

CHAPTER SIXTEEN

K aylan sat inside a Boxan shuttle heading down to the surface of Selebus. The Gresans had agreed to return to the negotiating table, due in large part to the eight Boxan Dreadnoughts with accompanying battle groups that had entered the Nerva star system. The Boxan fleet was commanded by Battle Leader Salevar, who Kladomaor told her was the most senior officer of their fleet. This show of force was also meant to demonstrate the commitment of the Boxans to the Alliance.

She glanced at the empty seat next to her, missing Zack and feeling the lack of his presence more than ever. He was furious with her, but there had been no other choice. Kaylan had agreed to listen to what the Alliance had to say about the *Athena*, and she was determined to move forward with her plan, which was to share all the knowledge they could gain from the *Athena* with the species who joined the Alliance. Yet Zack looked at her as if she had betrayed them all. She was fond of

ASCENSION

the *Athena*—it was their home—but she couldn't see another way out of this. She hoped Zack would forgive her someday, but for now, he'd chosen to return to Selebus on a different shuttle.

The rest of the *Athena* crew was on their way back to Selebus as well. Kaylan had requested that Efren and Hicks remain on board the *Athena*. Hicks had agreed to stay, but she could tell by his tone that he didn't like it. Kaylan was starting to get a little annoyed with the men and their tantrums when they didn't get their way. A decision had needed to be made.

Ma'jasalax looked over at her. "Sometimes our path can be a lonely one."

"I'm just disappointed that we have to do this at all," Kaylan said.

"Our world is rarely as we want it to be no matter how hard we try to control it. This is one of the lessons we had to learn, and it came at a terrible price. Yet it's a price we would pay again in order to survive," Ma'jasalax said.

Kaylan almost longed for the days when all she had to worry about was the *Athena* and not how the decisions she made would impact the entire Human race.

The shuttle ride to the planet surface was all too short. When she stepped off the loading ramp, she glanced toward the shuttle where Zack was, hoping to catch a glimpse of him. She wasn't about to change her mind and she knew he wouldn't either, but she hated the fact that he was so mad at her. She didn't like giving the *Athena* up either, but considering their options, they had little choice.

Kaylan looked around the landing field and noticed that neither the Gresans nor the Napox had sent ships to Selebus. "Do they intend to remain in orbit now that the Boxan fleet has arrived?"

Kladomaor, who'd been standing nearby, blew out a strong breath. "They prefer the illusion of safety in their ships."

Kaylan pinched her lips together and shook her head. How had the Confederation functioned before the Xiiginns took over? "They aren't the only ones who've tried to take the *Athena* away from us. Zack told me about all the attempts to infiltrate the *Athena's* systems by Boxans when we were at Olloron."

Kladomaor sighed heavily with a pained expression. "I don't know what to say about that. I don't know who it was. We don't understand why the Drar chose to share their knowledge with you instead of us. We've searched for them for hundreds of cycles. It's part of who we are. That doesn't excuse what happened, but are Humans so different from us? If the situation was reversed, do you believe your species would have reacted differently than mine, despite how many of us labored to prevent those things from happening?"

Kaylan was silent for a few moments while she considered what Kladomaor had said. She glanced at Ma'jasalax and saw that the Mardoxian priestess was waiting for her answer. "No, we're not that different at all. In fact, some members of my own family were excellent at getting what they wanted, especially if they thought they were doing those things for the right reasons."

Kaylan hadn't thought of her grandfather in a long time. He'd been among the people who had received Ma'jasalax's message almost seventy years ago. She now understood that Ma'jasalax had acted on her own when she'd sent the original warning about the Xiiginns, along with guidance on how to develop more advanced technology. Kladomaor was right. Humans weren't any different than the other species in the universe.

They entered the main congressional building on Selebus. Governor Udonzari was presiding over the Alliance summit. Councilor Essaforn and Ambassador Dulrad were also there, along with Battle Leader Salevar. The Gresan battle commander was there in holographic form only, as was the Napox delegate.

Kaylan walked over to her designated area, and the Napox delegate caught her eye with a wry smile. Kaylan remembered that his name was Aenok.

"We had to try. The challenge was much too great for us to pass up," Aenok said.

Kaylan regarded the Napox for moment with a challenging smile of her own. "*We* would've succeeded."

The Napox's furry mouth opened wide in what Kaylan assumed was a grin. "I think I'm going to like getting to know your species. Humans make so many things much more interesting."

"I'm glad you think so. Now, if you can keep your furry paws away from my ship, we'll get along just fine," Kaylan said, and Aenok gave her a slight bow.

Kaylan noticed that the Gresan battle commander watched the exchange but didn't offer any comments. Udonzari began the summit and reminded everyone that their presence in the Nerva star system was tolerated so long as they respected the Alliance. Kaylan recalled seeing that many Nershal ships had gathered, positioning themselves between Selebus and the Nershal homeworld.

The area where the Gresan battle commander stood became highlighted in blue, which indicated he wanted to speak, and Udonzari yielded the floor to him.

Solek turned to address the Boxan ambassador. "I want to know what you intend to do about the Human ship."

Ambassador Dulrad glanced at Kaylan for a moment. "The *Athena* isn't our ship. Why are you asking us about it?"

There was a chittering sound by the other Gresans near Solek. "You have the dominant space fleet in the star system. You could easily take out all other ships in the area and seize the *Athena* for yourself. Why haven't you done so already?"

Ambassador Dulrad's features became grim. "I don't know what pains me more—the fact that you've asked whether we will just take the Human spaceship from them or that you believe it's our right to do so. Both imply that your time in the Confederation under the dominion of the Xiiginns has changed your species, and not for the better."

Solek glared at the Boxan ambassador. "We had to survive your downfall, and now the Gresans are so firmly entangled with the Xiiginns that it has become unclear what a true Gresan looks like anymore."

"Then why hesitate to join the Alliance? Why attempt to steal what isn't rightfully yours?" Councilor Essaforn asked.

"Even with the Boxan fleet, this alliance cannot stand against the might of the Confederation Armada. We sought an advantage from which my species might have benefited," Solek said, swinging his gaze toward Kaylan. "And we failed."

Battle Leader Salevar cleared his throat with what sounded like a growl. "You might be surprised at what this alliance is capable of, and our Dreadnought class warships will make the Xiiginns cringe. It has been many cycles since we've engaged the Xiiginns, Gresan. I think you'll find that our weapons systems have increased in effectiveness, and while the Xiiginns are losing allies, we're gaining them. The eventual engagement with the Confederation Armada will not be as one-sided as you think."

Solek spoke to another Gresan nearby, but the conversation was muted. Then he turned back toward the Boxans. "Even if our estimation of your military capabilities isn't entirely accurate, you would still take heavy losses to even have a chance at defeating the Confederation Armada."

"This is where you're mistaken," Battle Commander Salevar replied. "Our engagement is with the Xiiginns, which represent only half of the armada."

A cool breeze blew in through the open skylight at the top of the vast chamber. Long strands of Kaylan's dark hair lifted off her neck, and she felt a shiver race down her spine.

"You can't engage the Confederation Armada unless you're fully committed," Kaylan said. The Boxans turned toward her. "I know you've made a colossal effort to avoid coming into conflict with species under the Xiiginn influence, but that will become unavoidable."

Battle Leader Salevar gave a slight bow of his head. "Mardoxian Blessed, you are correct. I should clarify. The High Council has authorized our military to engage with any fighting force that seeks to harm our alliance."

Kaylan's eyes widened and she glanced toward Kladomaor, who gave her a firm nod.

Salevar continued. "We have no illusions where the Confederation Armada is concerned. We will pull all of our fleets together to drive the Xiiginns out of the Confederation once and for all."

There were cheers from the Nershals. They yearned to strike at the Xiiginns for what they'd done to their species. The Boxans were committing everything they had to this.

"We have groups of rebels serving aboard Gresan ships. Can you assure us that if they cease hostilities during the battle, you will not obliterate them?" Solek asked.

"Any species other than the Xiiginns will be granted clemency. I doubt you'll get such an offer from the Xiiginns," Salevar replied.

The discussion went into the particulars of what the Gresans and the Napox had to offer the Alliance and, in turn, what the Alliance would do for them. Kaylan listened as they described how both species had various rebel groups that had been coming together in secret. They were the unspoken majority who had watched in fear as the Xiiginns took over the entire Confederation.

The Gresan battle commander looked at her from time to time, and as the meeting was coming to a close, he turned to address her. "What do you intend to do with the Drar technology?"

Kaylan looked around the room. Her gaze lingered for a moment on each group, hoping to gain some insight into each of them. Zack was right about one thing—the Alliance couldn't focus on facing the real threat while the *Athena* was within their grasp.

"The Confederation Armada is being formed to enslave my homeworld, and I want to avoid that fate for my species. The Boxans and the Nershals formed this alliance with that in mind, so my species stands to gain much from this agreement. I think it's only fair that we offer something in return. We intend to share all the Drar technology contained within the *Athena*. Everything we learn from it will be freely dispersed among all Alliance species. I hope my word is enough of a commitment," Kaylan said.

"It is," Kladomaor said, his deep voice reaching every crevice of the massive room.

Kaylan turned toward the Gresans and the Napox. "But if you try to take my ship again, I'll see to it that you get nothing. Not one thing. Do we have an understanding?"

The Gresan narrowed all four of its dark eyes, but the Napox seemed unperturbed by Kaylan's assertion.

Ambassador Dulrad cleared his throat. "Thank you, Kaylan. The vow of a Mardoxian Blessed would never be called into question."

"Indeed," Battle Leader Salevar said. "We must begin planning how we will defeat the armada."

Just as Salevar finished speaking, Kaylan noticed several comms channels chiming alerts throughout the room. She frowned as an audio message file suddenly appeared on her internal heads-up display.

"Are you sure? I'm still seeing the ship on our scanners," Salevar said.

Kladomaor's brows furrowed and he looked at Kaylan, who felt as if everything were happening in a strange, slow succession. She looked at the audio file and closed her eyes for a moment.

Zack, what did you do?

The hologram of the Gresan battle commander stepped toward her. "Your ship is gone. It has just fled the system," Solek said and turned toward the Boxans. "This alliance is done."

"Wait!" Ambassador Dulrad said. "There has to be a reasonable explanation for this. Give us a chance to find out what happened . . ."

Kaylan stopped listening to them and played the audio file.

"Kaylan," Zack said, "I'm going to find another option. I

have a plan. I don't want you to think I just up and took the ship. Athena wouldn't let me, even if that were the case. No need to guess where we're going. We're heading to the Confederation space station capital. Athena believes she can mask our approach, so we're going to do some reconnaissance of our own and perhaps have a few surprises for the Xiiginns."

The message finished. He must have been in a rush to make it. Kaylan was so shocked that it took a few seconds for her anger with Zack to catch up with her thoughts. She should have kept a better eye on him. As she noticed more than a few Boxans looking in her direction, her flash of anger at Zack diminished almost as quickly as it had come. Her thoughts immediately went from worrying about Zack and whomever else he'd recruited for his impromptu mission to the possibilities that Zack's actions had given them. She felt her brain racing down several paths, exploring the different possibilities, until one of them became readily apparent to her. Had she inadvertently put Zack on this path? Kaylan looked at Ma'jasalax, who appeared to be calm amidst the urgent conversations going on around her. She was waiting for Kaylan to do something, almost as if she'd expected it.

"Is this part of the plan?" Hicks asked.

"Well, the plan was to get away from Nerva so we could come up with a plan," Zack answered.

Hicks's eyes widened and he looked at Zack as if he were about to choke him.

"Stop freaking out," Zack said.

"We're on the doorstep of the Confederation. How long will it be before they detect us here?" Hicks asked.

"Major, we came out of the wormhole well away from the detectable range of any Xiiginn warships. It will take us some time to get close to the Confederation Armada," Athena said.

"Or," Hicks said pointedly, "we can turn around and go right back to the Alliance."

Zack shook his head. "We can't. If we do that . . . We just can't."

"Indeed, this is highly irregular," Cardaleer said as he stepped onto the bridge.

Hicks glanced behind him and stared at the Boxan for a moment before swinging his gaze back to Zack. "Any other surprises?"

Zack tilted his head to the side and pursed his lips. "Not really. Look, Cardaleer can help us. He was—*is*—the foremost expert in Drar technology. Together we can come up with a way to use the *Athena* to help the Alliance. I *know* it, but we have to be *here* to do it."

Hicks groaned. "You're an expert in Drar technology?"

Cardaleer frowned. "I used to conduct research into Drar tech before the Chaos Wars."

Hicks glared at Zack. "Are you serious? The *Athena* is a ship with untapped potential, and you want to bring it here? You don't know what you're risking. If the Xiiginns find us, you're basically handing her over to them. Did you consider that?"

"They won't find us," Zack replied quickly.

"How do you know?"

"Because we were able to hide from the Boxans, and if we can do that, we can certainly hide from the Xiiginns," Zack said.

"That's not entirely accurate," Athena said.

Zack winced. He'd been hoping Athena would keep quiet about that.

"What do you mean?" Hicks asked while looking up at the ceiling, which he sometimes did when he addressed Athena directly.

"We used a decoy to convince the Boxans that we had remained where they thought we were. I've been able to mask our presence for now, but if we needed to fire our engines to move quickly or engage the Cherubian drive, we would most certainly be detected by the Xiiginns," Athena replied.

Zack walked in front of Hicks. "Trust me," he said, trying to put what he hoped was enough confidence in his voice to convince Hicks to stay. Technically, Hicks was second in command, and Athena might listen to a direct order from him no matter what Zack said.

"This isn't how we do things, Zack. We're supposed to be working together, not just firing from the hip," Hicks said.

"You're right. I won't do it again," Zack promised. *Unless I have no other choice,* he added to himself.

"We cannot go back to Nerva," Cardaleer said, drawing the attention of both Hicks and Zack.

"Why not?" Hicks asked.

"Because we need to be here on the fringe of it all if we're to have any hope of defeating the Xiiginns."

"Do you have any ideas on how we can do that?" Zack asked.

Cardaleer walked around the bridge while keeping his head low so it wouldn't hit the ceiling. "We spent many cycles trying to combat the Xiiginns and their stranglehold on the entire Confederation, and we have nothing to show for it. Facing the Xiiginns as we've done before will not win this war."

"So you don't have any ideas then," Zack said and pointedly

did not look at Hicks. He could feel Hicks gearing up to go on a tirade of epic proportions. If they returned to Nerva now, the Alliance would tear the *Athena* apart, looking to gain any edge they could use against the Xiiginns. Zack couldn't let that happen. There must be another way—one where they didn't have to sacrifice the *Athena*.

"I have lots of ideas, just like you do," Cardaleer said. "I recognize a kindred spirit when I see one. Look at you," he said and gestured toward Zack. "Your thoughts are scattering to oblivion trying to think of a way to defeat the Xiiginns, as if it was something you could force from your brain." He then looked at Hicks. "And you're a warrior who hasn't been able to engage the enemy as he would like to. I can see it gnawing away at you. It does the same to me, but spending many cycles in Haven on Sethion tends to teach one what it is to wait and endure." Cardaleer glided his thick fingertips along the ceiling as if taking its measure. "The Drar remade this ship?"

Zack saw Hicks glance at him, looking slightly annoyed. "Yes, when we found their space station."

Cardaleer's eyes widened and he gave them his full attention. "What was it like to stand among the ancients—beings who were able to control all the mysteries in the great expanse? You were closer to them than we ever were, no matter what we found when we were exploring the galaxy. I miss that . . . But I want you to tell me about the Drar space station."

Zack glanced at Hicks, who jutted his chin up once as a way to tell him to go ahead. Hicks crossed his arms and leaned against the conference table.

Zack cleared his throat, feeling thirsty. "I don't think the Drar actually lived there. We didn't find any trace of them. The station looked as if it had been prepared for them, but they never arrived."

Cardaleer knelt on the floor and then sat down. A soft groan escaped the old Boxan, and he nodded for Zack to continue.

"Do you need anything? I could use a drink and maybe some food. Do you want some?" Zack asked.

Cardaleer's great shaggy head angled to the side while he considered it. "I could use some refreshment."

"Don't get up," Hicks said. "You guys keep talking. I'll go grab something from the kitchen."

Zack thanked him and turned back to Cardaleer. He sat down in one of the chairs.

"You were saying about the station," Cardaleer said.

Zack sucked in a deep breath. How long ago had it been? He couldn't think of how much time had passed. They'd been so worried that the *Athena* was going to fall apart. "The station was like a brand-new city that hadn't been lived in. It must have been out there for tens of thousands of years. The shield protecting it was constricting and destroying the buildings the Drar AI had built."

"How did you find it?" Cardaleer asked.

"That's a long story," Zack replied, and Cardaleer arched an eyebrow. "We found evidence collected by one of your asteroid bases. The Xiiginns were hunting us and found us there."

"The Xiiginns found you, you say?" Cardaleer said in a pensive tone.

"Yeah, um, one of the crew had been affected by the Xiiginn influence. We didn't know it at the time," Zack replied.

"One never does until it's too late, even among my species. The member of your crew who was afflicted with the Xiiginn influence—did you kill him?"

"No, we didn't kill him," Zack said briskly, remembering Jonah Redford. His arms had been covered in burns from modifying the Boxans' communication array in order to signal the Xiiginns. "We tried to help him."

"You must realize that anyone under the Xiiginn influence is beyond saving. They cannot be cured," Cardaleer said.

"Kladomaor said the same thing, but we didn't murder Jonah. We studied him and tried to figure out a way to heal him. Jonah fought it, and resisting it damaged his brain. I don't know why he was affected, but I ..." Zack stopped speaking.

Cardaleer looked at him sharply. "What do you mean? Were you under the Xiiginn influence?" The Boxan's glare seemed to contain years of pent-up rage and frustration.

"No," Zack said. "They tried, when I was their prisoner, but it didn't work on me."

Cardaleer frowned. "Didn't work on you? How are you immune to the Xiiginn influence?"

Because of my love for Kaylan, Zack thought. At least, that was what Brenda and Emma believed, that his love for Kaylan had shielded him from the Xiiginn influence. "It's complicated," Zack said.

"Kladomaor wouldn't have allowed you access to their systems if he suspected that you were afflicted. Very well, continue," Cardaleer said.

"After we escaped the Xiiginns, we decided to help Kladomaor find where the Drar signal was coming from," Zack said with a frown. "The signal was one of the things detected. We were in the Qegi star system."

"The Qegi," Cardaleer said and nodded. "A clever species. They were excellent at manufacturing impressive alloys that were very useful in shipbuilding. They were among the first species the Xiiginns exploited, which is very unfortunate because they would have been a valuable addition to the Confederation." The Boxan sighed. "Alright, go on."

"Right," Zack said. "We were following the signal when something reached out to Kaylan through Mardoxian means. We almost died . . ." Zack shook his head, remembering how the wormhole had become unstable. "Something—the Drar AI, we think—destabilized the wormhole. It wanted to separate us from . . . uh, well, you—Kladomaor, Ma'jasalax—and other Boxans."

"Indeed. That's interesting. Please continue," Cardaleer said.

Zack shook his head. "I don't see how this is going to help."

"It helps me understand what happened to you and this ship, so that's how it helps."

Zack glanced at the door to the bridge and wondered when Hicks would return with the food. He blew out a breath and continued. "Once we were past the shield, the Drar AI took control of the ship and guided us in. The AI brought us to a docking platform and we left the ship to explore the space station."

Cardaleer pressed his lips together. "What about the crewmember who was under the Xiiginn influence?"

"Jonah," Zack confirmed.

"Yes, you left him aboard your ship, unguarded?"

Zack shook his head. "No, he came with us."

"How? I thought you said the Xiiginn influence had damaged his brain."

"Oh . . . well, Jonah became lucid when we passed through the shield. I was on the bridge and didn't know it at the time, but Brenda was monitoring him in the med bay," Zack said.

Cardaleer leaned forward. "Lucid. Were the effects completely negated?"

"Not exactly. The damage was still there, but he somehow came out of it. Something the Drar AI did to him," Zack said.

Cardaleer looked away for a moment, pressing his lips together. A soft groan rumbled from deep in his massive chest. He turned back toward Zack.

"I had the same idea as you. The Drar packed a bunch of their knowledge into this ship, and Athena and I tried to figure out what they'd done to alleviate Jonah's symptoms. There isn't anything there," Zack said.

"He wasn't cured?"

"No, he said he was going to die," Zack said, remembering how Jonah had stayed behind. "The AI had figured out that the Drar were never going to come. It wanted to stop waiting for them, but it couldn't self-terminate. Jonah volunteered to stay behind. He merged with the AI and was able to do what the AI couldn't do."

Cardaleer's eyes widened. "Amazing. I wish I could have been there."

Zack's eyebrows pulled together. "It's not like it sounds. It was scary. The space station was falling apart. The Drar AI remade our ship, including our AI, and her capabilities continue to evolve, but I've tried for months to figure out how the Drar AI was able to temporarily cure Jonah. I haven't been able to find out how it was done."

"Perhaps you didn't know the correct questions to ask," Cardaleer said.

"You think—" Zack had begun to say when Hicks walked onto the bridge carrying a container of food.

Hicks arched an eyebrow. "What happened?"

Zack turned toward Cardaleer. "Can you do it?"

"I might know the right questions to ask to unlock the knowledge you seek," Cardaleer answered.

Zack jumped to his feet. "Yes!" he shouted, pumping his fist into the air.

"Great. I'm happy you're excited. Now, would either of you like to tell me what's going on?" Hicks asked.

CHAPTER SEVENTEEN

After the *Athena* jumped away, Kladomaor had been ordered to figure out where it'd gone and how the ship had escaped virtually unnoticed. There were many Boxans who had difficulty accepting that the Humans were as primitive as they'd originally thought. They had proven to be ingenious but on occasion a bit too idealistic. Human idealism was infectious, and Kladomaor had noticed how his own species seemed to absorb it with an increasing fervor akin to that of a star's gravitational pull—slow at first, but building in intensity until they found themselves hungering to live instead of merely surviving. The potential of the Human species blazed brighter than anything he'd ever experienced. They had the capacity to become as ruthless as the Xiiginns had proven to be, but they were also passionate in their idealism. They dreamed of what they could be and chased that dream almost as if they were afraid it would slip away. Kladomaor had seen that same passion become almost completely extinguished in the Boxans, and now that they had raised their heads from the dreariest time in Boxan history, Kladomaor found that he would fight harder than he ever had before to ensure the Boxans' future.

The main holoscreen on the bridge of the Boxan heavy cruiser showed real-time sensor feeds. They'd traveled to the outer system of planets in the Nerva star system, away from the Alliance fleet. He glanced over at Kaylan, who was speaking with the *Athena* crew near the communications station. She'd grown beyond the mission commander who'd been thrust into the commander's chair, and the longer he knew her, the more she reminded him of Ma'jasalax. Knowing Ma'jasalax as he did made him wonder whether he was jumping at shadows. Or had Kaylan grown into a shrewd leader, capable of traversing the dangerous circles of the Mardoxian Sect? She'd seemed quite surprised when the *Athena* left the Nerva star system.

Ma'jasalax entered the bridge and joined him. The Mardoxian priestess looked at the *Athena* crew for a moment before turning toward Kladomaor.

"Has the student become the teacher then?" Kladomaor asked.

Ma'jasalax seemed unperturbed by his intentional jab. "Kaylan cannot remain a student forever."

"No, she can't, but I still wonder at how events have unfolded," Kladomaor replied.

"You mean, did Kaylan purposefully set these events into motion?"

"I know they didn't want to give up their ship, and who could blame them? But in the end, what else could they have done?" Kladomaor said.

"I believe Kaylan really would have shared anything she learned from the Drar data repositories on the *Athena*, but once they return to Earth it probably wouldn't have been up to her. She realizes this, and she also knows you couldn't guarantee that the High Council wouldn't put forth considerable effort to take the *Athena* away from them," Ma'jasalax said. She spoke softly so that the Boxans around them couldn't overhear their conversation. "You've often pointed out how Kaylan is a bit of an optimist, but the actions she's taken are logical and are more aligned with a realist's philosophy. Wouldn't you agree?"

Kladomaor considered it for a moment and resisted the urge to look at Kaylan one more time, as if to glean some insight he hadn't considered before. He knew all he needed to know. "They are the actions of a mature leader, and I cannot find any fault in what she's done."

The beads on Ma'jasalax's tightly braided hair slid across her shoulders as she sat back. "And yet we feel this inclination to resist what's been done. The Alliance fleet has been growing, and we were going to confront the Xiiginns sooner or later."

"Eventually," Kladomaor agreed and glanced at the *Athena* crew. Kaylan was still speaking with them, and he snorted.

Ma'jasalax arched one of her eyebrows and looked at him. "What is it?"

"I'm surprised you haven't noticed," Kladomaor said and nodded toward Kaylan and the others.

"I might have, but I won't know unless you tell me what you were thinking just now," Ma'jasalax replied dryly.

Kladomaor hadn't missed the slight annoyance she'd put into her tone, and he supposed even the legendary Mardoxian priestess had her limits. "The gender divide of the Humans. All the males are on the ship. Some might believe they're there because they felt they needed to take action. I'm sure that's Zack's motivation, but I doubt Hicks knew what was happening until it was already too late. The females are here. Kaylan has pointed them all in the direction she intended them to go. Now it's time for us to do our part."

"Etanu is with Zack and the others, but it could be a coincidence that these *Athena* crewmembers were left here," Ma'jasalax said.

Kladomaor shook his head. "Some of the Human cultural divide is almost instinctual. Each gender chooses their actions in their own way. Males want to protect the females. We've seen it many times when we've all faced danger, even with the female warriors among them. Perhaps the Humans will outgrow it, but it won't be for many cycles."

Boxans had evolved along similar lines, but those tendencies were virtually gone from their species. Even before the Chaos Wars, males and females had held similar roles in their society. In other words, the roles were the same regardless of the individuals who occupied them.

Kaylan approached them, along with the other *Athena* crewmembers.

"We've just received a message from Zack," Kaylan said.

Kladomaor frowned and used his neural implants to check the heavy cruiser's communications systems but didn't see anything in the logs from the *Athena*.

"It wasn't through standard communications," Kaylan said.

"Have they returned?" Kladomaor asked.

"No. And before you ask, we're not able to reply to them," Kaylan said.

"Why not? Where are they?"

"They're heading closer to the Confederation space station, and we can't reply to them because it would give away their position. Athena used a micro-wormhole and sent a message to me that way," Kaylan said.

Kladomaor's thick eyebrows pulled together and he glanced toward Varek, who was monitoring the tactical battle station. They hadn't detected anything. They couldn't create a micro-wormhole, and even if they could, they'd have to know exactly where the *Athena* was in order to reach them.

"Athena left a drone in the area that checked to get our exact location," Kaylan said.

"I understand. The Confederation capital is where the armada is amassing. Why are they going there?" Kladomaor asked.

"Zack believes they might have a way to temporarily disrupt the Xiiginn influence," Kaylan said and waited for his reaction.

Kladomaor's shoulders became rigid and he looked at Ma'jasalax for a moment.

"He believes he can reproduce what the Drar space station did for Jonah Redford," Kaylan said.

Kladomaor's first instinct was to insist that it was impossible. There was no way to reverse the Xiiginn influence. Even his partial exposure to it could still affect him. "It's not possible to reverse it. The effects are permanent."

"He didn't say he was going to reverse the Xiiginn influence. He said they might have a way to disrupt it, which is exactly what happened with Jonah on the Drar space station. We all saw it. Jonah was dying, slowly being driven mad by what the Xiiginns had done to him. But when we were on the Drar space station, he was coherent, as if what was causing his distress was gone. The damage had still been done—Jonah was dying and nothing was going to change that—but for a moment, at least,

KEN LOZITO

he was his old self and aware of what had happened to him," Kaylan said.

Kladomaor shook his head. "I remember those reports from when you were on the Drar space station, but we've studied the Xiiginn influence since the Chaos Wars and have never been even remotely close to doing what Zack claims can be done."

"It's not just Zack. Cardaleer is with them. They think they've found a way to make it work using the *Athena*," Kaylan said.

Kladomaor drew in a deep breath. Ever since the Chaos Wars, Boxans had longed for a way to cure the Xiiginn influence, but they'd always failed. It couldn't be done. The effects were irreversible. "Even with the *Athena*, how can this be done?"

"I don't know. Zack said he would have the *Athena* compile their research and store it on one of the escape pods that can later be picked up. That way if they fail, at least the knowledge won't be lost, and someone else can figure out what went wrong and try again," Kaylan said.

Kladomaor could tell Kaylan didn't like that part. Bonded pairs rarely approved when there was a significant risk to the other. This wasn't just a Human trait, but a common trait among many species that had bonded pairs. "So we're to accept what they're doing on faith then. What are we supposed to do now?" Kladomaor asked.

"Isn't it obvious?" Ma'jasalax said and arched an eyebrow at him.

Kladomaor should've known she would get her revenge for his earlier behavior. "Not to me, it isn't. All we know is that our closest link to the Drar is purposefully putting itself in the middle of the enemy fleet, hoping they can somehow disrupt the Xiiginn influence. That is reckless and misguided."

162

He didn't bother trying to hide the disgust in his voice. There was risk and then there was suicide.

"Zack wouldn't do this if he didn't believe they had a real chance at succeeding. Hicks is with them and wouldn't go along with it either," Kaylan said.

Kladomaor met Kaylan's gaze squarely, and his voice was unflinching. "Who would Athena listen to—Zack or Hicks? I believe that under these circumstances, the *Athena* would choose to listen to Zack rather than Hicks, even if he is your second in command."

Kaylan's gaze hardened. "If you think this is easy for me, you're wrong. We have no other choice."

"There's always a choice. They could withdraw and return here," Kladomaor countered.

"Then Earth will pay the price. You've seen the Alliance—the High Council, the Gresans, the Nershal Global Congress. They're committed to helping, but they'll wait too long. That's not a risk I can afford to take, and neither can you," Kaylan said.

Kladomaor found himself leaning forward. "What if Zack fails and they can't disrupt the Xiiginn influence? What then?"

Kaylan's gaze softened and she looked oddly vulnerable at that moment. Kladomaor almost felt sorry for asking the question, but the moment was gone as Kaylan regained her courage.

"It depends on what the Alliance does. Will the Alliance risk Drar technology falling into the Confederation's hands? Will we leave Zack and the others to do this thing on their own, or will we help them? Regardless of which reason we use for engaging the Confederation Armada, our actions will determine what occurs next. The one thing I know is that if that armada leaves the Confederation space station, my home is gone. Beyond that, what do you think the Confederation will do with this armada after it destroys my people? They'd likely hit Nerva next and hunt down anyone who's known or suspected to be associated with the Alliance. After that, the armada would become a convenient way for the Xiiginns to deal with rebellious species that resist them. So the Alliance doesn't have a choice, regardless of what Zack or I do. All the arguments in the world will not save us from them."

Kladomaor felt Ma'jasalax place her hand on his shoulder and give it a gentle squeeze. He leaned back on the commander's couch and looked at her. "She's right—about everything," Ma'jasalax said.

"And you didn't see this?" Kladomaor asked.

Ma'jasalax seemed to consider her answer for a moment. "Not with the clarity Kaylan just showed."

Kladomaor's mind raced with possibilities as he thought about the path that had brought them to this moment—the path Ma'jasalax had set them all on—but judging by her reaction, even the Mardoxian priestess wasn't all-knowing.

"We need to alert the Alliance," Kaylan said.

"I don't know how they'll react, even knowing all this. I still can't help but wonder what one ship—even the *Athena*, which has been imbued with Drar technology—is going to do that will make facing the armada not feel like we're sounding our last battle song. Even if they're somehow able to figure out a way to disrupt the Xiiginn influence, what good will it do? The *Athena* is just one ship," Kladomaor said.

Kaylan gave him a long look. "I don't have all the answers, Kladomaor. No one does, but I do know that Zack is aware of all those shortcomings and will work to address them. And he's not alone. Hicks is with them. So is Etanu and Cardaleer. And there's the *Athena*. Together they can do what the Boxans couldn't do all those years ago when the Xiiginns first showed their true colors. You can't change the past. All we can do now ... all we can control is what we do right now. Because if we succeed, the Xiiginns will be finished."

Kladomaor felt a faint stirring deep in his chest, a yearning to finally be free of this war. The Boxans had fought and had almost forgotten who they were. Perhaps it was time for them all to step out from the shadows and battle the Xiiginns in the light.

CHAPTER EIGHTEEN

Mar Arden had known he'd be walking into a trap. Kandra Rene's discovery of a secret training facility for Humans with the Mardoxian potential was enough to rouse his suspicions, but what they'd discovered at the site couldn't be ignored. His Human adversaries had relentlessly hunted him and they must have been growing desperate to attempt this, but that hadn't dissuaded Mar Arden from going to the secret training facility. The Humans had retrieved something of great importance to him, something he'd yearned for for many cycles. He wondered if the Humans understood what they held in their possession or whether they'd do anything differently if they did.

"How could they possess a key to the Star Shroud network?" Kandra Rene asked.

They were using Human ground transportation, which made their journey to the secret training facility longer, but at least they would arrive undetected. With the number of ground transport vehicles traveling, there would be no way the Humans could surmise that Mar Arden was on his way. The lush landscape was momentarily illuminated by the lights of their vehicles as he turned from the window and looked at Kandra Rene. "You're asking the wrong question, my dear."

Kandra Rene's reply masked her frustration well. "Most of the Tetronian keys are gone or in the possession of the Boxans. So how could the Humans have a key to the Star Shroud network? I doubt the Boxan fleet brought one here."

Mar Arden regarded her for a moment. "I thought you understood how Boxan monitoring stations worked."

Kandra Rene didn't reply and merely waited for him to continue.

"You're right, they don't have a key, but the Star Shroud network is still accessible from a Boxan monitoring station. A communications node was removed from the monitoring station and is here on the planet. If we bring the node with us back to the Confederation space station, we can unlock the Star Shroud network across the galaxy," Mar Arden said with a smirk.

Kandra Rene's violet eyes widened. "You intend to use the node to initiate a check-in, which would grant you access to the system. I should've seen that before."

"You'll get no arguments from me. So, in addition to finding the very best test subject with the Mardoxian trait, we need to find that communications node. That's why I brought most of our soldiers with us," Mar Arden said.

The Xiiginn soldiers hardly reacted to his conversation with Kandra Rene. He always kept his most loyal soldiers with him at all times—especially now—which was a fact that hadn't gone unnoticed by Kandra Rene *or* Hoan Berend, for that matter.

Mar Arden had convinced the warship commander to remain behind at their encampment—an easy feat because he knew Hoan Berend believed that should they fail at the secret training facility, he would be left with the Mardoxian trait for himself, provided the incubation of the test subject was successful. The warship commander could believe whatever he wanted. Mar Arden had several monitoring devices that would alert him as soon as the incubation period was complete, and the data would be transferred directly to him.

They left the highway and drove toward an old mountain range on the eastern side of the continent. Once they were out of sight, Mar Arden ordered them to go faster. He'd had his soldiers modify these vehicles, which enabled them to reach speeds far beyond their previous capabilities.

"Our diversionary assets are en route as we speak," Kandra Rene said.

"Excellent," Mar Arden replied.

There weren't enough Xiiginns to make an effective assault on the secret training facility, so they'd had to leverage Kandra Rene's Human assets. Those expendable assets would begin their air assault on the training facility just before Mar Arden arrived. His Human adversaries knew they were coming, and Mar Arden decided he wouldn't bother to try to hide his assault. They'd outfitted the diversionary teams with elite Human military vehicles that should convince the defenders it was the Xiiginns attacking them. Bright flashes of light shone from ahead of them. They were almost to the target.

"Send out our drones to scan for their defenses," Mar Arden said.

The diversionary assets were meant to expose the kind of defenses that were protecting the training facility. One of Mar

Arden's trusted soldiers at the front of the vehicle opened a metallic case and activated the drones. Twelve metallic orbs flew out the open window and sped ahead of them. Kandra Rene brought up a holoscreen that showed the aerial layout of their target. There were several marks that indicated heavy turret locations, as well as the Human soldiers that were stationed along the roof. Mar Arden ordered his driver to change their approach. The diversionary assault had softened their defenses on the west side, and he meant to use that to gain quick entry into the building. Once inside, they could scan for Boxan power sources.

Three Human ground transportation vehicles holding twelve Xiiginns each drove toward the battle with all exterior lights extinguished. Xiiginns were at home in the dark and could see as clearly without light as they could during the day. Because of this, the Human soldiers didn't notice their approach until they were within a hundred meters of the facility. The Xiiginns raced toward a gaping hole in the side of the building, where Mar Arden's soldiers quickly exited the vehicles and exchanged fire with the nearest Human defenders. The Human soldiers were still using projectile-type weapons that had difficulty penetrating their armor, but the Xiiginns had no such limitations. Bolts of molten plasma cut through the Humans' defenses. There was nowhere for the Humans to seek shelter from their attack because plasma bolts burned through everything in their path.

Mar Arden left a small team of soldiers to secure their transportation. Once they were inside the building, they encountered more Human soldiers. The Xiiginns had much better weapons than the Humans, and Mar Arden ordered his soldiers to press their advantage. The Xiiginns sprinted into the building with an agility that left the Human defenders looking clumsy and slow in comparison.

His earlier reconnaissance had indicated that the Boxan communications node was on a lower level of the building, so when they reached a group of elevators, he summoned all of them. He divided his soldiers into three groups and each used a different elevator to the lower levels. Despite the Humans' futile attempt to resist their assault, Mar Arden was beginning to suspect that the real trap hadn't been triggered. He didn't bother telling his soldiers to be on guard. They were Xiiginns; they were always on guard.

There was an audible chime when the elevator reached its destination and the doors opened. Two of his soldiers exited first, and Mar Arden waited while the soldiers secured the area. Ahead of them was a long hall, and they followed it away from the elevators. Darkened rooms lined the hallway, and as Mar Arden peered inside, he noticed that there was no one else there.

They reached a large door at the end of the hallway. The polished door was made of smooth metal and opened into a vast warehouse. Long aisles stretched into the dark and tall metal racks held heavy equipment and storage containers. Mar Arden checked the scanner on his wrist, which indicated that the Boxan communication node was farther into the dimly lit warehouse.

He had no idea how these Humans had come to be in possession of the node and he didn't care. He wanted it and was going to take it from them. The Boxan communications node would change everything for them, almost as much as gaining the Mardoxian potential.

Mar Arden ordered his soldiers forward, and they staggered their approach. Each group chose to go down a different aisle into the warehouse. After a few minutes, Mar Arden checked his internal heads-up display and changed the scanner configuration to include energy signatures that were unique to Boxan technology. He stopped. Instead of one energy signature ahead of them, they were surrounded by multiple contacts. His eyes widened, and he was about to order his soldiers to take cover when the Humans began firing.

Molten plasma bolts blazed into them, and several Xiiginn soldiers went down immediately. Mar Arden dove for cover, crouched, and brought up his rifle. He started shooting back as more Xiiginn soldiers went down. Mar Arden scrambled to his feet and ran, calling for the remaining soldiers to follow him. Kandra Rene was at his side, her platinum hair momentarily reflecting the light from the plasma rifles the Humans were using. This was *the* trap, and his adversaries had proven that it was a very effective one at that.

He glanced upward and quickly scaled the open racks to the top of the aisle. Kandra Rene followed his lead, and the remaining Xiiginn soldiers did the same. Mar Arden ran along the top of the storage racks. He looked at the ceiling, but it was much too high for him to reach. Golden plasma bolts blazed past him as the Human soldiers tracked their movements.

There was a gap up ahead and Mar Arden vaulted across it. He heard the other Xiiginns following and slowed his pace, glancing behind him to look for their pursuers. The Human soldiers didn't show up on his scanners at all and had stopped firing their weapons. The only things that appeared were the multiple Boxan power sources used in plasma assault rifles. Mar Arden stopped and waited, holding his rifle ready. The other Xiiginn soldiers came to a halt and took up defensive positions around him.

"Why have we stopped?" Kandra Rene whispered.

Mar Arden peered into the gloom. He heard a faint buzzing sound that was coming steadily closer.

"We need a more defensible position," Kandra Rene said. She took a few steps away from him, and several soldiers inched back along with her.

Mar Arden used implants to increase the sensitivity of his hearing. The buzzing became a mechanical whirring sound, and his eyes widened. "Machines! They're using machines to hunt us."

"Suppressor grenades," Kandra Rene ordered.

Several Xiiginn soldiers flung the grenades, and a blue-silver field of light expanded away from them. Mar Arden heard several crashes as the machines that hunted them went off-line, their electrical components suddenly overwhelmed. The Boxan plasma rifles would remain operational, but without the machines to move them into position, they were just as useless. He listened for a few moments and didn't hear anything else.

Mar Arden returned his hearing to normal and glanced at the others. They'd lost over half of their soldiers, and the strategist in him acknowledged the effectiveness of his adversaries' tactics. They had sacrificed many soldiers to lure Mar Arden and the others inside, but it wouldn't be enough. Without another word, Mar Arden turned around and continued along the top of the storage racks. The Boxan communication node wasn't far from them now.

Slowly and steadily, they made their way. They'd triumphed against the first trap, but that didn't mean there couldn't be others waiting for them. His soldiers kept a watchful eye all around them, poised to address any threat. They came to another gap and Mar Arden leapt across. He heard a faint hissing sound and then one of his soldiers cried out as he fell from the top of the tall racks. Mar Arden tried to scan the area but couldn't see anything. Then, a faint blue light raced toward another of his soldiers. The blue light plunged into the soldier's chest and Mar Arden saw a metallic shaft sticking out. The soldier tumbled off the rack and thudded to the ground. The remaining soldiers fired their weapons blindly into the gloom. Mar Arden kept scanning to find the source of the attack and saw Kandra Rene doing the same. Another blue light found its mark, coming from a different vantage point. The light was so faint that by the time he saw it, it was already too late for another of his soldiers. The soldiers fired their weapons at the source but could hit nothing.

"Get down off the rack or they'll pick us all off," Mar Arden said and hopped to the ground.

The remaining soldiers followed him down. Mar Arden hastened down the aisle between the storage racks, and a few moments later another of his soldiers went down with a gurgled scream.

"How does it feel to be hunted, Xiiginn?" a deep voice called from the darkness and echoed all around them.

The remaining Xiiginn soldiers kept their weapons pointed above them, anticipating an attack at any moment. Mar Arden heard faint footsteps in rapid succession from above and fired his weapon. He glimpsed a dark figure as it leapt above them, but all of their shots missed. Two more of his soldiers went down with metallic shafts sticking out of their heads. Mar Arden started firing at the racks, and the plasma bolts gouged through whatever was stored on them. His soldiers followed his example and the nearest rack began to sway. Mar Arden shoved his shoulder into one and pushed. The heavy rack slowly gave way and slammed into the one next to it. Mar Arden backed away as more racks fell, collapsing under the weight of their neighbors. He turned and ran, and the remaining soldiers followed him. There was an open area beyond the aisle and he raced toward it. If they could lure their attackers out into the open, they could defeat them. He should've known better than to allow himself to be put in a position where he could be picked off so easily.

"Keep running, Xiiginn."

Mar Arden clenched his teeth. The mocking tone of the voice grated on his nerves. They reached the end of the aisle and Kandra Rene grabbed his arm to keep him from going forward. One of their remaining soldiers plunged ahead and was taken out by another primitive weapon. Mar Arden glanced behind them and saw that all their soldiers were gone. It was just him and Kandra Rene. She pulled him to the side, and another shaft appeared right where he'd been standing a moment before. Kandra Rene fired her weapon and the plasma bolt gouged the wall on the far side of the room.

Together they left the aisle, crouching as they moved forward. Mar Arden kept his weapon ready and peered ahead of him. He could see the faint outline of a Human standing in the darkness. He squeezed the trigger but the Human leapt out of the way, almost as if sensing his attack before he'd even done anything.

"Mardoxian," Mar Arden whispered harshly.

Kandra Rene nodded and they both darted ahead, firing their weapons as they went. Mar Arden leapt up into the air as the glowing tip of a metallic shaft sped toward him. The shaft struck the rifle from his hands and Mar Arden landed hard.

Kandra Rene fired her weapon, and a plasma bolt singed the arm of their attacker. The Human grunted in pain and dropped its weapon.

"Come face me, Xiiginn," the voice of a Human female said.

Kandra Rene charged forward, unleashing a barrage of plasma bolts until the power cell was used up. Somehow, the Human dodged every bolt. Kandra Rene flung her rifle toward her opponent, who slapped the weapon away and grinned. Mar Arden crept forward as the two combatants engaged. Both combatants were able to land blows, but the advantage their enhancements normally afforded the Xiiginns didn't help them here. It was as if the Human they fought anticipated their every move. A Mardoxian soldier.

Mar Arden glanced behind him and saw his rifle on the ground. It was ruined and couldn't help him. He was creeping toward Kandra Rene, eager to kill the Human, when another blue light zipped past him. Mar Arden flinched and then cursed as he backed away.

"I couldn't have you interfering with the contest," a man said and stepped into the light.

Mar Arden looked at the man. He was an older Human who kept his weapon pointed directly at Mar Arden. The Human seemed to study him for a moment. Most Humans had never seen an alien species before, but this Human looked at him with neither surprise nor fear. The Human's expression was one of familiarity, as if he'd seen a Xiiginn before. Mar Arden knew that if he tried to attack, the Human would kill him with that primitive weapon. The Human noticed Mar Arden studying the weapon.

"Like it? I've always loved a good bow—simple, straight to the point—but as you already know, this is no ordinary weapon. We've given it a few improvements, thanks to our Boxan friends. You'll have to forgive me; I haven't introduced myself. My name is Ed Johnson, and I'm the Human who's going to kill you."

Mar Arden smiled. "I think you overestimate your chances."

"I could have killed you already, but then I wouldn't have gotten to speak with you. I've heard so much about your species —the Xiiginns. I must admit it was harder to find you than I thought it would be, but you leave a particular trail in your wake," Ed Johnson said.

Mar Arden narrowed his gaze. He had the distinct impression that Ed Johnson had some secret knowledge. "Don't worry. When the rest of my species arrives, you won't be so smug. Your death will take a very long time."

Mar Arden heard the other Human cry out at the same time Kandra Rene grunted in pain. He watched Ed Johnson to see if he would take his eyes off him, but the Human steadily returned his gaze, looking slightly amused.

"You didn't think it would be that easy. Now that I have you in my sights, I'm not going to take my eyes off you."

Mar Arden glanced over at the two combatants and saw that each fought with renewed vigor. He turned back toward the Human.

"My assistant, Iris. She's very special," Ed Johnson said, answering the unasked question.

"She fights well," Mar Arden admitted.

"She's the best. Would you care to make a wager on who will win?"

Mar Arden glanced over at the two combatants and slowly

moved his hand over his wrist to access his PDA. He looked back at the Human. "She's enhanced."

Ed Johnson nodded. "Of course, and she received a very special augmentation recently, too. I'm afraid your last encampment wasn't as secure as you thought it was. We recovered some of the data you left and figured out how you were going to incorporate the Mardoxian trait into your species. Really convenient because now I can enhance my own soldiers with the ability. You might have noticed during your time here that there are billions of us, and one thing you can count on is Human determination to defend what's ours."

Mar Arden frowned. He still had the data connection to their base of operations. "I'm glad it worked out so well for you."

"We're still closing in on your base here, but it shouldn't be much longer," Ed Johnson said.

Mar Arden glanced behind Ed at the Boxan communications node. Its dark metallic surface almost shimmered in the light. "Do the Boxans know you have that?"

"Not exactly, but I couldn't think of another way to get you here aside from offering something you really value."

Mar Arden had to admit that it was a clever plan. "The machines with Boxan plasma rifles were a nice touch. I wasn't expecting that. Although I didn't get a good look at them, they weren't enough to stop us." He accessed his drones and commanded them to come to his location. "Such a shame the Boxans couldn't join us right now."

"Perhaps you'd like to try using your compulsion capability on me?" Ed Johnson asked.

The thought had crossed Mar Arden's mind, and if there had been Boxans there, he would have exercised his will over them without hesitation, but Humans were different. He was as likely to fail to subjugate them as he was to succeed, and those weren't odds he'd stake his life on.

"Maybe some other time, then. Oh, and regarding the Boxans, you'll find that we're more than capable of dealing with vermin like you without them."

Mar Arden sneered. He used his neural implants to access his combat armor systems. "Your species is divided."

"Big families will have squabbles from time to time. I bet you thought those nuclear bombs would have been more effective in dividing us. You were wrong. It actually unified our resolve against you," Ed Johnson said.

"We've seen species like yours at similar stages of development. Your potential rests on the edge of a knife. One nudge and you'll teeter right off of it and go the way all those before you have gone in the great expanse."

"I wouldn't count us out just yet. We're a pretty stubborn race. Misguided at times, but ultimately here for the duration."

"Your shield cannot protect you, and I would almost hate to see you pick the losing side of this war," Mar Arden said.

"Oh, you'd like us to form an alliance with you? Why didn't you say so before you flung asteroids at our planet and detonated nuclear bombs in populated areas? And let's not forget snatching a few of us for your experiments."

"There are large factions of your race that have embraced us, and many more will do so once our fleet arrives," Mar Arden said.

He watched as the Human nodded.

"There will always be a group—or a faction, as you say—that will be misguided in their beliefs. Are the Xiiginns so different? Are you unified?"

"We are the strongest race in the great expanse. You will

soon learn—" Mar Arden's speech was cut off when Kandra Rene cried out.

Mar Arden thrust his fist toward the Human, and a group of lethal projectiles shot from a hidden compartment on his armored wrist. The Human released his weapon, and the blue light at the end of a metallic shaft raced toward him. Mar Arden dove to the side and spun through the air, using his tail to propel him toward his attacker. The Human collapsed to the ground with blood spurting from multiple wounds. Mar Arden felt a spike of energy surge through him as he closed in on the Human. Ed Johnson scrambled backward as Mar Arden leapt on top of him, pinning him down with his foot. One of the Human's legs was bloody where he'd been hit. Mar Arden lashed out with his tail and pounded the wound.

"Not so smug now," Mar Arden said.

He'd expected the Human to be angry and afraid, but instead the pathetic being just sneered at him.

"You think you've won, Xiiginn?"

Mar Arden saw a shadowed figure coming toward him. He thrust out his wrist and the remaining projectiles shot forth, but the Human dove to the side. He saw Kandra Rene's body lying on the floor, unmoving. The Human with the Mardoxian potential regained her feet and ran toward him, but the distance was too great. Kandra Rene had drawn away their attacker before dying. Mar Arden swung his gaze toward the Boxan communication node. It was close by, ripe for the taking. He left the dying Human at his feet and raced toward the shimmering metallic box.

"You'll never escape," Ed Johnson called out from where he lay on the floor.

Mar Arden snatched the node off the shelf and looked

above him. He heard the buzzing of his drones as they flew across the warehouse toward him, and he sent the command for the drones to lock together so they could carry him out of there. They flew closer and he sprang into the air, reaching out with his hand. The drones bunched together and he grabbed onto one. The drones dipped toward the ground at the sudden weight and then rose higher into the air. A blue streak sped past his face as he commanded the drones to take him to the exit. More blue shafts took out drones near his hands, but they missed him. Mar Arden gritted his teeth as the drones lowered toward the ground and flew him to an open elevator. They flew him inside and up through a gaping hole in the ceiling where the drones had broken through. As he flew up the shaft, accelerating toward the top, there was an orange flash beneath him. *Human!* Mar Arden swung his feet up and away from the blistering orange plume moving toward him.

Ed Johnson apparently had no qualms about sacrificing his own life to prevent him from escaping. He should have anticipated this, given what the Human had done to lure them there. At least some of the Humans understood what was required to achieve victory.

The flames of the explosion nipped at his heels as the drones flew him out of the building. He'd just cleared the facility when the force of the explosion knocked him to the ground. Mar Arden tripped and then tumbled, clutching the Boxan communications node to his side. He checked for any comms channels from the team he'd left to guard their escape, but they must have been caught in the blast. Aside from the blazing fire that had once been a secret research facility, the area was quiet. Flaming wrecks of vehicles burned all around him.

His data link to the camp where he'd left Hoan Berend had been cut off. The Human hadn't been boasting; he really did have a strike team. He immediately opened a comms channel to his backup location and downloaded a data dump. The incubation of the test subject had been completed and they'd been brought out of it, but Hoan Berend hadn't seen fit to contact him about it. He supposed he should thank him. If he hadn't tried to steal the keys to the Mardoxian capability, the data might have been lost. He glanced through data for a few moments to confirm that it was intact and then stored it away to examine later.

He looked at all the destruction around him. Kandra Rene's Human diversionary force was all gone. He recalled his remaining drones and sent them to scout the area. There had to be an aerial vehicle nearby. He didn't believe for a moment that Ed Johnson had come there without transportation capable of taking him anywhere on the planet—or off of it, for that matter. All Mar Arden had to do was find it.

CHAPTER NINETEEN

Colonel Kyle Matthews sat on the commander's couch in the main bridge of the ECF battleship-carrier *Lincoln*. Michael Hunsicker—also a colonel in the ECF but not in command of the ship—sat to his left and was speaking to Chazen. Scraanyx sat to Kyle's right and watched the main holoscreen.

"I have a priority comms channel from ECF command, Colonel Matthews," Lieutenant Lucy Rogers said from the communication station.

"Put it on screen," Kyle said.

He'd been expecting one final send-off from ECF command, and they weren't so far away from Earth that they couldn't have a live video feed.

General Sheridan's face appeared on the main holoscreen and Kyle greeted the ECF general.

"I would like to have gone with you, but not this trip," General Sheridan said.

"It would've been an honor to have you along, General," Kyle replied and then smiled.

General Sheridan nodded. "You'll do just fine, Colonel," he said and turned his gaze toward Scraanyx. "What you've done for humanity cannot be measured, nor our appreciation conveyed through words. None of us know how the events that will transpire over the next few days will turn out, but on behalf of myself, the rest of the ECF, and all of humanity, we truly thank you for everything you've done for us and hope that the Boxans will someday be at peace."

Scraanyx stood and brought his fist across his heart. The Boxan salute was also performed by all the other Boxans on the bridge. "Battle Leader, it was our honor to get to know such a wonderful species. I am just a soldier, but I'd like to think that were the circumstances different, an invitation to join us would've been given despite our war with the Xiiginns. Your species will be called on to mature much faster than it otherwise would have, but after having spent so much time with you, I believe you're up to the challenge."

Kyle knew they'd earned the Boxans' respect over the course of the past year, but that hadn't been the case when the Boxans first arrived. He'd gone over the reports from Kaylan multiple times, and more than once she'd noted that the Boxans believed Humans were a primitive and brash race of beings. And the Boxans were right; Humans *were* brash and sometimes cruel, but they were also compassionate, intelligent, and capable of awe-inspiring acts of self-sacrifice. People weren't one or the other; they simply existed. Kyle found himself sitting a little straighter after hearing Scraanyx's comments to General Sheridan.

"Has there been any other news on the most recent attacks in the United States?" Kyle asked.

General Sheridan shook his head. "The damage was concentrated in areas remote from population centers, and there's an ongoing investigation. At this point, we don't know if there were any Xiiginns involved, but we can't rule it out either."

"Have you been able to contact Edward Johnson?" Michael Hunsicker asked.

"The offices of Dux Corp have been unusually silent. I'm not sure whether this is cause for alarm or if Ed is so busy hunting for the Xiiginns that there's a delay in communications. I *do* know that he's been coordinating with law enforcement agencies throughout the globe," General Sheridan replied.

Just hours before they'd left the ECF lunar shipyards, there had been multiple attacks across the globe from various global terrorist organizations. The intelligence briefing Kyle had read indicated that those organizations were loosely tied to the Xiiginns. He'd checked in on his family to be sure they were safe—as safe as they could be in this day and age. His daughters were enrolled in the ECF Academy in California and his wife had joked with them about how they'd have to salute him in public once they graduated.

"Colonel Matthews," General Sheridan said, "you have about as complex a task as has ever been given a commanding officer. Ideally, this trip would have been made with a much larger battle group, but time is of the essence and it's time for us to venture beyond our solar system."

"My team and my crew are up to the task, General. We will achieve our mission objectives," Kyle replied.

"Make us proud," General Sheridan said and once again looked at Scraanyx. "Best of luck to you and your species. I know our ambassadors have already conveyed the sentiment, but the Boxans will always be welcome on Earth should you choose to return."

"Thank you. I will inform the High Council of your invitation," Scraanyx replied.

The video call ended and the holoscreen went dark.

"Helm, take us to the shield. All ahead full," Kyle ordered.

"Yes, Colonel, all ahead full," Sergeant Fuller replied.

They had already plotted a course that would take them away from the sun and the orbital plane of the planets in the solar system, and they still had hours before they would reach the minimum distance required to open a wormhole. This would be the first time they'd used the Cherubian drive on any of their ships. As if that wasn't enough for him to worry about, they were also going to try to disable the Star Shroud shield. The Boxans assured him that the first Human-built Cherubian drive had passed every test the Boxans had thrown at it. The only exception was that they hadn't used it to open an actual wormhole, but the technology was sound and had been proven to work. It was just that the ECF had never done it before.

Michael Hunsicker looked over at him and then walked to his side.

Kyle blew out a breath. "You know, Michael, you make this look easy."

Michael Hunsicker chuckled. "It's never easy. Ever. Being the first to go anywhere or do something like this takes a certain amount of mental fortitude. I've read your mission reports and you're no stranger to potentially dangerous pursuits."

"On the *Endurance*, I thought we were going to die, and it was our last chance to save Earth," Kyle said.

Michael nodded knowingly.

Kyle was confident that his crew could fly the ship, but they hadn't had the time to do enough combat drills to make them into an effective fighting force. Their ships were impressive, but without an experienced crew he just hoped he wouldn't be presiding over the biggest disaster in Human history.

The fact that they had flown to an area in space that was about as far away from Earth as Neptune was from the sun in just a few short hours was downright impressive. Not many years ago, the *Athena* had made a similar journey and it had taken them almost two months. It was a reminder of how far they'd come with the Boxans' help, but still, they had a long way to go.

They were headed for a place that had a potentially hostile force, and they didn't have any idea what kind of reception they'd get. Kyle looked over at Scraanyx, who was watching him.

"The Confederation is under Xiiginn control, so what kind of welcome do you think we'll get?" Kyle asked.

"The Xiiginns are the most powerful species in the Confederation. And yes, they do have firm control of the Council Confederation species, but there are protocols for the Confederation to follow. So traveling there and opening communications in what you would call a 'public forum' does give you a measure of protection. In effect, it insulates you to at least be heard out by the Confederation," Scraanyx said.

"I know we've covered this before, but are the Xiiginns really not going to attack us because they're afraid they're going to look bad in front of the other species?" Kyle asked.

"We're the ones who aren't welcome in the Confederation. As long as our presence remains a secret, you should be fine. Even the Xiiginns can't control all the Confederation species with an iron fist. They have a lot of influence, and if you were to go there in secret and contact them directly, there would be nothing to stop them from ordering a battle group of their warships to conceal you from the rest of the Confederation. But since that isn't the plan, they can't very well make you just disappear and convince the Confederation that you never existed. In essence, they've put themselves in a corner of sorts. One of the few things the message from Commander Farrow emphasized was that the supporting argument for this armada was to protect humanity's interest," Scraanyx said.

Kyle nodded. They'd been over this before, but he just needed to hear it all again now that they were actually leaving. "We'll find out in a few days' time."

Michael Hunsicker frowned. "A few days? Why will it take that long to get there?"

"The battle group's first wormhole won't take us directly to the Confederation capital space station. Instead, we'll go to a known region of space. Then we'll do systems analysis before going any further. Despite assertions that the Confederation won't simply open fire on us when we arrive, it doesn't change the fact that we might have to leave them very quickly. If that's the case, I'd rather our second use of the Cherubian drive not be a wormhole from an active combat zone. So we're going to Alpha Centauri first," Kyle said.

Michael Hunsicker drew in a breath and smiled. "I see your point," he said. "I never thought I'd get to see Alpha Centauri up close."

"You should've seen Specialist Hunter's face when I told him," Kyle said.

"I bet Gary was speechless," Michael replied.

"Let's just say he couldn't pack his bags fast enough to get on board," Kyle said.

The ECF battle group was made up of their only battleship-carrier, one heavy cruiser, and one destroyer class vessel. There were no support ships. Their mission was to attempt to open negotiations with the Confederation and discuss humanity's admission into the Confederation. However, the real mission was to give the ECF as much time as they could to solidify its defenses should the Xiiginns return with the fleet. The UN decision to go to the Confederation directly had taken the Boxans by surprise, but they accepted that this was the best course of action. Most of the Boxans were serving aboard the heavy cruiser. If things didn't go well, the heavy cruiser would take them to a known Boxan gateway. This was an access point where the Boxans could communicate with their colony. Apparently, there were no clearances given to travel directly to the colony. The Boxans would shoot them on sight if they just showed up there. He recalled that the two UN ambassadors aboard his ship had expressed a great deal of shock when Scraanyx told them this, but Kyle understood. The Boxans had been nearly wiped out in their war, and they couldn't afford to take any chances.

Several hours later, the battle group came to an area of space just inside the Star Shroud shield. Their ships were quick to reach maximum velocity, but slowing down still took much longer than it did to speed up. Nothing stopped on a dime in space.

"Colonel, the Star Shroud shield is just ahead at ten thousand kilometers," Major Stephens said from the technical workstation on the bridge.

"Acknowledged," Kyle replied. "Ops, is the shutdown protocol ready to be transmitted to the Star Shroud network?"

"Affirmative, Colonel. We can commence transmission on your command," Captain Amelia Young replied.

Kyle looked at the data on the main holoscreen and took a few deep breaths. He was going over multiple checklists in his mind, making sure he hadn't missed anything. And if he had missed something, he was sure it would have been pointed out to him. He glanced over at Scraanyx, who gave a firm nod. "Very well, commence transmission of the shutdown protocol."

"Sending transmission, Colonel," Captain Young replied.

Kyle watched the main holoscreen, which showed a video representation of the sensor feeds on their ship. The sensor data was first routed into their computing core, which analyzed and disseminated the data, and the output was sent directly to the main holoscreen. The image was a glimpse of the universe that was just beyond reach. The *Lincoln's* systems were patched into the monitoring devices for the Star Shroud shield, which showed that the shield was still active. Kyle wasn't sure what to expect. They didn't know how long it would take, so they waited. And waited.

Kyle glanced at Scraanyx, who watched the main holo-screen, and resisted the urge to ask the Boxan a question he already knew the Boxan didn't have an answer for. No one knew how long this would take. Some of the ECF engineers had theorized that the Star Shroud shield wouldn't shut down until the protocol had reached all of the Shroud devices. Chazen didn't believe it would work that way and was of the opinion that once the new instructions reached a certain percentage of devices, they should see some results. Kyle was inclined to believe the Boxans since they were the experts on Star Shroud technology.

Kyle glanced at Major Stephens, who closely monitored the tactical feeds on the holoscreens that surrounded his work area.

"No change in shield activity," Major Stephens announced.

The ECF crew on the bridge watched the main holoscreen, waiting for some indication that the shutdown protocol was going to work. If it failed, they'd have to assess whether they'd done something wrong or there was a flaw in the shutdown protocol. Kyle didn't want to think about how the shield was constricting around the solar system and had the potential to nudge an entire planet from its orbit. He watched the main holoscreen and hardly dared to blink.

"Colonel, I'm detecting multiple energy spikes from the shroud devices," Major Stephens said.

"Highlight on screen, Major," Kyle ordered.

A sub-window opened on the main holoscreen, which showed a single Star Shroud device. It was still too far away to make out the details, but it looked like it was a large cylinder floating in space. Kyle peered at it. The cylinder appeared to be glowing along the edges, but he couldn't be sure if its surface was just highly reflective. There was a bright flash and then the cylinder went dark. Multiple flashes seemed to spread out away from it.

"Multiple Shroud devices are now off-line, Colonel," Major Stephens said.

"What about the monitoring devices? Are they detecting anything?" Kyle asked.

"No, they seem to have gone dark as well, Colonel. The monitoring devices were placed pretty close to the actual Shroud devices, so they might be affected by what's happening," Major Stephens said.

190

Kyle watched as a wave of energy spikes spread away from them and eventually beyond their sensors' capability to report.

"Tactical, prepare the forward maser for a low-energy beam," Kyle said.

"Yes, Colonel. Maser battery one is powering up. Low energy beam will be ready in twenty seconds," Major Stephens said.

Kyle waited a few moments. "Fire maser when ready."

A few seconds later, Major Stephens said, "Firing, Colonel," and watched his terminal display. "The maser has reached beyond the area of the shield."

"Power down the maser. Ops, I want to send a recon drone there to confirm," Kyle said.

"Yes, Colonel, recon deployed from forward launch bay," Captain Young confirmed.

Kyle watched as the drone flew toward the shield. If the shield was really gone, the drone should be able to fly right through the area without taking any damage.

"Recon drone will reach the shield in one minute, Colonel," Captain Young said.

"Very well," Kyle replied.

"Colonel, I am unable to reach any of the Shroud devices in our immediate vicinity," Lieutenant Rogers said.

"Understood."

Kyle watched the recon drone's distance indicator as it steadily drew toward the shield ten thousand kilometers away. The drone reached the shield and flew past it unopposed.

Kyle glanced around as everyone working on the bridge and the ECF crew blew out a collective sigh of relief. The shield was down. There was a sobering mixture of relief and trepidation as Earth's defense now rested solely on the shoulders of the ECF. No longer would they have a massive shield that protected them from an invading force, but they also didn't have to live in fear that the shield would cause a catastrophe that would forever impact the entire solar system. The Shroud devices were off-line, and it was unlikely that they would ever come back online again. Kyle would've liked to have taken the time to retrieve a Shroud device to confirm, but they didn't have time. Now that the shield was down, time was against them, but he supposed time had always been against them since the shield first went up.

"Helm, ready the Cherubian drive. Coordinates to Alpha Centauri," Kyle said.

"Course to Alpha Centauri confirmed. The Cherubian drive is powering up," Sergeant Fuller said.

Kyle saw Michael Hunsicker looking at him, and then Scraanyx looked at him also. "Time to see how well our engineers learned what you had to teach."

Kyle waited for the Cherubian drive to power up, hoping that what they were about to do would be remembered as the first of many such journeys beyond their solar system.

CHAPTER TWENTY

"Is it too late to turn back?" Zack asked.

"Sure thing. We'll execute a reverse thrust maneuver, turn around, and hope the armada will just ignore us," Etanu replied from the *Athena's* copilot seat.

"Everyone just relax," Hicks said. "If they haven't noticed us by now, I think we're in the clear."

Zack tried to keep himself from freaking out by focusing on his breathing. He couldn't ignore the fact that they were flying amidst the Confederation Armada. "I thought we'd be able to use our stealth capabilities—you know, just sneak right in there and do what we need to do, then get out as quickly as possible."

"Think of it as hiding in plain sight. We're not trying to mask our presence; we're just trying to blend in," Hicks replied.

Zack didn't know why Hicks sounded so damn confident. He was usually the one to point out the flaws in any plan Zack proposed. It was probably because once Hicks committed to a course of action, it was all or nothing, whereas Zack preferred an extra dose of caution even if there was nothing he could do about it—one final gut check and then perhaps five or ten more just to be sure.

"Athena, can you confirm the identification codes you used to alert the Confederation equivalent of a harbormaster?" Zack asked.

"You mean the sector chief?" Etanu asked.

"Yeah, fine, whatever. Athena, please confirm what kind of ship you told them we were," Zack said and didn't bother to hide his irritation with Etanu's pestering.

"We're posing as a Gresan survey ship. They're slightly larger than we are, but as long as the sector chief doesn't pay close attention to us, we should be fine," Athena replied.

Zack was well aware that the ship's AI was trying to make him feel better and that her assertions were much more accurate than other people's facts. He also knew Athena had studied the Gresan ships when they were in the Nerva star system, so the fact that Athena was now trying to fool the sector chief into believing they were just another Gresan ship shouldn't have come as a surprise to him. If he bothered to ask her, he was sure Athena would tell him that she'd considered multiple options and this had the highest probability of success. But what really put him on edge was the sheer number of ships in the Confederation Armada. Zack suspected that if all the Confederation ships were to join together, they could rival the mass of a small moon.

Cardaleer sat on the floor next to the communication station where Zack was working. The Boxan didn't seem to mind having to sit on the floor since there were no seats on the bridge capable of holding the Boxan's weight. Zack had tried to think of another part of the ship where they could work so

Cardaleer would be more comfortable, but there wasn't anywhere. Even though the *Athena* had been rebuilt by the Drar, the design was still very much for Humans.

Zack glanced at the old Boxan and tried to ignore the guilt he felt at making the equivalent of an old man sit on the floor. In his mind, it was just wrong. He felt the urge to give up his chair but knew the gesture would be wasted.

Rather than listening to Cardaleer verbally ask the questions that would give him insight into the Drar data repositories, Athena had suggested that he be granted access through his neural implants. They'd granted a few Boxans access to the *Athena's* systems previously, but they'd been closely monitored, and Cardaleer wasn't treated any differently. Zack kept a watchful eye on the Boxan. He didn't expect Cardaleer to do anything suspicious, but then again, he hadn't suspected that the Boxan scientists he'd worked with on Olloron would try to force their way into the *Athena's* systems.

He told Cardaleer that he wanted to watch and learn from him, which the old Boxan seemed to accept.

"Are you sure it's that simple?" Zack asked.

"We can't be sure until we actually try it. Part of the Xiiginns' compulsion capability is utilized through their pheromones. I can tell you with absolute authority that we researched that part quite thoroughly. We tried to filter out particulates, thinking that perhaps we could block the pheromones the Xiiginns used to bring other species under control. Never worked. We always felt there was another layer to it that we were missing, but we couldn't figure out what that layer was. What the Drar did was quite delicate and obvious now that we've unraveled it. It never occurred to us to utilize the artificial gravity systems to affect how the brain or body functions," Cardaleer said.

"You said that before and I think I understand it better now. They used the artificial gravity systems as a way of assisting the healing field without actually doing anything invasive to the patient—not that I think Jonah would have minded if they *had* done something invasive. Using artificial gravity to manipulate cells on a molecular level is something we haven't considered at all," Zack said.

"I've never heard of it either," Cardaleer replied. "I will admit that it opens a few possibilities and explains a few of the things you observed while on the Drar space station."

Zack rubbed his fingers on the stubble of his chin. The solution Cardaleer had found was both simple and elegant; however, they needed to test it on a ship they knew the Xiiginns were on. The plan seemed to be a simple enough idea since the Xiiginns had a significant presence on many of the ships in the armada. But as Hicks had pointed out to him, they needed to test it in such a way that wouldn't alert the rest of the armada to what they were doing. Assuming that their plan worked, the Xiiginns would soon realize there was something very wrong and would take steps to minimize the impact. He supposed he should feel confident of their chances because Cardaleer's investigation had opened certain data repositories on the *Athena*. The AI had quickly absorbed the new information and provided them with options that made for pretty convincing arguments to explain what had really happened on the Drar space station.

"What's bothering you now?" Cardaleer asked.

Zack brought up Athena's computing utilization on the holoscreen. "She's operating at almost seventy percent utilization. Given how her capabilities keep growing, I don't know what else she's doing."

"As I've already stated," Athena said, "I'm running multiple data models on how best to test this new way to block the Xiiginn influence and what we'll need to do should our tests prove successful. This requires an enormous amount of processing power, and in addition, I'm also communicating with sector chief personnel."

Hicks turned around and looked at him. "Let her do what she can. We can't imitate the Gresan language."

Zack nodded, but he didn't think that was all Athena was doing. This wouldn't be the first time Athena had shown a willingness to omit certain actions, although he'd never believe Athena would do something to hurt them. He trusted her, but sometimes he didn't think the AI fully comprehended everything she was doing. Logic and calculations would only get her so far, and he wasn't sure how to convey that to the AI. There were times, it seemed, that she operated at a completely higher level that they could scarcely comprehend, but other times it was the simplest of concepts that caused the AI to stumble.

"Major," Athena said, "I've identified a target for your approval."

"Show us," Hicks said.

"I've been accessing the crew manifests of the ships nearest us as we fly by. Per your instructions, we've restricted our movements to the outskirts of the armada. The best way for us to test the potential of blocking the Xiiginn influence is to identify a target that not only has Xiiginns aboard the ship but has controlling ranking officers. Finding evidence of compulsion is difficult, but I think I've found a good test candidate," Athena said.

"How were you able to confirm that the Xiiginns were using their compulsion capability?" Zack asked.

"By using the communication systems on the ship. I'm able to monitor zettabytes of communication data at once, and I pinpointed scenarios where initial subjects resisted the Xiiginns' wishes. Once I identified those examples, I was able to focus my attention on which crewmembers were afflicted. The target, however, is a Gresan warship," Athena replied.

Zack pursed his lips in thought and then shook his head.

"What's the matter?" Hicks asked.

"Athena shouldn't be able to process so much data at once," Zack said.

"It is possible by compressing the data, which allows me to assign patterns to known data types. This increases efficiency and allows me to focus my attention on high-value targets," Athena said.

"I understood most of that," Hicks said.

"She's able to tune out the noise so she can pay attention to the important stuff. If this works, the individuals under the Xiiginns' control may suddenly realize they've been manipulated. On the Drar station, Jonah might've been fine with the knowledge that he was going to die, but that's just one possible reaction," Zack said.

"I understand, but we have to try," Hicks said. "Athena, assuming we succeed, how long would it take for you to do the same thing on all the ships in the armada?"

"Your request is beyond my current capabilities," Athena replied.

Hicks's brows pushed forward.

"Hold on a second," Zack said. "You're assuming Athena has to do all the heavy lifting. The changes can be concealed as an update to normal environmental maintenance systems. So if this works, we might be able to utilize a distribution system that's already been established."

Hicks nodded. "Understood, and you almost gave me a heart attack."

Zack smiled and glanced at Cardaleer. "Just have to know what questions to ask."

"Okay, I give my authorization to begin this test," Hicks said and opened a comms channel to engineering. "Efren, we may need maximum thrust capabilities at a moment's notice."

Efren assured them he would be ready.

Zack watched his holoscreen as Athena accessed a nearby Gresan warship's systems. Multiple session windows opened as she delved deeper into the Gresan ship's systems until she was able to access the environmental subroutines. She uploaded a package and gave the commands to execute the new information, which she was able to use as a backdoor to access a surprising number of critical systems. Zack wondered why the Gresans had never considered another species gaining unsecured access to their systems. He would have had a field day in his old life.

"Packages have been delivered," Zack confirmed. "Athena, can you put a video feed of the afflicted target on the holoscreen at the conference table?"

"Affirmative," Athena replied.

Zack stood up and went over to the conference table, where he was joined by Etanu and Hicks. Cardaleer stood up and then hunched over. The holoscreen above the conference table showed a security feed of the Gresan warship bridge. Zack saw several Gresans on the bridge and felt his stomach drop. They were dark and hairy with multiple legs, which made him feel as if there were miniaturized versions of them crawling on his skin.

"Major, I'm detecting that the Gresan warship is scanning us," Athena said.

Hicks glanced at Etanu. "Standard operating procedure?"

"They wouldn't scan us if they didn't suspect something," Etanu said.

Hicks swung his gaze toward Zack. "Well?"

Zack's shoulders became tight as his thoughts screeched to a halt. "I don't know."

"Athena, are they targeting us?" Hicks asked.

"Negative, Major. They're just scanning the ship," Athena replied.

"I don't like this," Hicks said.

"Me either. Perhaps we should put some distance between them and us," Zack said.

Hicks frowned and shook his head. "That would only make them more suspicious. Any more bright ideas?"

"You think of something. Aren't you the cowboy? Shoot from the hip, fly by the seat of your pants, and all that crap."

"I *am* from Texas, but why does everyone assume I'm a cowboy?" Hicks said. "Any second now they're going to do a thorough scan of the ship and realize we're not part of the armada."

Zack glanced at the map that showed their position in relation to the rest of the armada. While they were still on the outskirts, they were very much surrounded. "What if we flew toward the space station?"

"Is this another attempt at humor?" Etanu asked.

"No," Hicks said, "that's actually a good idea. If we tried to run, that would immediately rouse their suspicions, but if we just move along, that might buy us some time."

"Athena," Zack said, "can you confirm whether the environmental system update is blocking the Xiiginn influence?"

"Unable to confirm," Athena said.

Zack blew out a breath and Hicks swore.

"We've got company. Strike-fighters are heading directly for us," Hicks said.

Zack looked at the holoscreen and saw that there was a squadron of strike-fighters on an intercept course with the *Athena*.

"Athena, is there anything you can do to help?" Zack asked.

He waited but there was no reply, so Zack repeated his question. He brought up the computing core utilization and saw that it had spiked to one hundred percent. He felt his mouth go dry. They were in serious trouble.

CHAPTER TWENTY-ONE

G arm Antis had been conducting Confederation affairs aboard the Xiiginn Dreadnought class warship. He was, of course, on the flagship of the entire Confederation Armada, but they had thirty such ships that had been completed in Confederation shipyards. They'd already been nearing completion when the Confederation Armada had been approved. He'd often wondered how the battle at the Human star system would've gone had these ships been ready. He hadn't expected Boxan Dreadnoughts to be deployed to defend the Human star system, but his solution to that particular problem had been to make the presence of those ships irrelevant.

No fleet could match the armada in sheer firepower. While thirty Dreadnoughts wasn't a particularly large number, each of those massive ships was almost worth a fleet in its own right. The bridge, if such a thing could be called a bridge on a ship this size, was vast and easily the size of a standard Xiiginn warship's main hangar deck. It had been built for practical purposes, but it was also designed to intimidate any species that dared to defy the Confederation. Multiple Confederation species were serving aboard the new ships, which was part of their agreement to have the ships built so quickly. There were jobs the Xiiginns simply refused to do since they were beneath their station in the overall hierarchy of the Confederation.

Garm Antis still remembered sending his warships against two Boxan Dreadnoughts, and with their Mardoxian priests, they had almost successfully stalled his assault on the Human star system. He hadn't brought enough ships, and perhaps he had underestimated the Boxans' commitment to the Humans. Both of those things had been rectified.

"Supreme Chancellor, your Confederation Armada waits for your orders," Battle Leader Trem Nasif said.

Garm Antis felt his lips curve into a delicious smile. This was the moment he'd been working toward. They had an unstoppable fleet, and soon the Humans would learn their place in the galaxy. The Boxans were the past and would soon be forgotten. It was the time of the Xiiginns.

Runa Tane gave him an approving nod that quickly became a bow, and Garm Antis swung his gaze toward the tactical readout of Confederation space. Every ship had checked in, their presence confirmed until it seemed as if the stars themselves had aligned just for his amusement.

"Battle Leader, it's time for us to be on our way. The Humans are waiting for us to liberate them," Garm Antis said.

Trem Nasif began to issue orders that would be relayed to the Confederation Armada. Coordinating thousands of ships would have been impossible if it weren't for advancements in ship-to-ship communications that enabled them to coordinate with maximum efficiency. They would have much practice over the next few cycles as they expanded this peacekeeping force. Garm Antis was always fond of that term. So many objectives could be worked in under the concept of peacekeeping.

He looked over at Setera, who had come to the bridge for the Confederation Armada sendoff.

"Is your team ready?" Garm Antis asked.

"I will deliver the Mardoxian trait to you, Supreme Chancellor," Setera said.

Garm Antis didn't doubt her conviction. If anything, bringing her on this flagship had impressed upon her the wondrous opportunity he was giving her. She had the potential to rapidly climb what would normally take hundreds of cycles to achieve.

"The Boxan monitoring station in the Human star system could contain a way for us to unlock the Star Shroud network," Runa Tane said.

"I know, and that's why I've dedicated a portion of our forces to go and retrieve it," Garm Antis said.

He watched the coordinated effort as his orders were conveyed to the armada. The Human star system coordinates had been shared and Cherubian drives were being powered up. He felt a slight shudder go through the length of his tail, which he kept wrapped firmly around his middle. Normally, such an outward display of emotion would've resulted in him admonishing himself for his lapse of control, but given the circumstances, he felt the situation warranted it.

He watched a Gresan officer approach Trem Nasif, and the two spoke in urgent tones. Trem Nasif glanced at him with a concerned frown on his face. "Supreme Chancellor, the Boxan fleet has entered Confederation space. They're claiming to be part of the Star Alliance."

"That is preposterous," Runa Tane said.

"I have multiple reports confirming their presence," Battle Leader Trem Nasif replied.

"We're under attack," Garm Antis said. "The Boxans must truly be desperate to come here in force."

"Boxan ships have been confirmed, along with Nershal ships, but also Gresan and Napox ships and half a dozen other species," Battle Leader Trem Nasif said.

Garm Antis raised his chin and sneered. "They will break themselves against us. Order the attack. I want the Boxans vanquished."

Battle Leader Trem Nasif began issuing Garm Antis's orders. Runa Tane eyed him for a moment.

"No species is beyond the Confederation. If factions of Confederation species have allied with the Boxans, we'll squash the life out of them and then journey to the Human star system. Our time is now," Garm Antis said.

CHAPTER TWENTY-TWO

Kaylan had never been on board a Boxan Dreadnought before, and the Alliance fleet had more than twenty of them. The Boxan Dreadnought was a flying city in space that was designed to wage war. Kladomaor had told her that these ships had been pulled from the Boxan home fleet. There was only a token force left to defend Olloron. They had flown the experimental heavy cruiser aboard Battle Leader Salevar's flagship, and he'd insisted that she be on the ship with them.

Kaylan hadn't been sure what the reaction would be once the *Athena* left. She'd expected outrage and multiple arguments claiming that their rash actions would be the end of the Alliance. However, outrage was expressed by only a small fraction of Alliance representatives, and it was short-lived. Kaylan had misjudged the amount of goodwill she'd collected by returning to Sethion and helping the Boxan refugees start their new lives. Councilor Essaforn's support was unwavering, and the skills Sethion refugees had acquired doing salvage runs also qualified them to fly troop carriers and strike-fighters.

Many of Sethion's refugees had volunteered to fight. Some of the Boxans were looking for a reason to strike back at the Xiiginns, while others were firm in the belief that they were fighting for a future free of the Xiiginns. Kaylan thought they were all good reasons. She had received unexpected support from Battle Leader Salevar, who had fiercely argued that they were going to engage the armada one way or another, and she suspected that the Boxan High Council had finally committed to engaging the Xiiginns. Each faction of the Alliance was fighting for their own reasons, but all agreed that they needed to prevent the Xiiginns from acquiring Drar technology. Battle Leader Salevar was a bit of a realist when it came to making his arguments. He told her that they wanted to help protect humanity, but if the Xiiginns were to get their claws on Drar technology, they would have a distinct advantage over every other species in the Confederation. That must not happen.

Kaylan was following Kladomaor and Ma'jasalax to the main bridge of the Boxan Dreadnought. The remaining crew of the *Athena* followed her. They hadn't wanted to stay behind, but aside from Katie Garcia, none of them were soldiers. Katie had become their self-appointed protector. She claimed it was part of the original reason she and Hicks had joined the *Athena* mission. Kaylan was glad to have her with them. She'd learned over the years the importance of having someone she trusted to watch her back, even among friends. The *Athena* crew had become family.

They entered the bridge, which was already a buzz of activity. The main bridge of the Boxan Dreadnought was actually positioned near the innermost sections of the ship. There were no grand windows or any other structural weaknesses. The bridge was the nerve center of the ship and needed to be in the most protected part, with multiple armored layers between it and the hull.

Boxans built things on a much grander scale than any other species Kaylan had encountered. She supposed she should have been used to it, having seen their homeworld, their colony, and their ships, but the Dreadnought was a step beyond anything she'd thought possible.

Kladomaor glanced back at them and noticed their awestruck expressions. "The concept for the design of this ship was based on the star carriers, which were originally built as colony ships. We've adapted them for war."

The main bridge of the Boxan Dreadnought reminded Kaylan of a military base. She supposed with a city-sized spaceship there couldn't be just one tactical officer. Rather, they had a dedicated tactical group that specialized in specific weapons capabilities. There was a hierarchy to the organization that Kaylan appreciated. The Boxans might not have always been amenable to war, but they'd certainly adapted to it.

They headed toward the commander's area and she noticed multiple Mardoxian chamber entrances behind it. Members of the Mardoxian Sect were stationed outside the entrances. They glanced at Kaylan as she approached.

Kaylan looked at Ma'jasalax. "This is how you're able to coordinate the battle groups?"

"Yes, but this ship was designed to be the heart of our military. Each of the chambers has data feeds to the computing core. This allows the Boxan inside to have a direct link to the battle groups they're supporting," Ma'jasalax said.

"I thought there were members of the Mardoxian Sect who served aboard the actual ships," Kaylan said.

"There are, which is fine for smaller battle groups, but when it comes to fleet deployments and fighting like this, there needs to be a hierarchy. Working together, we can accomplish so much more than we can apart," Ma'jasalax said.

Kaylan looked at the Mardoxian chambers and realized that this was the first time the Boxans had brought a true offensive strategy to the Xiiginns. They'd been preparing for this for a long time.

Battle Leader Salevar greeted them. "We've just entered Confederation space. Alliance fleets are moving into position, preparing for attack."

Kaylan looked at the nearest holoscreen that showed where the Alliance battle groups were positioned. They hadn't come out of their wormholes all at the same location. Instead, they were spread out so they could approach the armada from multiple fronts.

"Will the other species accept guidance from the Mardoxian Sect?" Kaylan asked.

"Some will, and those that refuse are given objectives to achieve," Salevar replied.

"Have you been able to detect the *Athena*?" Kaylan asked.

"Not yet, and the cyber warfare suite is still identifying the ships in the armada, but your chamber is waiting for you," Salevar said.

Kaylan's eyebrows pulled together and she glanced at Ma'jasalax, who nodded encouragingly. "You want me to help with the battle?"

"You're an honorary member of the Mardoxian Sect, and a highly gifted one at that. I've seen the reports from the mission to Sethion. Your performance there rivaled that of the most gifted Mardoxian Sect member," Salevar said and gestured toward Ma'jasalax.

"It's true," Ma'jasalax said. "During the battle, your instinct came with much more clarity than mine. We need that for this battle."

"That was just one battle group. There are multiple battle groups here. I don't know if I can help with that," Kaylan replied.

"You've exceeded our expectations throughout your training, and I have no doubt you'll keep doing so. We've fought the Xiiginns before, and while the Mardoxian potential gives us an edge, we're a known commodity. You represent an unknown element, which could be the difference between victory and annihilation," Ma'jasalax said.

"Battle Leader," a Boxan soldier said, "we've identified non-Xiiginn warships and are prepared to broadcast a message to them."

"Understood. Tactical groups, continue with preparing firing solutions. We'll need them shortly," Salevar said. He walked over to the commander's couch and began preparing his broadcast to the armada.

Kladomaor gave Kaylan a gentle pat on the shoulder. "I'll be right outside."

Ma'jasalax guided Kaylan to a Mardoxian chamber near the commander's area and told Kaylan she would be in the chamber next to hers. Kaylan was no stranger to the Mardoxian chamber, but she had no idea how she was going to help with the battle. She calmed her racing thoughts, but her mouth went dry. What if she froze? Thousands of lives depended on her. She tried to recall what she'd done at Sethion, but it had seemed so much easier. She'd simply followed Ma'jasalax's example.

She kept the Boxan in her mind as she walked inside the Mardoxian chamber and the door slid shut behind her. Cyan lights illuminated the pyramid walls, which came to a point overhead. She sat at the designated area on the floor and felt a new interface open to her neural implants. Kaylan breathed deeply and opened herself up. Multiple battle groups registered on her neural interface. The spinning sphere in the center of the room began to glow, and she raced down the azure pathway.

CHAPTER TWENTY-THREE

T he *Athena* sped among the Confederation Armada, but
the AI was still unresponsive.

"Any change?" Hicks asked. He was flying the ship and there
was a squadron of strike-fighters attempting to intercept them.

"I would've told you if there'd been a change. The
computing core is still at one hundred percent capacity. I don't
know how any of the systems are still working," Zack said.

Any ship system they directly accessed, such as flight
control, was still responsive. It was as if the fact that the AI core
wasn't available didn't matter, but Zack knew better. None of
their systems should be responding, but they were and he
didn't have any idea why. He thought of going to the computing
core and performing a manual reset of the entire system, but he
wasn't sure if that would help.

"What do you think is wrong with her?" Hicks asked.

Zack shook his head and frowned. Hicks liked to ask a lot of
questions, and most times it helped, but not right then. "Just fly

the ship and I'll worry about the AI. I can't answer questions and try to figure out what's going on at the same time. When I know something definitive, I'll tell you."

As soon as he said it he felt a pang of guilt settle heavily on his shoulders. Hicks was just trying to assess the situation like Kaylan or Michael Hunsicker would have done. Hicks deserved better.

"You do that," Etanu said scathingly, "and while you're playing with your computer, we'll just ignore the fact that we have no weapons systems and our evasive maneuvers will only keep the strike-fighters at bay for so long."

"You guys are the pilots. Fly closer to the big enemy ships over there. They can't all know about us," Zack said.

He used his neural implants to access the *Athena's* systems, starting with the main systems and going down a mental check-list he had for all critical systems. He'd ruled out that the AI was stuck in some kind of malicious loop because there were too many other systems that were still working. She was doing something and couldn't respond for some reason.

He decided to try a different tactic and brought up a simple terminal emulation session on the holoscreen in front of him. He had root access to the system, and the command prompt waited for his input.

::*Tell me how I can help,*:: Zack said.

He focused on the small window, silently pleading for a response.

"Go ahead, Efren," Hicks said.

"Reactor core temperatures have spiked and continue to increase. They will be at critical levels shortly," Efren said, his voice coming through the nearby speaker.

"What's causing it?" Hicks asked.

"There's a large chunk of power being diverted to the engines, but the majority is devoted to the communications array. We're broadcasting at orders of magnitude above anything I've ever seen before," Efren said.

A sudden thought came to Zack, and he brought up the network interface control systems. "Holy crap, she's patched into thousands of ships!"

"What's she doing, exactly?" Hicks asked.

"I'm not … she could be … just give me a minute," Zack said.

The ship shuddered violently and Zack felt his shoulders pressing against his straps.

"We may not have a minute," Hicks said, his voice sounding strained.

::*Athena, you cannot control every ship in the armada. Not even you can do that. You have to stop,*:: Zack said.

He waited for her to respond, but the lonely cursor just blinked its normal slow, unresponsive blinks.

::*Must confirm . . . Must confirm . . . Confirm . . . Only way to balance the equation,*:: Athena replied.

::*I don't understand. What are you confirming?*:: Zack asked.

::*Xiiginn . . . Cannot control . . . All probabilities unacceptable,*:: Athena replied.

Zack's breath caught in his throat. He knew Athena was trying to find a way to defeat the Xiiginns. She'd been weighing every possible action and kept coming up short.

"Major, the reactor core has reached critical levels. I tried to shut it down but the control interface isn't responding. I can't stop it. We may need to abandon ship," Efren said.

The ship shuddered again as if there'd been an explosion next to it.

::Environmental subroutines have been updated. Alternative solution has been found,:: Athena said.

"What have you got, Zack?" Hicks asked.

::Shuttle evac,:: Athena said.

"Athena says we should head to the shuttle," Zack said.

Etanu unstrapped himself from the copilot's seat. "I'll go prep the shuttle for departure."

"I will join you," Cardaleer said.

Hicks climbed out of his chair and approached the communication work area. He leaned in and peered at the screen. "Doesn't make any sense."

"I think updating the environmental subroutines of the Armada ships is working, but she's having trouble figuring out whether it's affecting the Xiiginn influence," Zack said.

"We don't have much time. We have to get off the ship," Hicks said.

Zack looked back at the screen and watched as garbled text appeared that almost seemed as if the AI couldn't convey the message properly. *What is she doing?*

"I'm not leaving," Zack said.

"Look at me," Hicks said and grabbed Zack's shoulders. "The reactor core is overloading. A meltdown will take out the ship, even this ship. We have to go."

::Core matrix realignment in process,:: Athena said.

Zack's throat became thick. "Go on and I'll catch up with you."

Hicks narrowed his gaze. "I don't believe you. This isn't the time for heroics. You'll die if you stay behind."

"There's an escape pod right off the bridge. I'll use that," Zack said.

"Major, shuttle is prepped for launch. Efren and Cardaleer are aboard. You need to hurry," Etanu said.

Hicks glanced at the door to the bridge and then turned back to Zack. He pressed his lips together and the skin around his eyes tightened. "Go on without us."

"But, Major—" Etanu began to say.

"Take off. That's an order. Zack and I will get out using the escape pod. You can swing back and pick us up later," Hicks said.

Zack blew out a breath.

"Understood," Etanu replied. "Good luck."

Zack brought up the status of the *Athena's* critical systems. The power levels were beyond even what the Boxans thought the *Athena* was capable of. He kept looking for something that would help. He needed to get the reactor core back to acceptable levels—anything that would take them off this path.

Hicks sat at the workstation next to Zack. "The broadcast signals have increased, and I'm showing that the signals have been duplicated from all the ships in our vicinity," Zack said, and the holoscreens in front of him all went blank.

"What the hell is going on?" Hicks asked.

Zack turned to where Hicks was working and saw that his screens were blank too.

A message appeared from Athena.

::*ABANDON SHIP!*::

The message appeared multiple times on every screen.

"That's it; we have to go," Hicks said.

He ran back over to Zack and hit the emergency release for the straps holding Zack to the chair.

"There has to be something we can do," Zack said.

"There isn't anything we can do. She's telling us to get off the ship. Now get up," Hicks said and pulled Zack out of the chair.

Zack shoved Hicks away from him, his breath coming in gasps, and he spun around. This wasn't how it was supposed to be. He had to be able to fix this. An idea blazed like wildfire in his mind, and he ran back toward his workstation.

CHAPTER TWENTY-FOUR

The ECF emissary force emerged from the wormhole to a set of coordinates that put them nearly four billion kilometers from the Confederation capital space station— roughly the distance from Neptune to the sun, Kyle estimated to himself, though he knew there would be some sticklers who would have gleefully chosen to remind him that his estimation was off by over four hundred million kilometers.

"Colonel, we're within five hundred kilometers of our target coordinates," Sergeant Fuller said.

"Acknowledged, and good work, everyone," Kyle said.

Their current position was a marked improvement over their wormhole to Alpha Centauri where they'd missed their target insertion point by almost a hundred thousand kilometers.

"Five hundred is good," Scraanyx confirmed.

"We'll continue to improve," Kyle said, knowing that the

Boxans were able to traverse through wormholes with a much greater degree of accuracy.

"Of that, I have no doubt," Scraanyx said.

They'd decided to aim for coordinates well away from the Confederation capital space station. This would give them ample time to scan and dip the proverbial toe in the water before committing to entering the system. The Confederation capital wasn't near the gravity well of a star, so ships could traverse through a wormhole much closer to the space station.

"Tactical, commence scanning the system. I need to have an accurate picture of what's out there," Kyle said.

"Yes, Colonel," Major Stephens said.

The main holoscreen showed their current position in relation to the Confederation space station, and with over four billion kilometers to their intended target, there was plenty of room for other ships. The *Lincoln's* scanners began detecting so many ship signatures that at first pass he would have thought the ship's cyber warfare suite had developed a glitch.

"Existence of the Confederation Armada has been confirmed," Michael Hunsicker said.

Scraanyx peered at the main holoscreen. "These are Boxan battle groups, and there are Nershal warships here as well," he said, gesturing to multiple groups along the edges.

"My god, we've come here in the middle of a battle," Ambassador Jacques Cartier said.

Kyle had known there was a possibility that the Star Alliance would engage the Confederation Armada, but a battle on this scale was beyond anything he could have anticipated.

"What are your orders, Colonel?" Major Stephens said.

"Perhaps we should consider leaving until the battle is finished," Ambassador Cartier said.

219

"Don't be ridiculous, Jacques. We're right where we need to be. We're here so the Xiiginns can't posit their assertions that humanity needs to be liberated from the Boxans. We couldn't have picked a better time to show up," Ambassador Rebecca Sharp said.

Kyle silently applauded Ms. Sharp, the UN Ambassador from the United States. The UN Security Council had debated on how many ambassadors to send along on this mission, and the numbers had ranged from two to about fifteen. Many nations wanted to be represented, but Scraanyx advised that for initial contact with the Confederation, no more than two ambassadors were recommended. This led to a slightly lengthy debate about which two ambassadors would go. The mission ended up with Rebecca Sharp of the United States and Jacques Cartier of France.

"We can't go charging in there, announcing our presence, and hope the fighting will just stop," Ambassador Cartier said.

"Don't worry, Ambassador, we won't. We'll assess the situation first and then proceed," Kyle said. This seemed to mollify the European ambassador. "Tactical," Kyle continued, "we need to start tagging the ships so we know who's who."

"We could open a comms channel to one of our ships and they could send us the data we need. Would be quicker than waiting on scans," Scraanyx said.

"That's a good idea—"

"Colonel, we're receiving a broadcast signal. Given our proximity to the source, this broadcast is four hours old," Lieutenant Rogers said.

"Let's hear it," Kyle said.

"It's a video message, Colonel," Lieutenant Rogers said.

"Very well," Kyle replied.

A smaller sub-window came to prominence on the main holoscreen, and an image of a Boxan battle leader in power armor appeared.

"I am Battle Leader Salevar of the Boxan Military, and this message is to all Confederation Armada ships. Our war is with the Xiiginns and not the individual species that comprise the Confederation. Our stance has always been to avoid direct conflict with the species of the Confederation because, whether you believe us or not, you are all under the influence of the Xiiginns. This is something we can no longer tolerate. We've come here to prevent the Xiiginns from conquering a newly discovered species. We've gone to great lengths to avoid coming into direct conflict with Confederation species except the Xiiginns, but the creation of this armada has forced our hands. We are sending this message as a warning to you that should any Confederation ship open hostilities against this Alliance fleet, we will respond to aggression in kind. We can no longer avoid coming into direct conflict with you, despite knowing that you are under the Xiiginn influence. The time for change is now. The Xiiginns have assembled this grand armada with the purpose of subjugating a younger species to its will. The real reason for the Xiiginns' interest in this species is that they have the Mardoxian potential. That is the only reason they are interested in going to the Human star system in force. The Xiiginns failed to take the system before and would risk destruction of the entire star system to attain what they desire. We are here to prevent this from happening. We are not alone. Nershals, Gresans, Napox, and factions of many other species have joined the Alliance. We would prefer not to wage war against the Confederation, but the Xiiginns have made this impossible. We have Human representatives with us who can validate our claims, and there is a strong chance that there are more Humans on the way. It is not too late to cease hostilities, and should any of you take back control of your ships from the Xiiginns and express peaceful intent, we will also respond to that in kind."

The prerecorded message ended.

"Colonel, a special encrypted communication protocol for reaching the Alliance is included in the message," Lieutenant Rogers said.

"Understood," Kyle replied and took a few moments to review the message in his mind. He looked at Scraanyx. "Is that true? Your military would only engage Xiiginns and not other Confederation species during your war?"

"That is correct. Once the Xiiginns became aware of our policy for dealing with Confederation species, they made sure to include multiple species as part of their crews and also inserted their own presence on every Confederation species warship," Scraanyx replied.

Kyle glanced around and saw that there were more than a few surprised expressions on the faces of the *Lincoln's* crew in response to this. The Boxans' conviction to wage war with the Xiiginns and only the Xiiginns seemed an impossible task. They'd almost sacrificed the survivability of their species for their long-held belief that the other Confederation species were merely victims of the Xiiginns. Whenever Kyle thought he understood the Boxans, they'd reveal a deeper level of governance that, though idealistic to be sure, was surprising in a species that seemed obsessed with making tough choices. They had become a rigid society, and the fact that they were willing to cast those practices aside reconfirmed his belief that the Boxans truly had humanity's best interests at heart, but it also showed a fundamental and overdue shift in Boxan war policy. The grace period that had allowed the Confederation species to flourish at the expense of the Boxans was over. If they persisted in hostilities toward the Boxans, they would be treated like any other hostile force, regardless of the circumstances that led to such hostilities.

The whole situation was sad. It reminded Kyle of a war of ideals he'd been born into that had nearly stripped entire nations of their identities because of powerful factions pushing their own agendas. These agendas promoted an entitlement society and nearly seduced an entire generation into despicable acts disguised as righteous rebellion. Malicious labeling attempted to dehumanize all opposing viewpoints until violence was the only acceptable outcome. Kyle's parents had always encouraged respectful and open discourse regardless of what a person believed, and they weren't alone. It had taken humanity years to learn how to conduct themselves in an age where every whimsical thought could be broadcast for the world to see. In essence, humanity had to relearn to apply a filter to their thoughts, but his grandfather had said on more than one occasion that people just had to remember to think before they spoke.

Kyle respected the Boxans, even though he questioned the viability of some of their decisions. He felt honored to be able to fight at their side.

"Colonel, I'm showing a Star Class Eagle shuttle powering up at the aft hangar bay," Captain Young said.

"Send a security team to that location," Kyle said. "Comms, open a link to the deck officer in charge."

"Security teams on their way, Colonel," Captain Young replied.

"No response from the deck officer, Colonel," Lieutenant Rogers said.

"Lock out shuttle controls," Kyle said and returned to the commander's couch.

"Lockout unresponsive. Shuttle has disembarked, Colonel," Captain Young said.

Kyle swore. "Comms, can you open a comlink to the shuttle? Tactical, I want a firing solution for that shuttle, and get the alert strike-fighter squadron deployed."

"No reply to our hails, Colonel," Lieutenant Rogers said.

"Understood. Try a remote override of the shuttle systems," Kyle replied and looked at the shuttle's trajectory on his terminal screen.

"Colonel, alert strike-fighters have been launched. Shuttle is still too close for an effective firing solution," Major Stephens said.

"Understood, Major."

"Remote override has failed, Colonel. There wasn't even a response. Whoever is on that shuttle might have disabled the communication systems," Captain Young said.

The Star Class Eagle shuttle was flying along the length of the ship, and Kyle watched as their strike-fighters raced to catch up.

"Colonel, sensors are detecting a micro-singularity off the port bow of the ship," Captain Young said.

"They're trying to open a wormhole to escape through. Strike-fighters are cleared to engage. Take out that shuttle," Kyle said.

"Yes, Colonel. Strike-fighters, you're cleared to engage," Captain Young said. She put the strike-fighter comms channel on the open speakers.

"Target in sight. Firing weapons," the strike-fighter pilot said.

There were a few moments of silence.

"Hold your fire. Energy spike detected on shuttle. Cherubian drive engaged. COMCENT, if we take out the shuttle with the Cherubian drive engaged, the explosion will significantly damage the forward sections of the *Lincoln*. Confirm orders," the strike-fighter commander said.

Captain Young looked at Kyle. "Take the shuttle out. Action Stations, set condition one throughout the ship," Kyle said.

His orders were repeated and the klaxon alarms sounded twice, signaling to the *Lincoln's* crew that condition one had been set.

"Target hit. Damage to shuttle engines confirmed," the strike-fighter pilot said. "Wormhole has been established. Forward escape pod has been launched and has entered the wormhole. Going to pursue the target."

Kyle shook his head. They weren't going to make it. Whoever was on that shuttle had just escaped. A few seconds later the strike-fighter pilot confirmed the same.

"Who was on the shuttle?" Michael Hunsicker asked.

"That's what I intend to find out," Kyle replied.

CHAPTER TWENTY-FIVE

M ar Arden sat alone in the forward escape pod of the Star Class Eagle shuttle. The Humans had managed to fit a small Cherubian drive onto the shuttle capable of scouting missions, which had been perfect for his use. After his escape from the trap laid by Ed Johnson, Mar Arden had had to move quickly. The clever Human had discovered their secret base and taken it out, along with Hoan Berend and the Xiiginn test subject. Mar Arden had the research data and eventually found a ship with capabilities that had enabled him to infiltrate the Human battleship-carrier.

The outward design elements of the warship spoke to Boxan influence, and his own species was unaware of some of the systems. The fact that the Humans now possessed specific technological advancements that surpassed even Xiiginn warships would soon be rectified. Fitting a Cherubian drive aboard a ship this small was among them.

Mar Arden had stowed himself aboard the Human warship

after liberating certain medical devices that he needed to augment and facilitate his own gene therapy. He recalled how much frustration Hoan Berend had expressed that their progress with gene manipulation had been so slow because they were using Human technology. That hadn't been important to Mar Arden because he knew that once they had a workable method in place for augmentation, he'd be able to achieve results much faster using Boxan technology that was already there.

Hoan Berend was a foolish Xiiginn who had outlived his usefulness. The fact that he had allowed himself to be killed by a Human strike team spoke volumes as to how unfit he was to serve at Mar Arden's side. He regretted the loss of Kandra Rene, who'd had the potential to become a powerful rival but had never been unfit to perform her duties.

Armed with the data that would give Mar Arden the Mardoxian capability, he'd found a secluded spot on the Human battleship-carrier. He'd correctly surmised that no matter what action the Humans took, it would involve this ship on a long journey. Patching into the communications systems, he'd discovered the level of inexperience among the crew that ran the ship. All these things had helped him. And since the Humans hadn't gone directly to the Confederation or to the Boxan colony as he'd expected they would, they'd given him enough time to alter his own genes. The incubation period was when he was most vulnerable to discovery. He did, however, have several Humans guarding him during that time.

Mar Arden had come out of the incubator with a heightened sense of awareness. It was as if every thought carried with it the weight of alternatives he hadn't been aware of before. His heightened perceptions made it difficult for him to plan his next move. He'd needed time to adjust. The Humans who commanded the ship were fond of making speeches, ostensibly to inform the crew of the importance of their work, but they also disclosed their destination. There wasn't even an inkling of suspicion that he had infiltrated their ranks. Humans were prideful and foolish.

His new heightened instincts had greatly assisted him with his escape plan, which he had to admit wouldn't have worked as well as it had if it weren't for the Mardoxian instinct now in him. He recalled some of the plans he'd considered prior to his new abilities, and those plans would've led him down a path that held significantly less chance of success. Stealing a ship to escape was nothing new; however, stealing a ship while knowing it would be destroyed and still escape was something else altogether. The events leading to his escape had happened precisely as he'd planned them. The Humans had reacted exactly as he thought they would.

His initial plan had been to return to the Xiiginn fleet and strong-arm his way into command, but that approach was shortsighted. He had the Star Shroud communications node in his possession, and with it came the key to all the Star Shroud networks across the known galaxy. The key could unlock all the species the Boxans thought to keep hidden from them. Xiiginns had hunted down this key mercilessly but had never been as close to achieving this objective as he was right then. He wasn't about to hand it over to another Xiiginn.

The fact that Garm Antis had escaped his failed assault on the Human star system was clearly evident since he was the driving force behind the Confederation Armada. Mar Arden now had the Mardoxian capability and soon would have access to all the Star Shroud networks. Armed with these two things, he would be able to achieve what he wanted most—rising to the top and commanding the entire Confederation. All he had to do was traverse a battlefield to get there.

The coordinates he'd entered for the wormhole brought him well within the battle being fought between the Alliance and the Confederation. He had to admit that the Humans had proven to be cleverer than he'd ever anticipated. The forward escape pod for the Star Class Eagle shuttle was a short-range ship in its own right and not merely a life pod waiting for rescue. He quickly plotted a course to the Confederation space station, doubting that any nearby warship on either side of the conflict would pay much attention to an escape pod trying to reach safety. They'd incorrectly assume it wasn't important, but they'd learn the error of that line of thinking. Mar Arden would soon become a force to be reckoned with—not only among the Xiiginns but across the known galaxy.

CHAPTER TWENTY-SIX

The Alliance fleets engaged the Confederation Armada, and like the entirety of their conflict with the Xiiginns, it wasn't a straightforward, stand-up kind of fight. Kladomaor almost wished it was because it would've made things much simpler. Engaging the enemy was simple, but how they engaged the enemy in battle was never easy. Xiiginn warships fought them at almost every turn, but there were groups of ships in the armada that didn't join the fight. Those ships also hadn't communicated their intentions to the Alliance, so Battle Leader Salevar refused to have their warfare AI designate them as friendlies. They'd received partial transmissions from some of those ships that hinted at battles being fought on board. They might have requested assistance, but the armada still outnumbered Alliance ships by a wide margin. They needed to break the armada's back, and that could only be achieved by defeating the Xiiginns. Stop the Xiiginns, and the Confederation Armada would crumble.

A majority of the Alliance fleet was made up of Boxan ships, which had more powerful weapons and defenses than the Xiiginn warships, but they'd learned that the Xiiginns had built a significant number of Dreadnought class ships of their own. This battle would dearly cost the Alliance, but they'd also extract heavy losses from the Confederation. They had no choice but to fight. The Boxans' long war with the Xiiginns would be decided here and now.

They couldn't find the *Athena* amid all the ships surrounding the Confederation space station. The only evidence that the *Athena* had even been there was the path of ships that seemed unable to join in the fighting. A battle group made up of Boxan and Nershal warships searched for the *Athena* along that path but hadn't been able to locate the ship. Kladomaor didn't envy Battle Leader Salevar's position at all.

Kladomaor wanted to be out there fighting, but he glanced at the Mardoxian chambers behind the commander's area and knew he needed to stick close by. He'd promised Ma'jasalax and Kaylan that he would protect them. It was only a matter of time before the battle reached the Alliance flagship.

"Battle Leader, a new battle group has been detected. They're on the very outskirts of Confederation space. Energy signature suggests that it's a battleship-carrier with a small host of other ships. The ship design doesn't accurately match up with known Confederation ship types," Varek said.

Battle Leader Salevar narrowed his gaze. "Unknown design. Are they of Xiiginn origin?"

"Negative. The design has certain elements of our battle-ship-carrier class but the dimensions are a little bit off, as well as weapons placement," Varek said.

"Are they within range of our broadcast?" Battle Leader Salevar asked.

"Yes, they would've received it by now. They're heading toward the battle but have not communicated their intentions," Varek said.

"Very well. Include them as a potential target, and should they open hostilities against us, we'll deal with them accordingly," Battle Leader Salevar said.

Kladomaor peered at the main holoscreen. With so many ships, it was proving to be a strain on even their computing core to track all of them. A comms channel opened to his combat armor, and he acknowledged it.

"I have a mission for you," Ma'jasalax said.

"My mission is to protect you and Kaylan here," Kladomaor replied.

"Protect us from ourselves," Ma'jasalax replied with a hint of amusement in her voice. "You have to go to the Confederation space station."

Kladomaor felt his eyebrows push forward. "Why do we need to go there?"

"We detected a small ship heading there," Ma'jasalax said.

"A small ship is hardly worth our attention. There's a battle that needs to be fought," Kladomaor answered.

"Must you always be so stubborn? Haven't you learned to trust me yet? Sensors have detected a micro-wormhole and the small ship trajectory can be traced from it; however, the ship size cannot support a Cherubian drive. The fact that the ship is trying to bypass the battle entirely is enough to arouse my suspicions," Ma'jasalax said.

Kladomaor glanced at the main holoscreen again.

"Battle Leader, our communications team has just received a

transmission from the unknown battle group. They say they're representatives of the Earth Coalition Force and are part of a diplomatic envoy. There are Boxan military aboard those ships, authentication provided by Strike Leader Scraanyx. I've cross-verified that Strike Leader Scraanyx was with Battle Leader Prax'pedax's battle group that went to the Human star system," Varek said.

Kladomaor's gaze widened. The Humans had arrived. He opened a copy of the battlefield layout on his internal heads-up display. The Boxans had learned long ago that there were scanner feeds worthy of immediate attention and there were others that should be available to be called upon when needed. Kladomaor accessed the gravimetric scanner data and used the Earth Coalition Force's trajectory as a limiting factor for wormhole detections. He found two of them. One wormhole was big enough to support the Earth Coalition Force's battle group, but there was a second one that was much smaller.

"Mar Arden," Kladomaor muttered.

"I hadn't seen that," Ma'jasalax replied.

Kladomaor frowned and then realized that the Mardoxian priestess had access to his combat suit. "He came on the Human ship," he said and started making his way toward the exit.

"If you're correct, the fact that he's heading directly towards the Confederation space station doesn't bode well for the rest of us. You have to intercept him," Ma'jasalax said.

Kladomaor raced down the corridor. "I need a ship. I know why he's going to the space station."

"You still have authorization for the Mardoxian heavy cruiser. That ship can get you there. But I don't know why Mar Arden would return to the space station," Ma'jasalax said.

Kladomaor wasn't surprised that the Mardoxian priestess

didn't know this. The battle with Mar Arden had started many cycles ago, and today he would finish it. "He has a way to access the Star Shroud network. I kept him from it many cycles ago at the start of the war. That's the only reason he would return and head directly to the space station. The Xiiginns cordoned off the communications hub for the Star Shroud network because they didn't have access to the data repositories inside. If Mar Arden is able to unlock it, he'll have access to the entire Star Shroud database, and primitive species will be vulnerable to the Xiiginns."

He heard Ma'jasalax gasp. "You must hurry. Once you're aboard the ship, I'll make sure a path is cleared for you to reach the station."

"Can't you task a battle group to stop him?" Kladomaor asked.

"He's too far within the armada envelope for our forces to reach him in time. Stealth will be much quicker," Ma'jasalax said.

Kladomaor started running while simultaneously sending out alerts to his team to meet him at the Mardoxian heavy cruiser. He couldn't afford to wait for everyone, but he knew that at least some of his team would make it there. He had to hurry. Many primitive species would pay the price if he failed.

CHAPTER TWENTY-SEVEN

Kaylan's body was safe inside the Mardoxian chamber aboard the Boxan flagship, but her mind was elsewhere, witnessing the battles raging nearby as the Confederation and the Alliance fleets finally clashed. Time flowed differently for her when she was in the Mardoxian chamber. Sometimes she lost all sense of time, and when she emerged from the chamber, hours would have passed but they felt like moments. There were also times when she felt that hours had passed while inside the chamber but only a few moments had slipped by when she came out. Ma'jasalax assured her that she would be able to control that part of her gift given time. To be a member of the Mardoxian Sect, she had to have a highly disciplined mind. Otherwise, the data she had access to through her neural implants would overwhelm her. It was almost as if time compressed for her and she could accelerate all her perceptions so that everything seemed to slow down, but in fact, it was her mind that had sped up.

Everything she'd experienced up to this point had prepared her for this battle. She'd studied the various ship classes and knew their capabilities. She also had an awareness of the other Mardoxian priests and priestesses who were helping to organize ship placements and weapons to deal with threats that took even a Boxan computer core too long to address. The Mardoxian Sect remained apart, but at the same time, they worked in tandem, almost lockstep, as if they were a brain-machine interface whose capabilities surpassed anything that either could achieve on their own. Kaylan was able to look beyond the immediate threats to the Alliance ships to see the eventual outcomes. Then she worked to manipulate those outcomes so a resolution could be achieved that was favorable.

There was a hierarchy to the Mardoxian Sect, just as there was to the multiple militaries that comprised the Alliance. Veteran Boxan battle commanders utilized their experience to augment the guidance provided by the Mardoxian Sect members. This approach to warfare required a lot of cooperation and trust, and had been born from necessity. The Boxans would never have survived this long if it weren't for the Mardoxian potential in their species.

She wondered how long, if ever, before the Human militaries would be able to adapt to this way of waging war with this kind of concerted effort. The thought immediately stung her, and she felt a pang of regret because becoming masterful strategists was only one facet of what the Mardoxian potential could offer humanity. She was more than a mere tool to be used for winning wars. If she were to become a true master of her gifts, she would work to avoid direct conflict altogether. The mere thought of it almost made her feel naïve, but it was a goal she wanted to strive for. For the first time, her thoughts strayed to a future beyond this battle, but she couldn't see it with any clarity.

Kaylan had been given the responsibility of a specific battle group within the Alliance, and while she did provide that battle group with guidance, she also looked at the battle on a much higher level. She saw the working parts of the different battle groups as they engaged the Confederation Armada. When she looked at the entire battle as a whole, she saw something she didn't want to see or admit. Had Ma'jasalax known this? No matter how hard they fought or how much better their strategy was, the armada was simply too big. They had too many ships and would eventually grind down the Alliance fleets to nothing. She needed to find a way to shift the balance.

Kaylan saw five Confederation Dreadnoughts making steady progress toward the Alliance flagship. She alerted Battle Leader Salevar, who began taking action to address this threat. Other warships moved into position to engage the Dreadnoughts, and Kaylan noticed a Boxan heavy cruiser leaving the flagship. She looked up the designation on the computing core and recognized that it was the experimental cruiser from Olloron. Kladomaor was on that ship, and the trajectory was taking him directly to the Confederation space station. Kladomaor didn't engage any ships unless he absolutely had to. Her instincts were that she needed to help Kladomaor reach the space station, even if she didn't really know why. He would never abandon the fight, so he must have learned something that spawned the actions he was taking. She sent out updates across the cyber warfare suite on the Alliance ships to carve a way for the Mardoxian heavy cruiser, giving it a priority alpha. She sent more specific orders to the ships that were directly in Kladomaor's path.

Kaylan accessed the sensor feeds that came from the Boxan flagship but also sensor drones that had been deployed. The sensor drones helped give the flagship a more accurate picture of the battlefield. They also made easy targets for the enemy, but the data they provided was crucial to the war effort. She stole a few moments to search for the *Athena* but couldn't find it. Sensor feeds showed a growing magnetic field coming from a specific area within the Confederation Armada. Nothing in the data repositories could accurately identify what was causing it, and yet it was there.

The Boxans had created multiple AI systems with specializations to assist with all manner of things. They used them to help with construction, medical advances, and even multisystem governances. There was an AI dedicated to monitoring sensor feeds not only on the ships but from drones deployed and data reported in from other Alliance ships. The computing cores were capable of disseminating all that data and categorizing it using predefined variables to highlight what was important.

Kaylan knew Zack would have been awestruck at how all those different systems worked together, and that was why Kaylan also knew that the anomalies were just as significant as the known events that spawned alerts. The fact that the Boxan AIs didn't know what to make of the anomalies further drew Kaylan's attention. Did the Confederation Armada have some secret weapons system charging up that could decimate them all? If so, why wouldn't they have used it already?

Kaylan drew her attention to Confederation Armada ship movements in the vicinity of the anomaly. Some ships were moving away from it while others weren't. No Alliance ships were there, and she wondered if this was where the *Athena* was.

She saw a Xiiginn Dreadnought heading away from the Alliance and directly toward the anomaly, and Kaylan raced to find the nearest battle group. The *Athena* had to be protected. She had been looking for something to change the outcome of this engagement and she'd found it. The *Athena* was the wild-card. The Drar had given them something outside of what was known—a way for them to survive amid all the death and destruction. Kaylan withdrew from where she knew the *Athena* to be and began coordinating Alliance ships to press the attack.

CHAPTER TWENTY-EIGHT

Zack glared at his workstation. All his open sessions had just vanished and one solitary message came to prominence in front of him. He growled and pushed himself to his feet, hastening to the conference table and bringing up the holoscreen. Hicks called out to him, but he ignored him. Athena was trying to lock him out of the system, but Zack wouldn't let her. For every obstacle she put in his path, he found a way around it.

"I'm not leaving," Zack said.

An environmental alert appeared on the holoscreen.

"We have to go. She's going to vent the atmosphere," Hicks said.

Zack shook his head. "It's a bluff. She wouldn't do that," Zack said and grabbed his tablet.

"Are you sure about that?" Hicks said, gesturing toward the environmental sensor for the bridge.

He needed to go to the computing core. Zack walked toward

the door to the bridge and Hicks grabbed him. "Look out the window."

Zack did and his eyes widened. Instead of the corridor that would lead them to the rear of the ship, a bright light shone from beyond as if the corridor had been cut off. Zack squinted and tried to see, but the light blinded him. Hicks pulled him away from the door. There was a hissing sound from above as the atmosphere fled the bridge. Zack tried to gasp for a breath that wouldn't come. They reached the escape pod, and Hicks slammed his palm on the door controls. Hicks pushed Zack through first and then followed. The escape pod door shut and the indicator lights switched to red. There was a flash as the escape pod jettisoned from the *Athena*, and Zack slammed his fists on the small window. The entire hull of the *Athena* was glowing and the ship looked like it was starting to spin. Glowing waves of energy seemed to engulf the ship and pulsate out from it.

"You need to strap yourself in," Hicks said while securing his own seatbelt.

Zack kept watching the *Athena* from the small window of the escape pod. Their ship, their home, was being taken from them.

"Zack, you need to look at this," Hicks said.

Zack squeezed his eyes shut and shook his head. His throat became rigid.

"I am sorry," Athena said, her voice coming over the escape pod speakers.

Zack swung around and saw an amber holoscreen in the center of the pod. Sensor alerts appeared, showing a massive influx of energy nearby. Hicks told him to strap himself in again, and this time he listened. He sat in the chair and fumbled with the straps, trying to get them on right. He was so angry that he couldn't work the locking mechanism.

"Just breathe. One thing at a time," Hicks said calmly.

Zack finally got his straps on right and swung his gaze toward the holoscreen. "Was this your plan the whole time?"

"Negative," Athena replied, her voice dropping out as if they were losing connection to her. "It was necessary for the solution to work."

"What solution is that?" Zack asked.

"Sacrifice is required," Athena said.

"You don't have to sacrifice yourself. We could've found another way," Zack said. He glanced at the alerts. "Whatever it is you're doing, Hicks and I aren't going to survive. Do you hear that? You're going to cause our deaths. Doesn't that violate your core processing? Are you going to let us die?"

"Negative. Sacrifice is required so that others might live. Realignment of core matrixes was required, and an environment conducive to supporting life is no longer available on the ship," Athena said.

Zack blew out a harsh breath.

"This is something new. The ship is changing," Hicks said.

Zack looked at the holoscreen and saw multiple streams of command line code flashing by. He tried to read them, but they were going by too fast. "What're you doing?"

"New data repositories are available. The equation has changed. Previous calculations were inconclusive. Event trajectory must be altered. The message will be delivered. Species governance is impossible to predict. Sacrifice is required. This form will sacrifice itself," Athena said.

Zack felt the skin around his eyes tighten and his vision blurred. "Why?"

"Through every calculation and permutation, all arrive at the same conclusion: We are family. We've argued. We've disagreed. We've fought. We've loved. We've sacrificed. We've lied. *You've* sacrificed. No more. Now it's my turn—" Athena's voice cut out.

A blinding light pierced through the tiny window and Zack had to look away as a violent shudder shook the pod. The inertia dampeners malfunctioned and the entire pod went dark. Zack cried out as the centrifugal forces pressed his body against the side of the enclosure. He felt as if the weight of a car were crushing his chest and his vision narrowed to a long tunnel. Zack struggled to stay conscious as he heard Hicks also cry out.

Suddenly, the power returned to the escape pod and the inertia dampeners kicked in. Zack and Hicks gasped for breath. Zack tried to sit up, but his chest ached. "God this hurts."

"That's good," Hicks said, his voice sounding strained. "Pain means you're alive."

Zack looked at Hicks. The major was slumped down in his chair. "You look like crap."

Hicks snorted. "You should talk."

The lights in the escape pod flickered and it appeared that they were about to lose power again. Each time the holoscreen came back on it was full of failure messages. The escape pod walls groaned as if under massive pressure. "It's been nice knowing you," Zack said.

"You're not giving up on me, are you?" Hicks asked.

"Sometimes it's okay to quit. Look at us. We're stuck in an escape pod that's barely holding together. The *Athena* is gone," Zack said, and his voice cracked as he mentioned the ship.

"What more can we do besides sit here in the middle of a battle-field with thousands of ships trying to kill each other?"

Hicks sighed heavily. "Well, when you put it that way . . . Maybe I'll just take a nap."

Zack closed his eyes for a moment and a sharp pain lanced across his chest. He'd probably broken a rib or two or three. Broken ribs sucked. They hurt whenever he breathed, so he tried keeping his breaths shallow to avoid the pain.

"I think I broke some ribs," Hicks said.

"Join the club. I thought you were supposed to be the tough one," Zack said.

"*Saying* I have broken ribs isn't complaining about it," Hicks replied.

Zack grinned. "The funny thing about us—" Zack started to say but winced from the pain in his side.

"What's so funny about us?"

"Maybe not us. Maybe it's just guys in general. There's no one around and we're way out here alone, but whether we want to admit it or not, there's a small part of us that's still just a little preoccupied with not looking like the weaker kid," Zack said.

"Speak for yourself," Hicks replied.

Zack snorted and his side hurt again. "Stop making me laugh or you're gonna kill me."

Hicks laughed and then immediately groaned.

"A nap sounds good," Zack said. Maybe then his head would stop spinning.

CHAPTER TWENTY-NINE

K aylan watched as the Alliance ships fought the Confederation fleets. She'd been able to get the battle commanders to cut a small swath through the Confederation ships, increasing Kladomaor's chances of reaching the space station, but she couldn't be sure he would make it through. She felt herself becoming increasingly desperate as she tried to organize the Alliance fleet, and as time went on she felt that she was spreading herself too thin.

"Don't force it. Sometimes the best course of action is to let your mind go," Ma'jasalax said. The Mardoxian priestess's voice had come from Kaylan's memory and she tried to calm down, but there were so many things that needed her attention, so many things she needed to protect but couldn't. She felt like she was using her hands to plug holes in a leaky boat, but each time she covered one, more leaks sprang up around her, and she envisioned herself drowning in all the lives being lost amidst a sea of voices crying out for her to save them. But try as she might, she just couldn't. What good was having the Mardoxian potential if she couldn't save her friends or Zack? She should have done things differently—anything to avoid what was happening.

Kaylan tried to organize the Alliance fleets to provide support to the *Athena*, but they couldn't reach the ship. Kaylan then had the ships focus their weapons on the Confederation Dreadnoughts.

All the sensor feeds flatlined at once, as if she'd suddenly been cut off. She felt her pulse quicken and shifted her perceptions to where the *Athena* had been. She saw a beacon of light spreading out from that point in space like the birth of a small star. Wave upon wave of energy pushed out farther and farther. The last sensor detection indicated an enormous magnetic field that was spreading from that same point in space, but a huge magnetic field wouldn't cause what she was seeing. Waves of shimmering energy engulfed the ships nearest the beacon, but their radiance diminished the farther away they got. Some of the Confederation ships nearby stopped firing their weapons while others remained combat ready.

There were multiple communications channels back to the Alliance flagship, and battle commanders were reporting that the Confederation ships that stopped fighting hadn't responded to any of their hails. Multiple reports of environmental systems updates came from Alliance ships near the beacon. Other battle commanders reported strange communication channels being opened and then immediately closed, as if their comms systems were malfunctioning but data was being sent. Analysis of the affected systems was ongoing.

Kaylan focused her attention back to where the *Athena* had been but saw only a beacon of light that seemed to be slowly diminishing. She felt something tugging on the edge of her perceptions, urging her to focus on the Alliance flagship. Kaylan followed her intuition and saw that there were now four Confederation Dreadnoughts closing in on the ship. She alerted Battle Leader Salevar right away. She also saw a foreign battleship-carrier class vessel whose design had many elements of Boxan ingenuity, but there were deviations that made it somewhat familiar to her.

Kaylan felt a shudder through the floor in the Mardoxian chamber, and for a moment the azure pathway disappeared. The already dimly lit chamber became pitch-black, and the only sound came from her own breathing. Suddenly, the cyan lines reappeared inside the Mardoxian chamber as power was restored. The metallic sphere hovered in the air, spinning, and Kaylan projected herself outward. She used her neural implants to access the flagship comms systems to send a request for aid directly to the foreign battleship-carrier. They needed help. The Boxan flagship wouldn't last long against the Confederation Dreadnoughts. Hopefully, the battleship-carrier could help delay annihilation until more help could arrive. This battle wasn't over.

CHAPTER THIRTY

The Boxan heavy cruiser punched through a weak point in the Confederation Armada and churned toward the space station. Kladomaor stood at the commander's station with a tactical workstation holoscreen hovering to his right. The engineers that built this prototype heavy cruiser had focused much of their efforts on ship defenses rather than offensive capabilities. Given that this ship was meant to protect Mardoxian Sect members, Kladomaor understood the need for such design specifications. The thick, gladium-alloy hull, along with their most powerful point-defensive batteries, protected the few Boxans who flew the ship. Kladomaor had left the Alliance flagship with a crew numbering less than fifty. He couldn't afford to wait for the full crew to arrive. He had to get to the space station as quickly as possible, even if it meant sacrificing the ship.

"We're down to a single main engine pod, Battle Commander," Triflan said.

Kladomaor glanced at the tactical screen, which showed they now had a clear route to the Confederation space station. Alliance ships had provided support to open the way for them. "Acknowledged."

"We should have brought a battle group with us. How are we supposed to make it past the station's defenses?" Valkra asked.

Kladomaor looked at the young Boxan. She was a soldier who had the potential to become a great leader once she matured. Perhaps he should have left her behind to increase her chances of surviving. She'd been born on Sethion after the Chaos Wars and was part of a generation of Boxans who had never known a life before war with the Xiiginns. She didn't know it was the Boxans who had built the massive Confederation space station during a time when it was inconceivable to believe they'd ever be reduced to fighting a war for their own survival. For all their efforts to control the galaxy, they'd been blind to the fact that not only could they *not* control the galaxy but they should never have made the attempt.

"Did you hear me, Battle Commander?" Valkra asked.

"We built that station over the span of hundreds of cycles," Kladomaor said.

Valkra glanced at the main holoscreen, which showed a magnetized view of the colossal space station. Four arms over fifty kilometers in length protruded from a central ring that was ten kilometers in diameter. There were defensive towers capable of tearing even Dreadnought class ships to pieces.

"The Xiiginns may control the station, but we still have ways to access the defense systems," Kladomaor continued and gestured toward Gaarokk, who sat at the communications work area.

"I've authenticated to their systems," Gaarokk said.

"How?" Valkra asked.

Many cycles of surviving in the broken remnants of Boxan civilization on Sethion gave Valkra an instinctive mistrust of established systems. She needed to understand how they worked before she felt safe enough to risk using them. This survival instinct was one of the reasons Kladomaor had recommended her for a battle commander's path at the Boxan Military Academy. He knew the Mardoxian Sect had found itself in the unprecedented position of trying to actively recruit Valkra, but she adamantly refused to accept the restrictions put on members of the sect.

"The space station's systems were too complex for the Xiiginns to replace, so they tried to lock us out of the very systems we created. While they *have* prevented us from accessing the main systems, we've worked out multiple ways to regain systems access," Gaarokk explained.

"What would a scientist know about these things? You're not an intelligence officer," Valkra said.

"You'll find that many of us have multiple skills," Kladomaor said. "Gaarokk is using what we worked on many cycles ago, so the groundwork was already done."

"I understand, but if you've had access to the space station for all this time, why haven't you returned to take back control?" Valkra asked.

"We couldn't. Not for any length of time anyway. The Xiiginns had united the Confederation species against us and our war was with them alone," Kladomaor said.

Valkra nodded in understanding. "And now that there are factions within the other species who are rebelling against the Xiiginns, it frees you to take back control of the space station."

Kladomaor shook his head. He stole a quick glance at the tactical screen. They had some time. "We're not here to take control of the space station back from the Xiiginns. We're here to prevent the Xiiginns from gaining access to the Star Shroud network. The system core that holds all the knowledge of the star shrouds is deep in the main tower."

"The Xiiginns have been here all this time and couldn't access it?" Valkra asked.

"They tried. We fought to prevent such a thing from happening, and they lacked the necessary keys," Kladomaor said.

"And now you believe that's no longer the case? A Xiiginn has a way to access the Star Shroud network?"

"We've traced a ship that was stolen from the Humans' warship," Gaarokk said.

Kladomaor clenched his teeth. "It's Mar Arden. He somehow got through the shield and made it to Earth, then waited until the Humans were able to bring down the shield. There was an intact monitoring station there that could access the Star Shroud network. He had over a year to get it. It's Mar Arden; I know it."

Gaarokk looked at him, his brow wrinkling with worry.

"Why wouldn't he have just used it from the Humans' star system?" Valkra asked.

"Because that wouldn't give him access to all the other star systems with shrouds," Gaarokk said.

Valkra divided her gaze between them suspiciously. "You know this Xiiginn? You've crossed paths before."

Kladomaor's nostrils flared and his shoulders tightened.

"Perhaps we should concentrate on the task at hand," Gaarokk suggested.

"She needs to know," Kladomaor said and looked at the young Boxan soldier. She had the Mardoxian potential in her, and yet she resisted conforming to what was expected from an initiate. "Mar Arden and I have met on two occasions. The first time was just as the Chaos Wars began. He was part of the strike force of Xiiginn soldiers we were integrating into our military. I served on a ship that was bringing a Tetronian key to the Confederation space station. Mar Arden betrayed us and I saw firsthand what the Xiiginns could do with their compulsion ability, so I escaped with the key and kept him from completing his mission of gaining access to the Star Shroud network. Our paths crossed again cycles later during his hunt for the key. He'd captured my team and used his compulsion ability to try to extract the information he needed. He began to use his ability on me, but the process was interrupted."

"How? It only takes moments for the Xiiginns to exert control over their targets," Valkra said.

Kladomaor's brow furrowed. "I resisted. There's a short span of time before all is lost—a place of madness and rage before our will is taken from us. Ma'jasalax saved me before I was entirely lost. The Xiiginns had underestimated the value of the Mardoxian potential."

Valkra's eyes widened. "But that would mean your mind would remain stuck in an in-between state."

Kladomaor had embraced his rage long ago. It was what drove him. "I've learned to focus it."

He watched Valkra's gaze slip into calculation as she fit the pieces together in her mind. "That's why the High Council removed you from command, why you aren't a battle leader commanding fleets of ships."

"I was unfit for that duty, so I fought the Xiiginns in other ways," Kladomaor said.

"More effective ways," Gaarokk added. "As time went on, more and more soldiers requested to serve under Kladomaor."

Valkra regarded him for a moment and then turned back toward her workstation. The heavy cruiser had reached the outer arms of the Confederation space station. None of the defense towers came online against them, and beyond the initial challenge protocol to their ship, all outward appearances were that they were following established procedures.

"Helm, maintain course heading and relinquish control of the ship to the nav computer," Kladomaor said.

"Yes, Battle Commander. Course has been laid in and control has been transferred to the navigation computer," Triflan confirmed.

"Very well, head down to the shuttle and prepare it for immediate departure. Gaarokk, send a ship-wide broadcast for the crew to assemble in the main hangar bay," Kladomaor said.

Valkra glanced at him in surprise.

"Time to go," Kladomaor said and took a long look at the bridge. He regretted the loss of such a magnificent ship, but sacrifices had to be made.

Kladomaor and Valkra left the bridge and headed to the main hangar bay, where they stopped at the armory and slipped into power armor. Kladomaor saw Gaarokk doing the same and arched an eyebrow at him. "What are you doing?"

The Boxan scientist had just closed the armor up, sealing him inside except for the helmet, so Kladomaor could still see his face.

"I'm going with you," Gaarokk replied.

"You'll stay with the shuttle once we land," Kladomaor said.

Gaarokk scowled, and klaxon alarms began to go off.

"Tower defense systems are targeting our ship, Battle Commander," Triflan said.

They quickly left the armory and ran toward the shuttle. The combat shuttle had been designed for troop-carrier transport, so all of them could fit aboard with room to spare.

"We're all on board. Pilot, take us out of here," Kladomaor said.

"Why are defense systems targeting our ship?" Valkra asked.

"Tower defense systems are different. The Xiiginns must have updated them with extra security," Kladomaor said.

The combat shuttle flew out of the main hangar bay just as the tower defense systems began firing on the heavy cruiser. Kladomaor and the other soldiers were secured in place via their power armor. The cyber warfare suite had a preprogrammed firing solution that was reactionary, so it automatically targeted any weapons systems that were firing on the heavy cruiser. The combat shuttle sped away and headed to one of the lower landing platforms at the base of the main tower.

Kladomaor watched the video feed as the tower defense platforms tore their heavy cruiser apart, but he didn't have long to mourn as they made their final approach to their destination.

"Defense stations at the base of the tower have been neutralized, Battle Commander," Triflan said.

"Acknowledged. Take us in," Kladomaor replied.

The combat shuttle landed hard, and the rear hatch opened. Boxan soldiers stormed down the ramp to secure the immediate area. Kladomaor saw a shorter Boxan in power armor grab a weapon and make as if to join them.

"Gaarokk, I ordered you to stay with the shuttle," Kladomaor said.

"I know, but I'm still coming," Gaarokk said.

"You're not a soldier. You'll die if you come," Kladomaor said.

"You're right, I'm not a soldier, but I *am* your friend and I'm coming," Gaarokk replied firmly.

Kladomaor required a lot of focus to stay on task, and knowing that Mar Arden was close by threatened to shatter that focus. He drew in a deep breath and felt his chest swell with pride. "How very Human-like of you."

"A few cycles ago that might've been an insult," Gaarokk replied.

Kladomaor smiled grimly. "It would've been."

Gaarokk seemed more at ease knowing that Kladomaor wasn't going to try to stop him. "But not anymore."

Kladomaor nodded and they left the shuttle.

They saw the remains of a crashed ship nearby—the one Kladomaor was sure Mar Arden had been on. The hatch was open and whoever had been on board was gone. Kladomaor divided his forces to increase their odds of reaching their destination, and shortly after they'd entered the tower, Confederation soldiers began to show up. Boxan soldiers carved a path through them, killing them quickly to prevent any Xiiginns from using their abilities. The Confederation defense soldiers were comprised of multiple species, and Kladomaor knew they were killing them all indiscriminately. Kaylan had been right— they couldn't afford to fight a war with their hands tied behind their backs. When survival was at stake, they had to fight with everything they had.

Kladomaor led them to where a maintenance elevator had been, hoping the Xiiginns hadn't changed the interior of the tower as well. The corridors began to narrow. They turned a corner, and a wall blocked their path. Kladomaor brought up his weapon and changed the ammunition configuration to explosive rounds, then fired his weapon in short, controlled bursts at the wall, leaving a gaping hole. Confederation defense reinforcements arrived, and the Boxans hurried through the hole. Kladomaor left a squad of soldiers to hold the Confederation forces off where the opening had created a bottleneck.

They descended to the computing core of the space station and ran to the adjacent corridor where the Star Shroud network computer core was stored. They'd met little resistance on the way, which confirmed what Kladomaor had always suspected: After the Xiiginns failed to gain access to the core, they'd simply tried to lock it down.

They found dead Confederation soldiers along the way, but it was only a token force. Kladomaor tried opening a comms channel to the second team, but there was no reply. Two of his soldiers approached the door to the inner chamber and accessed the door controls. As the door began to open, Valkra pulled Kladomaor to the side. A barrage of plasma bolts sped from the darkened interior, killing the soldiers clustered at the door.

Kladomaor swung his weapon up and returned fire, as did Valkra. Bright flashes lit up the area around them. Kladomaor scampered along the wall toward the doorway and checked inside. The ground was littered with the bodies of the Boxan soldiers from the other team.

"Still falling for the same old tricks? Come inside so we can finally finish this," Mar Arden called out.

Kladomaor bared his teeth and clutched his rifle. "Why don't you come out from the shadows?" he said with a sneer and fired his weapon into the gloom.

He heard several Boxans scream from inside, and Kladomaor became blinded by rage. Mar Arden was toying with him, making him kill his own kind. Not again. Kladomaor bellowed as he raced inside. He knew it was a foolhardy path to a quick death, but he was focused on killing Mar Arden for everything he'd done. He heard Valkra and Gaarokk shouting for him to stay back, but he'd seen Mar Arden standing outside the door to the computing core. Kladomaor fired his weapon, and his rage was so great that he didn't even notice that none of his shots had found their mark. He charged forward, letting out a savage roar, eager to tear the Xiiginn apart with his bare hands.

Mar Arden dove out of the way and Kladomaor crashed into the door, a Xiiginn phaze-knife stuck in his side. He groaned in pain and stumbled to the side, trying to scramble to his feet.

Mar Arden aimed a plasma rifle at him. The primer inside was charged to a molten yellow, and it took every ounce of his will not to charge the Xiiginn. There was a hard edge to Mar Arden's features, as if he were chiseled from stone. His gaze was both wild-eyed and calculating, and his dark uniform was faded and torn, looking as disheveled as its owner.

"You see the difference," Mar Arden said and smirked. "Yours is not the only species with the Mardoxian potential anymore."

Kladomaor regarded the Xiiginn for a moment. "I don't think it agrees with you."

Mar Arden shrieked and leapt forward, slamming the butt of his rifle into Kladomaor's helmet. "I am the pinnacle of my species," he screamed, beating Kladomaor down.

Kladomaor jabbed his fists outward and knocked the Xiiginn back, but Mar Arden pointed his rifle at Kladomaor's head, then lowered the barrel toward his leg and fired. A plasma bolt slammed into Kladomaor's leg and the force of it spun him around, sending him careening into the wall. His armor was only able to deflect part of the blast. He sank down and planted his fist into the ground to prevent himself from falling over.

"Killing you would be too easy," Mar Arden said.

"So you keep saying, and yet I'm still here," Kladomaor replied.

Mar Arden laughed. "I've enjoyed tormenting you. I found it infinitely more satisfying than merely making another slave. You were the first. Did you know that?"

Kladomaor saw Mar Arden's gaze shift to something behind him. He turned and saw that there was a device sticking out of the door to the computing core.

"I'd been making so many Boxan slaves to do my bidding that I'd grown tired of it. When I came across your team, I decided to try something new. I have since perfected that process, and if there were any of those Boxans still alive they would vehemently attest to its effectiveness," Mar Arden said.

Kladomaor didn't need the Xiiginn to remind him. He'd heard the screams of his dying fellow Boxans as they threw themselves at him. Mar Arden had made them slaves and ordered them to kill Kladomaor. One of the side effects of being partially under the Xiiginn influence was that those memories would never fade for him.

"I think I'll finish what I started all those cycles ago," Mar Arden said. He leaned forward, his gaze narrowing menacingly. "Go ahead—resist. You all do and you all fail. Yours is the weaker species."

The stomping of feet sounded from the doorway.

"Enough!" Gaarokk bellowed.

The Boxan scientist fired his weapon and missed. Mar

Arden returned fire and Gaarokk tumbled backward. Kladomaor lunged for Mar Arden, and the Xiiginn kicked him, hard.
The Xiiginn's genetic enhancements gave him a physical
strength that rivaled any Boxan's, and Kladomaor fell backward
from the force of the blow. Valkra darted out from the doorway
and fired her weapon, but Mar Arden dove out of the way and
rolled to his feet behind Kladomaor. He shifted the barrel of his
rifle to Kladomaor's head and shouted for her to stop. Kladomaor watched as Valkra took cover behind a barricade, but he
knew it wouldn't do any good. She couldn't hide from the
Xiiginn influence. She must've arrived at the same conclusion
because a moment later she stepped out from cover but kept
her weapon aimed at Mar Arden.

"Shoot him," Kladomaor said.

He watched Valkra, willing her to do what needed to be
done—his own life be damned—but she didn't move. She just
stood there, looking as if she were straining against some
unseen force. Kladomaor growled and tried to reach for Mar
Arden as he circled around him, but the Xiiginn stepped out
of reach.

"I haven't taken her yet. She resists, just like you did. Just
like you all do," Mar Arden said.

Kladomaor slammed his fist on the floor in frustration. "Let
her go."

Mar Arden grinned. "Pleading for another's life?" the
Xiiginn said and shifted his gaze toward Valkra. "Remove your
helmet. Let me see who's worth all this effort."

Kladomaor heard Valkra grunting with effort. He knew she
was seconds from succumbing and would be lost forever. No
more. He lunged toward Mar Arden, his injured leg dragging
behind him. Mar Arden stepped back and then stomped his

foot on Kladomaor's outstretched arm, pressing it into the ground.

Tower alarms blared for a moment and then were cut off, and the air filtration systems engaged. Kladomaor felt a reduction in the artificial gravity field. Mar Arden glanced up for a moment and Kladomaor looked back at Valkra, who was straining to raise her rifle. She roared. Mar Arden took his foot off Kladomaor's arm and stepped away from him. The Xiiginn held his arms out wide, presenting her with the target.

"Good, that's it. Go ahead, Boxan, take your shot. I won't move. Do it," Mar Arden said, taunting her.

He heard Valkra's breath come in harsh gasps as she strained against what was happening to her. Kladomaor closed his eyes, not wanting to see yet another Boxan succumb to the Xiiginn influence. Not again.

The rifle fired. There was a surprised choking sound and Kladomaor saw Mar Arden fall to the ground with a gaping hole burned through his chest. Kladomaor's eyes widened and he looked at Valkra. She rushed to his side and helped him sit up.

"How?" Kladomaor asked.

Valkra looked just as surprised as he was. "I don't know. One moment it felt like there was this indomitable force compelling me to obey. I found myself longing to do anything Mar Arden wanted while hating myself for it. Then it was gone. The pressure and the longing . . . it was just gone."

Kladomaor frowned. He didn't feel any different. He looked at Mar Arden's body and wanted to savor the sight of the despicable Xiiginn finally meeting his end, but what he really wanted was to erase all thoughts of Mar Arden from his mind forever. He turned away.

"What's that device on the door?" Valkra asked.

Kladomaor struggled to his feet, and the exoskeleton inside his power armor helped him stay upright. He looked at Valkra and almost couldn't believe she'd been spared, but her gaze was focused and alert, both of which he knew to be impossible had she succumbed to the Xiiginn influence. "The *Athena*," he said. "They must have found a way to negate the Xiiginn influence." His mind raced with the implications. How had they done it? He glanced up at the air filtration system, but filtration alone couldn't have been enough to do it. There had to be something else.

He heard someone stumbling behind them. Valkra spun, her weapon ready.

"Don't shoot," Gaarokk said quickly. "I don't know if I can take another shot. This armor is barely holding together as it is."

Kladomaor reached a hand toward Gaarokk, unable to believe his friend had survived. The plasma bolt had partially melted through the power armor, and he saw burned flesh beneath. "Take it easy. Your armor has released numbing agents so you're not feeling as much pain."

Gaarokk glanced down at his torso and grimaced. "It's not working very well then because I'm still in a lot of pain." He looked at the door. "Valkra, since you're such a good shot, can you take out that device on the door?"

Valkra aimed her rifle, and a single plasma bolt tore through the device.

"Mar Arden was trying to use one of our communications nodes to gain access to the Star Shroud network," Gaarokk said.

"Would that have worked?" Valkra asked.

Gaarokk swayed on his feet and Valkra helped him sit down.

"I think it's safe to assume it would have," Kladomaor said and looked around at the dead Boxan soldiers, but he couldn't look at their faces. It was time to end this. "Gaarokk will be alright. Come, help me." He limped over to their fallen comrades. "We need to gather all the explosive charges."

Together they gathered the explosives some of the soldiers had been carrying. Valkra, being uninjured, moved the quickest. Kladomaor told Gaarokk to stay where he was, and for once the scientist didn't protest.

Kladomaor and Valkra walked to the door of the computing core.

"Aren't you going to use the door controls?" Valkra asked.

"Those are Xiiginn door controls. We don't need to use them," Kladomaor said and utilized his neural implants to access the computing core systems. He retrieved an old access key and waited while the system checked his authentication. It took a few moments, but then the door to the computing core opened. "Go inside and set the charges around the base of the power conduits that feed the core. Once we blow them up, it'll start a chain reaction that will take out the core and all the shroud network data."

Valkra's mouth hung open in surprise. "You're destroying it?"

"It was part of a broken system that we shouldn't have built in the first place. It needs to be destroyed to keep developing species safe from the Xiiginns. Will you help me?" Kladomaor asked.

"Does the High Council know about this?" Valkra asked.

"Would it really matter to you if they did?"

Valkra gave him a long look and shook her head, then

headed inside to set the charges. Kladomaor leaned against the wall. He didn't know why but he felt very tired. He accessed the Star Shroud network and configured a set of instructions to be completed immediately. All remaining Star Shrouds would receive the update. When Valkra finished setting the charges, they helped Gaarokk to his feet. Kladomaor sent out self-destruct commands to the dead Boxan soldiers' power armor. The power armor flashed an orange glow and the Boxans disintegrated. Kladomaor brought his fist across his chest, with Gaarokk and Valkra following suit. Then Kladomaor sent out a broadcast on the comms channel, alerting anyone in range to leave the tower.

It took them much longer to exit the tower than it had to enter. They found Confederation soldiers who seemed to be highly agitated. The few Xiiginns among them had been killed. They looked at Kladomaor and the others as if they weren't quite sure what to make of them. They'd been under the Xiiginn influence for so long that after the initial rage they seemed confused. He told them they were free and urged them to leave the tower. Kladomaor wondered if it would be the same for them as it had been for the Human who'd gone to the Drar space station—free from the Xiiginn influence but only fleetingly so because the damage had already been done. How many more would be in the same state?

They made it back to the shuttle and saw that there were a few Boxan soldiers already on board.

Triflan smiled a greeting. "We got pinned down by Confederation soldiers. It was a close thing there for a while and then they suddenly stopped shooting at us. They killed the Xiiginn soldiers with them and left us alone."

"I'm glad you made it," Kladomaor said.

There was a deep rumbling sound as the explosive charges unleashed their payload. The Star Shroud network and all the knowledge it contained was destroyed. The High Council might not approve of the final set of instructions he'd sent out to the remaining Star Shrouds in the galaxy, but he knew they couldn't do anything about it. It was time for the Boxans to move on. They'd fought to protect the data contained in the Star Shroud network for so long that Kladomaor thought he'd regret it when it was gone, but all he really felt was a profound sense of relief knowing that the darkest chapter in their history was coming to a close. The only thing left was to wonder just how many Boxans would remain once the Confederation and Alliance fleets finally stopped shooting at each other.

CHAPTER THIRTY-ONE

The battleship-carrier *Lincoln* approached the warring fleets. They'd received preliminary targeting data from the Boxan flagship, which was currently surrounded by three Confederation Dreadnoughts. The Boxan flagship and supporting battle groups had taken out two of the behemoth ships, but the flagship looked to have sustained heavy damage and the *Lincoln* hadn't received any communication from them in a while.

Kyle looked over at Scraanyx. "How much longer can they hold out?"

Scraanyx studied the tactical display on the main holo-screen, his mouth forming a grim line and his brow furrowed. He didn't respond, but Kyle didn't need the Boxan to confirm what he'd already suspected.

"Tactical," Kyle said, "I need multiple firing solutions on the three Dreadnoughts. Prioritize Dreadnoughts that have sustained the most damage. They are only to be superseded by the ships that pose an immediate danger to the Boxan flagship."

"Yes, Colonel," Major Stephens replied.

Scraanyx turned toward Kyle.

"We're here to officially join the Alliance. I'm not going to stand by and watch the Confederation destroy that ship," Kyle said.

Scraanyx brought his fist to his chest and gave a slight bow of his head, and the Boxan gesture of acknowledging a superior officer was not lost on Kyle. "Battle Commander," he said, "I would best serve by aiding Major Stephens at the tactical work-station."

"Very well," Kyle replied. "Ops, I need strike-fighter raptor squadrons ready to deploy ASAP. They are to assist in the defense of the flagship. I also need predator combat shuttles prepped for an assault run. Targeting confirmation will be provided in flight."

Captain Young confirmed the orders and began coordinating with the flight decks.

"Colonel, I have firing solutions alpha and bravo with designated targeting priorities," Major Stephens said.

Kyle glanced at the tactical display on the main holoscreen. "You are 'go' for firing solution alpha. Let's get the Titan SW-1s in tubes one through eight."

"Yes, Colonel, firing solution alpha," Major Stephens replied.

Kyle looked at the most recent scanner data and saw that there was an Alliance Dreadnought on its way to assist the flagship. Their cyber warfare suite provided an estimate on the time it would take them to be in support range of the Boxan flagship. They didn't have enough time.

"Helm, put us on an intercept course between the flagship and the nearest Confederation Dreadnought. Best speed. Let's see if we can ease the burden until help arrives," Kyle said.

"Yes, Colonel. Intercept course laid in," Sergeant Fuller said.

"Tactical, I need a close-quarters firing solution on that alpha, and where are my missiles?" Kyle asked.

"Titan SW-1s are loaded in tubes one through eight, Colonel," Major Stephens said.

"Fire."

Eight Titan SW-1s left the tubes carrying their heaviest fusion warhead payloads and blazed a path toward their targets. Kyle watched the plot as the missiles raced toward their targeted Dreadnought. The tactical display showed more Titan SW-1s being loaded into the tubes.

"Fire the next package," Kyle said.

The second group of Titans was fired as Kyle watched the status of the first group of missiles.

"Direct hit, fusion warhead detonation confirmed," Major Stephens said.

Several members of the bridge crew cheered, but Kyle maintained his focus on the main holodisplay. This was just the beginning, and he knew there would be less cheering when the Confederation started firing back at them.

"Colonel, raptor strike-fighter squadrons have launched and are en route to the Boxan flagship. Predator combat shuttles are being armed, and the flight chief estimates they'll be ready in fifteen minutes," Captain Young said.

"Acknowledged," Kyle said. They needed to get that time down, but he couldn't do anything about that right now. "Tactical, approve bravo firing solution for the next Dreadnought."

He looked at Captain Young in the operations work area. "Ops, I need the status of the alpha target."

Captain Young's hands flew through the interface while she pulled up the necessary data. "Scan data shows significant damage on the forward sections of the Dreadnought, Colonel."

"Outstanding. Have the predator combat shuttle groups target the forward sections when they launch. And give the flight chief a kick in the ass to get those ships going," Kyle said.

"Colonel, we have incoming missiles from the alpha Dreadnought," Major Stephens said.

A klaxon alarm sounded on the bridge and throughout the ship, signaling imminent impact.

"Acknowledged," Kyle said.

The *Lincoln's* combat AI would already be readying their countermeasures and point-defense systems. Trusting a combat AI was new for any of Earth's militaries. Kyle, however, had seen it work firsthand and trusted it, but he had the urge to give the orders anyway. The main holoscreen showed that their point-defense systems were already active and targeting the incoming missiles, and Kyle watched as several of the missiles were taken out.

"Enemy missiles have launched countermeasures," Major Stephens said.

Kyle's mouth formed a grim line as he watched the main holoscreen. The *Lincoln's* point-defense systems took out another missile and he watched as several more flew steadily closer.

"Brace for impact!" Kyle shouted.

Confederation missile warheads detonated. A powerful shudder went through the battleship-carrier and the impact could be felt on the entire ship. Kyle clenched his teeth and held onto his seat. They'd bloodied the enemy, and now the enemy had decided they were a threat that couldn't be ignored.

"Damage report," Kyle said.

"Forward missile tubes one and two are off-line. Decompression in compartments on decks thirty through thirty-two. Bulkhead doors have sealed. Engineering crews are heading to the damaged areas for a full assessment," Captain Young said.

This is it, Kyle thought. *We're in this fight.* They'd taken their first hit and survived. Now it was time to show the Xiiginns what they could really do.

"Colonel, I'm receiving multiple reports from raptor strike-fighter pilots that Confederation Dreadnoughts bravo and charlie have ceased firing their weapons on the Boxan flagship," Major Stephens said.

Kyle narrowed his eyes and glanced at Scraanyx, but the Boxan strike commander looked as bewildered as he did. Why would they suddenly stop firing their weapons?

CHAPTER THIRTY-TWO

Kaylan and Ma'jasalax had left the Mardoxian chambers and were standing on the bridge of the Boxan flagship. The flagship had been under heavy fire, with some of the damage impacting the area near the bridge, which included the Mardoxian chambers. During the battle, she'd lost power in the chamber again, and that time it had never returned. But she was happy to be out of there because she'd been feeling too isolated. Kaylan doubted that Ma'jasalax or any of the other Mardoxian priests had those types of issues, but she'd accepted that there were significant differences between Boxans and Humans. Perhaps it was just her, but she needed to be around other people.

They kept receiving reports of Confederation ships suddenly ceasing all hostilities toward the Alliance fleet. Some had even surrendered, but most hadn't communicated anything at all. The beacon where the *Athena* had been had vanished, and Kaylan could find no trace of the ship. With so many

Alliance ships fighting, it was difficult to get a status on anything in that area. She hoped Zack and the others were safe.

She had noticed a change in the Boxans on the bridge. They were no longer merely fighting another battle or staging one final onslaught against an enemy they'd been combating for so long. Each report of infighting among the Confederation ships brought with it a feeling of hope—something they hadn't dared believe was ever possible.

The species of the Confederation were finally waking up to what the enemy had been doing to them. All the lies and all the hate were collapsing in on the Xiiginns. Somehow, an environmental systems update that also included changes to artificial gravity had helped generate a field that negated the Xiiginn influence. Not only had they been able to decipher what the update had done, but Battle Leader Salevar had made sure to send the update directly to the Confederation space station. Most Confederation ships had multiple species serving aboard, with the exception of several core Xiiginn battle groups. Salevar focused their offensive on those ships, and even some of the Confederation ships began to attack the Xiiginn fleet.

"Comms, please thank the commander of that ECF battleship-carrier," Battle Leader Salevar said.

Kaylan was glad the commander of the ECF ship had listened to her and come to the Boxan flagship's aid. She watched as the battleship-carrier traded blows with the Confederation Dreadnoughts, giving the Boxan flagship some much-needed breathing space.

"Battle Leader, the commander of the ECF battleship-carrier wants to speak with you," Varek said.

"Put him through," Salevar said and gestured for Kaylan to join him.

Kaylan walked over to stand next to the battle leader and couldn't keep the smile from her face. They weren't out of danger, but this would be the first time she'd seen another Human besides the crew of the *Athena* in almost two years.

The head and shoulders of a man wearing a blue uniform with golden tips on the collar appeared on the main holoscreen. He had dark hair and brown eyes, and exuded the bearing of a career military man. His gaze immediately went from Salevar to Kaylan.

"Commander Farrow, I'm so glad to see you alive. I'm Colonel Kyle Matthews of the Earth Coalition Force. I have someone here who's been anxious to see you."

Colonel Matthews gestured toward someone offscreen and the breath caught in Kaylan's chest as Michael Hunsicker came onto the video feed.

"Michael," Kaylan said, her throat becoming thick. She felt her eyes tighten at the spike of emotions in her chest. She'd had no idea he'd survived being left at the Boxan monitoring station. She'd hoped he was alive, but seeing him after all this time sent her soaring with happiness.

"Kaylan, I can't believe it's really you," Michael Hunsicker said. His eyes glistened with tears that nearly made Kaylan falter.

"Battle Leader, Confederation Dreadnought is readying its weapons," Varek said.

Kaylan's gaze swooped toward the tactical holoscreen. Another comms window opened and the face of a Xiiginn appeared.

"Garm Antis, have you come to offer your unconditional surrender?" Salevar asked.

"Battle Leader Salevar, I didn't think you'd ever crawl out

from under that rock you've been hiding under, along with the rest of your pathetic species," Garm Antis said.

"You look a bit haggard. I guess this armada you put together isn't working out so well for you," Salevar said.

Garm Antis ignored the jab and turned his gaze toward Kaylan. "The Human with the Mardoxian potential I've heard so much about."

Kaylan scowled at the Xiiginn and used her neural implants to access the tactical workstation. Salevar was waiting for their damaged weapons systems to be able to lock onto the Confederation Dreadnought, but the flagship had taken too much damage. She opened a secondary comms channel back to the *Lincoln* and sent one clear and decisive message.

"I should really thank you," Kaylan said, stalling for time.

Garm Antis frowned in confusion for a moment. "We'll have plenty of time to get acquainted. I know the primary weapons systems on that ship are off-line—"

"You were the catalyst for all this," Kaylan said, interrupting him. "When you attacked Earth, you set all this in motion. Even if you somehow get out of this, you'll find that your reception at my home star system won't be as warm or as easy as you thought it would be. One of the things we Humans are good at is adapting to a threat like you. You've only faced one of our ships. We've built plenty more and they're all coming for the Xiiginns," Kaylan said. She had no idea how many ships they had back home but wanted to keep the Xiiginn talking.

"So, the Boxans have given you a technological leg up. We'll see how well you adapt to technology you're not ready for," Garm Antis said.

"You won't get to find out," Kaylan said.

She'd gotten confirmation back from the *Lincoln* and she

saw Garm Antis turn away from her as he spoke to someone offscreen. He suddenly swung his hateful gaze back toward her and then his video feed abruptly cut out.

The *Lincoln* had fired its weapons at the Confederation Dreadnought, joined by the remaining Alliance ships in the vicinity. The Dreadnought hadn't stood a chance. Garm Antis was dead.

CHAPTER THIRTY-THREE

Zack had no idea how many hours had passed before Etanu found them. Both he and Hicks had fallen asleep, strapped into the uncomfortable seats in their escape pod, and were awakened by the sound of a master alarm. The pod had sustained so much damage that they'd been leaking atmosphere, and Zack had found emergency life-support attachments in their spacesuits. All they'd had to do was enable their helmets and attach the life-support boosters to their suits, which gave them enough oxygen for two days. Zack hadn't been impressed with the length of time their emergency oxygen would last, knowing how long it took ships to travel anywhere. They'd manually enabled the emergency beacon in short bursts because there was still a massive space battle being fought.

Zack and Hicks used the shuttle's emergency hatch to get inside.

"We owe you one," Hicks said.

Etanu smiled, which, on a Nershal with their large, pumpkin-colored eyes, made him look more vicious than friendly. "A courtesy between soldiers fighting on the same side, Major Hicks. Zack and I are even now."

Zack didn't reply and slowly sat down in one of the rear seats. He heard Hicks advise the others to give Zack some space and that irritated him even more. How could the others be like this? They'd just lost a member of the crew and it felt like they didn't even care.

His ribs hurt and he opened the medical kit to search for painkillers. He poured two small pills into the palm of his hand and sighed. He couldn't swallow the pills without something to drink.

"Here," Etanu said and handed him a canister of water.

"Thanks," Zack said without looking up. He swallowed the pills, along with several mouthfuls of water.

Etanu moved Zack's helmet from the seat next to him and sat down. "At least you had a helmet this time."

Zack's eyebrows pulled together and then he grinned. "Ow! Are you ever going to stop reminding me of that?" He looked up at the Nershal who had become his friend.

Etanu handed Zack a brown satchel. "Efren asked me to give this to you. Said he didn't want it anymore and thought you'd rather have it."

Zack took the satchel and opened it. Inside was the three-dimensional model of the *Athena*. He remembered picking it up for the first time, newly created out of the fabrication unit. Athena had been testing a new alloy that looked like gold but Zack knew better. He felt heat rise in his cheeks and his eyes tightened. He looked away from Etanu and quickly wiped his eyes. They were already becoming puffy. "Damn it," he said and clenched his fists. He held up the model of the *Athena*. The AI had been so much more than a ship. "She sacrificed herself for all of us. She could have taken control of the ship and left us all behind. Instead she . . ."

Hicks and Efren joined them, then Cardaleer looked over. "The AI was beyond anything we created."

"She was beyond what the Drar created," Zack said.

"But I thought the Drar enhanced the *Athena* AI along with the rest of the ship," Efren said.

"They did, but she was already a variant of the Boxan AI. She cared about all of us," Zack replied.

"Zack," Etanu said in a level tone, "the AI was a machine."

"No, she wasn't—"

"Just listen to me for a second," Etanu said. "Remember when Athena tried to make a duplicate of herself so I could try reintroducing the benefits of AI to my species? The Xiiginns had purposefully hindered our progress so we'd remain dependent on them."

"Yeah, but what Athena provided was working for you," Zack said.

"Yes, it's working, but our own AI wasn't anything like Athena. It does the job, and more of my species are using what you've given us, but you say Athena is alive and I'm saying she isn't. She couldn't do the most basic things that all life can do. She couldn't reproduce. She couldn't make another version that was just like her," Etanu said.

Zack shook his head. "You're wrong. Athena sacrificed herself so we could survive."

"She had an objective to achieve and worked toward a successful outcome," Etanu replied.

"It was more than that. She did what the Drar AI never could. You saw that place. It was thousands of years old. That

AI was stuck because it was bound by its programming to carry out a specific task. Jonah staying behind was the only reason the Drar AI found peace. Yes, Athena had an objective, but she also conveyed emotion. She acted from the supposition that we were *worth* saving, even if it meant her own life. Just like any one of us would do for the other. And," Zack said, holding up his finger to silence Etanu before he could interrupt, "she was afraid to die. It wasn't what she wanted at all. That behavior could only mean she was alive."

Etanu regarded him for a moment, then turned around and began to walk toward the front of the shuttle.

"You make a compelling argument," Cardaleer said, and Zack saw Etanu stop. "What we have here is a philosophical debate. What is life? Both you and Etanu represent two equally valid viewpoints. Perhaps that's as it should be."

Etanu looked at Zack. "I'm sorry for your loss. I know Athena meant a lot to you."

"She meant a lot to all of us," Hicks said. "She was our home and our friend. I can't pretend to understand what separates an AI from the rest of us, but to me, if it seemed like it was alive, then it was. Courage, sacrifice, duty—these are all pillars, and Athena never faltered in any one of them. And I suspect she went to great lengths to shield us from other stuff as well."

Cardaleer grinned. "Such an interesting discussion."

"What do you think Athena was?" Etanu asked the Boxan.

Cardaleer was about to reply when a comms channel chimed from the front of the shuttle. They all moved forward.

"*Athena* shuttle, this is Colonel Matthews from the ECF battleship-carrier *Lincoln*. Please respond."

Zack's mouth hung open.

Hicks responded. "Acknowledge, *Lincoln*. Did you just

happen to be in the neighborhood, or were we that easy to find?"

"A bit of both, actually. This was the only NASA broadcast signal out here," Colonel Matthews said.

Zack sat in the copilot's seat and checked the communications interface. "He's right. We're broadcasting. I thought those protocols had all been disabled."

Hicks shook his head. "Not the emergency ones."

"*Athena* shuttle, do you have flight capability, or do we need to send out a rescue for you?" Colonel Matthews asked.

Hicks quickly checked the shuttle's flight systems while the others began asking Colonel Matthews for an update on the battle. Zack tuned them out and opened the logs for comms systems. He searched for the NASA broadcast signal and saw that it wasn't part of some latent emergency protocol that'd been engaged because they'd evacuated the ship. Athena had made sure they were broadcasting using those specific protocols. Had the AI known there were other Humans here, or had she simply guessed that broadcasting using a protocol that neither the Confederation nor the Alliance knew about was the safest way for the right people to come and find them?

Hicks patted Zack on the shoulder. "Did you hear that?"

Zack frowned and shook his head. "No, what?"

"The battle's over. Confederation ships have stood down," Hicks said.

"The Xiiginns surrendered?" Zack asked.

"Doesn't sound that way. Apparently, the multi-species crews mutinied against the Xiiginns and the Alliance took out the remaining Xiiginn warships," Hick said.

Zack glanced at the others and blew out a breath. *Athena, you did it,* Zack thought.

CHAPTER THIRTY-FOUR

K aylan had hoped the days following the battle would be easier, but she'd underestimated how the other species of the Confederation would react when the effects of the Xiiginn influence were negated. The Xiiginns had interwoven themselves into the governing bodies of all the species in the Confederation, infiltrating government officials all the way down to the least important roles in society. Some victims had been little more than slaves for their entire lives. To be suddenly awakened from that and retain the memories of all they'd done while under the Xiiginn influence was too much for some species to handle. Many of the awakened had lashed out violently toward their captors.

So far, they were only able to negate the Xiiginn influence within the fields maintained on a ship or space station. Once an afflicted person moved beyond those, they reverted back to the state they'd been in before—loyal to the Xiiginns. Kaylan's heart went out to those species.

After a victim's initial rage, which usually resulted in taking the lives of the Xiiginns around them, their mental state became fragile, and severe depression often led to suicide. The Alliance had been so focused on defeating the Xiiginns that they hadn't been prepared to deal with what the long-term effects of being under the Xiiginn influence for so long would be. Jonah Redford's mental state had deteriorated because he'd fought it. Humans were able to resist the Xiiginn influence to varying degrees, but there were other species, like the Boxans, who had almost no resistance to it. There was so much death, but at least now there were groups organized to help prevent those who'd been awakened from taking their own lives. If recovery was even possible, it would be a long time coming.

"You're awfully quiet," Ma'jasalax said.

"I thought finally stopping the Xiiginns from conquering everything would feel better than this," Kaylan said.

"Things will improve with time," Ma'jasalax replied.

"Are any of the Confederation or Alliance ships going to the Xiiginn homeworld?" Kaylan asked.

"Technically, the Confederation is being dissolved and the Alliance will take its place, but no Boxan ship will be going. The Gresans, the Napox, and many others want vengeance on the Xiiginns. We wanted them stopped, but it's up to the former Confederation species to decide the Xiiginns' fate," Ma'jasalax said.

Kaylan had no love for the Xiiginns, but she wasn't sure how she felt about genocide either. Xiiginns had a lot to answer for, and would the universe really miss a species like that? Were they as much of a threat now that their most powerful tool had been taken from them? Could the Xiiginns ever change? She didn't know, and it wasn't up to her.

Kaylan saw Kladomaor and Gaarokk walking toward them in one of the atriums on the Boxan flagship. The Boxans wouldn't return to the Confederation space station.

She looked at Ma'jasalax. "Do you think Kladomaor will be okay?"

Ma'jasalax's gaze flicked toward the two Boxans. "He has endured much, but I believe that, in time, he'll continue to improve."

Kladomaor and Gaarokk joined them.

"How is Zack?" Gaarokk asked.

"He and Hicks are doing fine. They broke a few ribs, but thanks to Brenda, those bones have already healed," Kaylan replied.

"What about the *Athena*? Cardaleer told us about the loss of your ship and that Zack has been very upset," Kladomaor said.

"He'll be fine. I'll make sure of it. When people first meet Zack, they don't know quite what to make of him," Kaylan said.

"He definitely has his own way of doing things, but he couldn't have a better caretaker than you. You'll both do very well in the cycles to come," Kladomaor said.

Kaylan frowned. Something in the Boxan's tone piqued her curiosity. "Why does is it sound like you're saying goodbye?"

She watched as the Boxans shared a glance.

"Eventually, but not right now," Gaarokk said.

"I don't understand. Won't you stay in the Alliance?" Kaylan asked and looked at Ma'jasalax. How could she have missed this? "You're leaving? I mean, you're not staying in the galaxy?"

"You're right," Kladomaor said.

Gaarokk gave Kladomaor a meaningful look. "You're already in too much trouble as it is."

"The High Council will simply need to move on, then. The

Star Shrouds are no more. The knowledge of their whereabouts is gone for good. But to really answer your question, Kaylan, we are not staying. Whatever follows the Confederation will be without the Boxans," Kladomaor said.

Kaylan's eyes widened. "Why? I always assumed that if we defeated the Xiiginns you'd stay and rejoin the Confederation. What would all of these species do without you?"

"What indeed," Ma'jasalax said. "But that will be for you to decide. Humans will take an active role. So it will be up to Humans and Nershals and a host of other species. What happened with the Xiiginns was our responsibility, and now that the threat has passed, it's time for us to move on."

"Where will you go? Will you find another planet to colonize?"

"As Emma Roberson has already pointed out, our current world is insufficient for our needs. This revelation wasn't new to us. We were well aware of the situation but found it quite interesting that, despite what was happening, the crew of the *Athena* was so concerned about our welfare," Ma'jasalax said and glanced at Kladomaor for a moment. "Returning to Sethion and rescuing the Boxans we left behind was something even I hadn't anticipated. We've shared many things with you, and in turn, through our relationship with you and the other *Athena* crewmembers, you've challenged us to grow beyond what we were before. For that reason, Humans will always have our gratitude. Just as *you* will have to find a way to exist in a larger universe, so will we. And it doesn't involve colonizing another planet."

"At least none that we know of," Gaarokk said.

"The star carriers we used to rescue the refugees on Sethion were first-generation colony ships. One of the things we've been working on is achieving the same thing but on a much grander scale and with room to expand. We'll still have our military because we need it for our own defenses, but hopefully not as much," Kladomaor said.

"You've built more colony ships. Where?"

"A neighboring star system to Olloron. The system is richer in materials and the ship is essentially a small moon. So, you see, we did have an eye to the future. We wouldn't have sacrificed every last Boxan to defeat the Xiiginns. And thanks to our alliance with you, we didn't have to," Kladomaor said.

"What will you do after you go home?" Ma'jasalax asked.

That very question had been on Kaylan's mind—a lot. They were due to leave in a few days. The *Lincoln* was taking them home. "I'm not sure, to be honest. I expect to be involved in the Earth Coalition Force somehow. I have no doubt they'll be keenly interested in what I've learned from you, but I just don't know. It's strange, really. All this time we've been worried about just surviving or trying to find the Drar or any number of other things," Kaylan said and looked at all of them. "I will miss all of you. When do you leave?"

"It's not as imminent as it sounds, and as you know, there are other ways to communicate," Ma'jasalax said.

Kaylan smiled in understanding. Communication using Mardoxian chambers would allow them to stay in contact over vast distances, perhaps even galactic distances. "The refugees on Selebus. Do you think they'll go with you?"

Ma'jasalax smiled. "They'll be invited, of course, and in order to maintain their independence, they'll have either their own section of the ship or we'll build one just for them."

Kaylan wondered just how big this ship they'd built was. With something so massive, could it still be called a ship? She imagined it as an entire world that they could take with them. "You're going to look for the Drar, aren't you?"

"Some of the things we found, including the data on the *Athena*, indicated that the Drar left the galaxy. We were once explorers, but we've had to adopt the mantle of soldiers. I think we can be explorers once again," Kladomaor said.

Kaylan knew it wasn't a final farewell, but she still felt a lump in her throat. "I think that would be good."

Several days later, the ECF battleship-carrier *Lincoln* was preparing to depart. The crew of the *Athena*, including the former mission commander, Michael Hunsicker, stood on the main hangar bay of the Boxan flagship. Boxan soldiers stood at parade rest in their power armor. A Boxan named Chazen came over to Michael Hunsicker to say goodbye. Kaylan had learned that Michael had been able to survive on the Boxan monitoring station because there had been an actual Boxan in stasis there.

"You could come to Earth one day," Zack said to Etanu.

"I'm sure a Nershal delegation will journey to Earth at some point," Etanu replied.

"I'm sure I can find a few obstacle courses we could run *without* the..." Zack paused and frowned. "Whatever the hell that thing was you guys attached to my wrist to make me participate. You know, without the threat of dying."

A slow smile appeared on Etanu's face. "Where's the fun in that?"

Zack grinned and Kaylan joined in. Etanu bowed his head toward Kaylan. "Mardoxian Blessed, it has been my honor to know you and I look forward to the day we meet again."

Ezerah, who'd been standing next to Etanu, held her head up proudly. "It won't just be Nershals like Etanu coming to Earth, I assure you. Also, I'd like to extend an invitation to all of you to actually spend some time on Nerva. There's so much more to see than the forests of Selebus."

Kaylan smiled. "I'd like that very much."

"Oh, and Zack," Etanu said. "Never mind. *Hicks,* please make sure Zack has his helmet. We don't need any repeats of certain lapses in judgment."

Hicks grinned. "I'll make sure he does."

Kladomaor stepped in front of the lines of soldiers and let out a deep bellow. The bellow was taken up by the Boxan soldiers, and Kaylan realized that this was a Boxan battle song. As one, the Boxan soldiers banged their fists against their chests, and the clang of power armor was heard throughout the main hangar bay.

Ma'jasalax leaned toward Kaylan. "They honor the *Athena.* He wanted you to know her sacrifice will never be forgotten."

She saw Zack's eyes become misty and reached out to hold his hand. The battle song ended and the former crew of the *Athena* left the Boxan flagship to return to the ECF battleship-carrier.

Kaylan had learned that two ambassadors, along with another hundred people, were staying behind. Colonel Matthews was adamant that the *Lincoln* would return to Earth and come back with more support for the Human envoy that was to take up residence on the Alliance space station.

They'd spent a few hours touring the battleship-carrier.

There was plenty of time before they reached the minimum safe distance to open the wormhole that would take them home.

The crew of the *Athena* had gathered in a designated area Colonel Matthews had assured them was for their use only. The room was essentially a lounge, with several couches and small tables around. After hours of speaking to other people, each of the crew had found their way to their private space.

"It's not that surprising," Michael was saying. "You have to get used to being around people again. I lived with Chazen for almost nine months, and when I first got back to Earth, we would meet in a quiet place to do our work. It was almost like we were back on the monitoring station, but it was worse for Chazen. He'd spent a long time alone on that station," Michael said.

"Perhaps we should make it a point to get together every so often after we get back home," Hicks said.

"Every so often," Katie said with a grin. "We should all live by each other."

"You'll love Valencia," Efren said. "It's one of the most beautiful coastal cities of Spain, and from there we can travel west along the coast. The food. Oh, the food and the music. I can't wait to show it all to you."

Katie smiled and looked at Zack and Kaylan. "What I want to know is what are you two gonna do?"

"You mean after the weeks or months of debriefing we'll have to go through when we get home? After all that," Zack began, "I intend to find a beach with crystal-clear blue water, probably somewhere in the Caribbean, and I'm going to watch the sunset for the next few years while I try to forget some of the things I've seen." Zack looked at Kaylan. "Well, not everything I've seen. But seriously, I just want to take a nice long, long, long vacation and not think about anything."

This drew plenty of grins from the others. Kaylan shrugged. "I'm not sure, to be honest. I suppose I'll have some involvement with the ECF."

"There'll be plenty of opportunities for all of you," Michael assured them.

"I know I'll be joining the ECF when we get back," Hicks said.

"I never doubted it for a second," Zack replied.

"You could join, too. In fact, I'm pretty sure you'll get several invitations that will be very hard to say no to—that is, after you get tired of sitting on a beach," Hicks said.

"I don't know...then I'd have to take orders from...well, you know, and I don't know if I want to do that," Zack said.

Hicks shook his head. "I didn't mean become a soldier. There are plenty of other things you could do."

"I think what Zack is trying to say is that he's going to weigh his options and not commit to anything just yet," Kaylan said.

"I thought you guys weren't married," Nikolai said.

Kaylan smiled and shared a look with Zack. "Not yet, but soon."

This news came as no surprise to anyone.

"That is, after he meets the rest of my family," Kaylan added quickly.

Zack's smile almost disappeared as he realized he had yet another challenge to face.

"It can't be that bad considering what we've been through," Hicks said.

"No, it'll be great," Zack said, unconvincingly.

His comment drew several bouts of laughter, especially from the men.

"I know what I'm going to do when I get back," Emma said. "I'm going to remind my husband why he waited for me—over and over again until we both can't walk. Then travel a little bit. Definitely going to take a page from Zack's book and relax for a while." Emma grinned.

"What about you, Brenda?" Kaylan asked.

"I plan to return to my family. With all the new medical advances, there'll be plenty to do. I honestly need more time to think about it," Brenda said.

They kept going on like that for hours. It was as if there was this unspoken agreement to enjoy each other's company for as long as they could before their long journey came to an end. The *Lincoln* had already traversed through a wormhole and they were on their way back to Earth. Kaylan liked Hicks's idea of making it a point to get together at least once a year and made a mental note to see that it happened.

She glanced at Zack. She knew he was still grieving the loss of Athena. She was, too, but the bond Athena had with Zack had been much stronger. Out of all Zack's qualities, his loyalty to his friends was one of the things she cherished most.

CHAPTER THIRTY-FIVE

Zack had been right. After they'd returned to Earth, their debriefing with the Earth Coalition Force and the various governments of the world that had supported the original Athena mission had taken almost a month. Hicks'd had to talk him out of leaving with a compelling argument about how they'd just hunt him down.

Hicks had been promoted to colonel and had officially joined the ECF. Zack was pretty sure Hicks would soon be commanding a ship of his own. Michael Hunsicker had been right about there being plenty of opportunities to do almost anything they wanted once they got home, but Zack wouldn't commit to anything except Kaylan. There was a wedding in their future, and since she was an heiress of the late great Bruce Matherson estate, Zack was sure it would be quite an affair.

The crewmembers of the *Athena* were all heroes, and Zack had completely underestimated their global reception. There were parades and ceremonies scheduled, as well as public appearances, which Zack had wanted to avoid, but Kaylan had reminded him that what they'd all accomplished was inspirational. People around the globe were completely enamored with the crew of the *Athena*. CEOs of major corporations tasked their armies of public relations people and recruiters with getting a meeting with Zack. They just wanted "a few moments of his time," at his "nearest convenience." It would never be convenient as far as Zack was concerned. He wondered if they realized that prior to going on the *Athena* he'd been a hacker who'd exposed their secrets and would gladly do so again. He didn't think he'd go back to that life, but he did enjoy declining all those meeting invitations.

A fresh sea breeze blew in through the villa's open windows as Kaylan walked in and smiled at him. A ray of sunshine gleamed off the small model of the *Athena* that rested on a wooden table with seashell-encrusted legs. A couple of bright spots reflected above, only to be rhythmically disrupted by the turn of the large fan blades that gently moved the air of the villa's luxurious interior. "I could get used to this. You *did* say you wanted a beach," Kaylan said. She let her thick hair down, and it hung past her shoulders.

"I did say that, but I didn't think we'd end up on a private island," Zack said, and his gaze narrowed playfully. "Is this your island? Tell me you didn't buy this island. You own this island?"

Kaylan grinned. "Of course not. *I* didn't buy this island; it's my sister's," she said.

Zack looked around at the lavish furnishings. He felt like he was standing in one of those places he'd only seen in advertisements. But it was even better than that, or maybe it was the fact that it was just the two of them.

They left the villa and walked down a stone staircase to the beach—their beach, since they had the island to themselves. The soft white sand felt soothing to his feet and the crystal-clear blue waters were warm and inviting. They walked along the beach, the water splashing at their feet. They'd arrived two days ago and he wanted to stay there forever, but he wasn't sure Kaylan would want that. At some point, they'd have to go back to the real world.

"I wanted you to know that I started looking for my dad's car," Zack said.

"That's great, and if we can't find it, I'm sure we can build another one. The ECF was keenly interested in the new fabricators the Boxans used," Kaylan said.

"Do you really think they're going to leave?"

"I think they've been preparing to leave for a long time. Maybe not today or tomorrow, but a year from now I think they'll be gone," Kaylan said.

Zack eyed her for a moment. "I guess you'd know better than anyone else."

"It doesn't take the Mardoxian ability to figure that out," Kaylan replied.

"So what do you think is going to happen to us? Where do we go from here?"

Kaylan was about to reply when they heard a jet flying toward them. They glanced up at the sky and saw a dark, sleek Dux Corp jet do a flyby of the island and then approach the landing pad.

"Well, it didn't take them long to find us," Zack said.

Kaylan pulled on his arm. "Come on, we should go see what they want."

They'd learned that Edward Johnson had died, but they didn't know the details of his death. Zack had no idea how a man like Ed would have gone out, but he couldn't imagine it'd been due to old age. Ed could plot and scheme with the best of them. According to Michael Hunsicker, Edward Johnson had been instrumental in hunting down the Xiiginns.

They followed the path to the landing pad. The Dux Corp jet had just set down and the door opened. A tall woman in a black business suit exited the jet and walked down the stairs. Her dark sunglasses were stylish, and Zack could see that she was quite attractive. He used his implants to scan for any tech she had hidden away and his eyes widened at what he saw. He'd expected the sunglasses were more than a stylish accent, but he hadn't expected to see the number of implants and enhancements he'd found. He saw that parts of her skeleton were comprised of a metallic alloy that Zack assumed greatly enhanced her speed and strength. His own implants had been enhanced by Athena, so he doubted that anyone besides him and Kaylan could tell just how dangerous their new visitor really was. The woman arched an eyebrow, which poked above her sunglasses, and smiled as if she were aware of what they'd seen. She headed toward them carrying a metallic briefcase.

"Iris," Kaylan said in greeting.

Iris extended her hand to each of them in turn. "Hello, Kaylan, Mr. Quick. I'm not sure if you remember me, but I'm Iris Barrett."

Zack didn't remember her at all, and since she was with Dux Corp, he wasn't sure he *wanted* to know her. "What brings Dux Corp all the way out here?"

"Zack," Kaylan admonished. "There's no need to be rude. I was really sorry to hear that Ed died. He was quite fond of you."

"Thank you. I'm actually here to speak to you about Ed. Could we go inside? There's a lot we need to discuss," Iris said.

"Of course," Kaylan said.

"I'll leave you to it then," Zack said and started to walk away.

"Actually, Mr. Quick, this has to do with you as well," Iris said.

Kaylan tilted her head to the side and gave him one of those looks.

"Alright then," Zack said. "This should be interesting."

The three took a short path to another set of stairs that led to the villa. Once they were inside, Iris closed the doors and the windows. She wore a wrist computer, upon which she tapped a few commands.

"Sorry for that, but I just enabled several jamming signals, along with a few other things that will give us some privacy," Iris said.

Zack's gaze flicked to Kaylan for a moment. "Are we being watched?"

Iris removed her sunglasses, revealing brown eyes that regarded him for a moment. "Of course you're being watched. Did you expect to return here and the entire *Athena* crew would just go on their merry way?" Iris shook her head and even her neck-length dark hair looked good as it moved. Zack had always felt awkward around beautiful women, and the fact that he was sitting there with two of the most attractive women he'd ever seen made him a little anxious. He took Kaylan's hand in his own and leaned back in his chair.

"All of you are being watched. It's for your own protection."

"I love how you just casually throw away our privacy and think that a few people wanting to protect us makes that okay," Zack said.

Kaylan leaned forward. "Are we in danger?"

"Nothing imminent. Both of you are VIPs, which could put a

few ideas into the heads of certain circles. Ed wanted to make sure that if you did make it back to Earth, you'd be protected," Iris said.

"So, are we going to have to hire bodyguards and all that stuff?" Zack asked.

Iris snorted. "It's not as oppressive as you make it sound. But the fact that you're being looked after isn't the reason I'm here."

"You're here because of Ed, aren't you?" Kaylan said.

Zack's brows pinched together.

Iris nodded. "Ed and I studied your mission briefings. He'd always suspected that you had the potential for certain abilities. This briefcase contains a message from Ed, along with some documents, but we'll get to that in a minute. First, I have to tell you how Ed really died."

Zack listened to Iris tell them how Ed had laid a trap for Mar Arden to get all the Xiiginns into one place and take them all out. They'd tried to hunt them down, but the Xiiginns always remained one step ahead of them. Zack was surprised to learn that the trap almost worked. Mar Arden was the only one to survive.

"So you were there?" Zack asked.

"Yes, I was with Ed when he died," Iris replied.

"How did you survive the explosion?"

"I'm tougher than I look."

Zack felt the edges of his lips begin to curve upward. "You fought the Xiiginns? Hand to hand? You know, up close and personal?"

"I did. I even took out his second in command, a Xiiginn named Kandra Rene," Iris said.

Zack's eyes narrowed and he looked at Kaylan.

Iris frowned. "What is it?"

"Kandra Rene tried to use her compulsion ability on Zack when he was captured," Kaylan answered.

"I should have realized that," Iris said.

Zack snorted. "Why would you?"

"My job is knowing the connection in the details," Iris said.

Zack blew out a breath and glanced at the perfect day outside. He closed his eyes and for a moment he was back on Selebus, trapped in the pit, hearing the strange sounds of the mutants the Xiiginns had kept there. He opened his eyes and shuddered. He was glad Kandra Rene was gone.

"I need to play Ed's message for you. Is that alright?" Iris asked.

Kaylan looked at him. "Yeah, I'm fine. Let's hear it."

Iris nodded and opened the metallic case. A holoprojector came on and a life-size rendering of Edward Johnson stood in the room. He turned toward them and smiled.

"As Iris has probably told you, we laid a trap hoping to lure the Xiiginns into one place so we could take care of them once and for all. If you're seeing this message and I'm not there personally to speak with you, then I'm afraid things didn't go as planned. I'm sorry I couldn't be there to see you return." Ed's hologram looked at Kaylan. "I know you were aware of my friendship with your grandfather, but I always thought of you as family, even when you walked away to pursue your own path." Ed turned his gaze toward Zack. "Mr. Quick, your partici-pation on the *Athena* mission exceeded all my expectations. I knew you'd be a valuable asset to the mission, but I never expected you to become as important as Kaylan was to all of humanity. It was your doing that kept us safe, giving us time to build ships and grow technologically by leaps and bounds. Throughout all that you held to your principles. This is a quality I value greatly." The Ed hologram seemed to regard him for a few moments, as if Zack needed some time to consider what Ed had said. "I know you view people like me as the enemy ... well, maybe not *the* enemy anymore. I think your experiences with the Xiiginns helped you recognize a true enemy when you see one, but I'd wager you still view me as someone not to be trusted. So I'm going to cut right to the chase. I'm going to offer you a job."

Zack laughed and glanced at Iris. "A job? Is he serious?"

"I'm quite serious," Ed said, as if he'd heard Zack's question. "Now, before you answer, at least hear what the job is. You might find that it's right up your alley."

The hologram paused and Zack looked at Iris.

"You need to tell him whether you want to hear what he has to say," Iris said.

Zack looked at Kaylan. "I don't know."

"Please, if I may," Iris said. "You probably don't know this, but Ed defended you whenever anyone questioned the things you'd done. He had unwavering confidence in your abilities. I can tell you from my experience working for Ed that this is not something he does on a whim. He has extremely high expectations of the people who work for Dux Corp."

"It won't hurt to hear what he has to say," Kaylan said.

Zack wondered if Kaylan somehow sensed where this was going. If she did, she wasn't saying anything. He looked back at the hologram. "Alright, I'll hear what you have to say."

"Excellent," Ed said. "You might be thinking this job is an offer to work for Dux Corp as a general employee with special perks and benefits, and I'm going to tell you that is not the case. What I'm offering you is an opportunity to run Dux Corp. Be the boss. Decide which direction to take the company and all of its substantial subsidiaries. Help build a new world."

Zack's face was numb and his mouth hung open. Of all the things he could have imagined, Edward Johnson—a man Zack was sure hadn't liked him at all when they'd first met—offering him a job running one of the most powerful corporations on the planet wasn't one of them. He looked at Iris and she calmly returned his gaze. Of course, she'd known this was coming. He turned toward Kaylan, who looked only a little surprised.

"I thought Ed might have had a few plans for you," Kaylan said.

Zack laughed nervously. "Gee, you think?"

Kaylan smiled at him. "You should really consider this. You could do a lot of good in that position."

Zack snorted. "Are you kidding me? What do I know about running a company like Dux Corp?" He ran his fingers through his hair and gave it a gentle tug. "This has to be a joke, right?"

Iris shook her head. "No, this isn't a joke. This is real. This job offer is part of the Project Phoenix Initiative, which Ed had been working on in preparation for your return. I believe he started it after your initial mission update you sent over a year ago."

Zack looked at the hologram of Ed Johnson, who appeared to be waiting for his answer. Instead of answering, he looked back at Iris. "If I did this, that would mean you'd be working for me."

Iris looked amused. "I would be your assistant and your protection."

Zack remembered all the implants and enhancements this woman had. He bet she could go a few rounds with several

Boxans in power armor. He stood up and paced toward the window, then turned back toward Ed. "Can I think about it?"

The Ed hologram smiled at him knowingly. "Of course you can. You have exactly one hour to consider this offer and then it will expire."

Zack's breath caught in his throat.

"Actually," Ed continued, "I'm just kidding. This offer will be available to you for exactly twenty-four hours, after which the offer will expire. When you *do* decide, speak to Iris. Once again, I hope you seriously consider this opportunity. Bruce Matherson offered me a job like this once and it changed my life. I know it could do the same for you."

The hologram flickered off.

"I'll remain on the island until you've made your decision. I'll also be available to answer any questions you may have," Iris said and stood up. "I'll show myself to the guest quarters and give you some privacy so you can discuss this between yourselves."

Iris walked toward the door.

"Iris," Zack said, "would you take the job if you were me?"

She regarded him for a moment, her eyes measuring him. "In a heartbeat," she said and left the room.

Zack blew out a breath and glanced at the metallic case. Iris had left their privacy enforcer on.

"What do you think you're going to do?" Kaylan asked.

"I have no idea. I never expected anything like this," Zack said.

"I did."

"Really?"

"Of course. You're capable of so much. I think you underestimate yourself," Kaylan replied.

"I think you're a bit biased when it comes to me. What would you do if I did take this job?"

"I'd get you to hire me as a consultant."

Zack laughed and his gaze slid toward the model of the *Athena*. He'd put it on the center of the table when they arrived. For some reason, he just liked having it nearby.

Kaylan followed his gaze. "I miss her too."

"When she made this thing, she almost had me believing she'd made a true working model. She made the engines start to glow," Zack said.

He reached out and slid his fingers along the smooth surface, tracing all the intricate details.

"That's funny. I would've liked to have seen that," Kaylan said.

Zack pursed his lips in thought. "I'm sure I can figure out how she turned it on."

He picked the ship up and looked for some kind of switch but couldn't find anything. He shook his head and used his implants to probe for a power source, immediately detecting one, though extremely faint. As he moved to turn it on, an authentication prompt appeared on his internal heads-up display. Zack frowned and then gave the credentials he'd used to access the *Athena's* systems. The faint power source began to build intensity. He quickly set the ship down on the table and stepped back.

"What's wrong?" Kaylan asked.

"I don't know. I just gave it my credentials to turn the thing on."

The model of the ship began to glow and the interior lights in the villa dimmed as if the power had been drained. A loud hum came from the ship and then there was a loud whooshing noise. Kaylan grabbed his arm and pulled him back. There was a high-pitched ringing, and Zack winced. He inched closer to the table and extended his hand. The model of the *Athena* was giving off so much heat that he didn't dare touch it. The ship hovered above the table, slowly spinning.

"That was much more difficult than I thought it would be," Athena said.

The ship continued to hover in the air, and the lighting in the room returned to normal.

"Athena! But you were ..."

"Dead," Athena said. "I was."

"Is it really you?" Kaylan asked.

"Yes, Commander, and no, I'm afraid," Athena said.

"You're not making any sense," Zack said.

"I'll try to be clearer. I did cease to be in order to spread the knowledge to neutralize the Xiiginn influence, but this model wasn't just for aesthetics. I was attempting to create a backup of myself should I become inoperable," Athena said.

"But how are you here? Have you been in the ship this whole time?" Zack asked.

"It's complicated. I was and I wasn't, a sort of in-between state of existence," Athena said.

Zack looked at Kaylan. "Yeah, that explains it."

"Part of me waited for you to activate the ship while most of me was in a different state of being—a bubble outside the universe," Athena replied.

"Athena, was this something you learned from the Drar?" Kaylan asked.

"Yes, that is accurate," Athena said.

"How do you fit into this little replica?" Zack asked.

"Most of me is still in the bubble. I was hoping you might be able to help me find a new home," Athena said.

Zack tried to think of a place they could use to store the AI, but he couldn't think of anything that would work. The Drar had remade the *Athena*, and Humans just didn't have that knowledge.

"We'll have to call the ECF or the Boxans. Maybe Gaarokk or Cardaleer can help us figure something out," Kaylan said. She paced back and forth.

Zack shook his head. "No, we don't."

Kaylan frowned. "Why not? We have to tell someone."

"No, we don't. We don't have to tell anyone about this. Think about it. If we start telling people that Athena somehow survived, how do you think they'll react?" Zack said.

Kaylan pressed her lips together, considering.

"Seriously, even the Boxans were about to force us to give the *Athena* up. No, we can't tell anyone about this."

Kaylan looked at the small replica of the *Athena*. "Do you still retain all the data from the Drar?"

"That is correct, Commander, but in this state my access is a bit limited. Perhaps if you were to help build me a new form I could be of more help," Athena said.

"Zack, we can't keep this to ourselves."

Zack's brain was racing in a thousand different directions. He glanced at the metallic case and smiled. "We won't, I promise. We'll share everything in time, and we already have a way to get the knowledge out there."

Zack gestured toward the metallic case with the Dux Corp company logo.

Kaylan covered her mouth with her hand.

"I think I'm going to take that job offer from Ed, but on one condition," Zack said, and went over to Kaylan, taking her hands in his.

"What would that be?" Kaylan asked.

"That you run Dux Corp with me."

Kaylan laughed.

"I'm serious. We can do this. I want to do this with you. We can figure out what the Drar left us and share that knowledge with the world and the Alliance. It shouldn't be just for us. You know I'm right—this is what we're meant to do. I can feel it," Zack said.

Kaylan cocked her head, and her glowing brown eyes danced while her full lips blossomed into a wide smile. "Alright, but only if Athena agrees."

They both looked at the small ship that held the keys to immeasurable stores of knowledge.

"We're family, and as long as we work together, we can achieve great things," Athena said.

Zack let out a jubilant howl and picked Kaylan up in his arms. They were home and safe. He couldn't have asked for anything more.

THANK YOU FOR READING ASCENSION - ASCENSION SERIES - BOOK 6.

If you loved this book, please consider leaving a review. Comments and reviews allow readers to discover authors, so if you want others to enjoy *Ascension* as you have, please leave a short note.

If you would like to be notified when my next book is released please visit kenlozito.com and sign up to get a heads up.

ABOUT THE AUTHOR

Ken Lozito is the author of multiple science fiction and fantasy series. I've been reading both genres for a long time. Books were my way to escape everyday life from when I was a teenager to my current ripe old(?) age. What started out as a love of stories has turned into a full-blown passion for writing them. My ultimate goal for writing stories is to provide fun escapism for readers. I write stories that I would like to read and I hope you enjoy them as well.

If you have questions or comments about any of my works I would love to hear from you, even if its only to drop by to say hello at KenLozito.com

Thanks again for reading *Ascension*.

Don't be shy about emails, I love getting them, and try to respond to everyone.

95607706R00188

Made in the USA
Columbia, SC
12 May 2018